A HERO FOR SUMMER (SPECIAL FORCES: OPERATION ALPHA)

REINA TORRES

Dear Readers,

Welcome to the Special Forces: Operation Alpha Fan-Fiction world!

If you are new to this amazing world, in a nutshell the author wrote a story using one or more of my characters in it. Sometimes that character has a major role in the story, and other times they are only mentioned briefly. This is perfectly legal and allowable because they are going through Aces Press to publish the story.

This book is entirely the work of the author who wrote it. While I might have assisted with brainstorming and other ideas about which of my characters to use, I didn't have any part in the process or writing or editing the story.

I'm proud and excited that so many authors loved my characters enough that they wanted to write them into their own story. Thank you for supporting them, and me!

READ ON!

Xoxo

Susan Stoker

CHAPTER 1

Sitting with the SEAL Team on the beach, Kai Akina couldn't help but wonder at the odd turn his life had taken in the last few months. A joyous peal of laughter turned his head and he saw his good friend, Elodie Webber, try to avoid her husband's half-hearted attempt to lift her up onto his shoulder in a fireman's carry.

He wasn't sure if she'd actually stumbled or if she'd shortened her steps to give him a chance to catch up, but a moment later, Mustang lifted her up against his chest, cradling her as if he was about to carry her over the threshold, and walked into the waves, calf deep. He sank down to his knees in the sand and surf, the two of them lost in each other's eyes.

Kai turned away when they started to kiss.

To say that Elodie and Mustang were in love was too bland an expression. He'd seen the terror they went through to be together.

He'd seen the incredible faith and hope that helped them fight for each other.

Seeing them laugh and joke around was heart-warming,

but he'd also seen those quiet moments when the two seemed to focus in on the other person.

It wasn't done to exclude those around them. It wasn't a selfish thing. He doubted that they were conscious they were doing it.

One moment they were laughing and enjoying the present and then a moment would pass between them, closing out the rest of the world.

He'd seen it with his parents while his father had been alive. The way they could be in the middle of a huge group but lost in each other.

That was the kind of love he wanted.

That connection to another person that made them *the world.*

Standing up, Kai dashed some of the sand from his legs and tried to ignore the twinge in his back.

It wasn't nearly as painful or prominent as it had been before.

The lifesaving surgery that removed a mob assassin's bullet from his back and repaired the damage it had done to his muscles and blood vessels had been nothing short of a miracle. The weeks of physical therapy had done wonders for his range of motion.

But with all of that, the thing that healed him the most was seeing Elodie happy with her husband.

Heading down to the water's edge, he saw movement on either side of him. Turning around, Kai saw that two of Mustang's SEAL team had followed him. Midas and Jag, like the others on the team, had become friends with him over time. Partly because they went with him when he swam in the ocean.

He shook his head at the two. "I think I'll be okay if you'd rather stay on the beach." Kai had noticed all the local wahine and tourists watching the group from their nearby blankets.

Midas shook his head. "A swim sounds good." He stretched his arms and Kai was reminded of the fact Midas got his name from all the gold swimming medals he had earned in school.

Kai looked at Jag. "I've been swimming all of my life, since I was a keiki." He explained even though they probably knew that about him. "You both don't have to come out with me."

Jag's expression barely changed as he started for the water's edge, completely undeterred by his words. "We're not worried about you." The Seal moved out until the water coursed around his calves. "Smile for the nice lady before she has a heart attack, hmm?"

Kai turned to look at Elodie and saw the worry plainly displayed on her face.

She worried about him.

Had hovered over him almost as much as his mother had ever since he'd been shot by the man who'd come to Hawaii to kill Elodie for his boss.

Even though he only had one more week of PT before the doctor signed off on his recovery, he knew she'd likely nag him until he let the others tag along.

So, he cut to the chase. Gesturing at the SEALs standing nearby he called out to Elodie. "We're going for a swim."

Smiling, she gave him a little wave.

Eager to get into the ocean, Kai waded in deeper. Midas was at his side. "See? That wasn't so hard, right?"

Kai shook his head. "She doesn't have to worry about me."

"That's the key though," Midas added as Jag dove in ahead of them and came up a few yards away, "she doesn't have to, but she does. Elodie considers you family."

Jag shook his head, sending droplets of water in a wide arc. "And that makes you our family too."

Kai found the comments humbling, but he understood how the guys felt about Elodie. He felt the same way.

Family.

The three of them dove into the water and swam through the ocean parallel to the beach. It felt good to be out in the water. Long smooth strokes cut through the familiar current.

Every breath he took gave his body the oxygen it needed to continue. The further they went, the easier it was to let instinct take over. He felt the periodic twinge in his back. Felt the stretch of his muscles as he tested his limits. So close to normal, he could almost taste it.

But close, as they said, only counted in horseshoes and hand grenades and he didn't know what to do with either.

Kai slowed his movements through the water and then a few minutes later he stopped all together, treading water as he took mental stock of his remaining strength.

He was good. There was more than enough in him to make it back safely. Kai knew he just needed a few minutes to recover before heading back.

Midas and Jag had surfaced nearby, and they were talking to each other in quiet tones.

Life had changed so much since Elodie started working with him on board the Fish Tales. Even his close call was just another bump in the road.

Midas popped up beside him, pushing him to the side and into an immovable object that Kai knew had to be Jag.

Kai laughed at Midas. "Pushy much?"

He tilted his head back to the group on the beach. "Let's head back."

"Okay."

Midas looked over at Jag and then back at Kai. "Race back?"

Rolling his eyes, he looked at Jag. "Is he serious?"

Jag looked between the two of them. "Racing and swimming? Deadly."

Without wasting another second, Kai slipped underwater

and started swimming back toward the beach. He wasn't sure he'd be able to beat Midas, but he was alive to give it his best shot.

He'd count that as a win any day.

Summer Maitland reached for her camera, wrapped her fingers around the all-too- familiar body and lifted it up to her eye. Adjusting the aperture for the long shadows of her jungle like surroundings, she fired off a few shots of the open grave site.

Something bothered her about the scene she'd spent the better part of the morning excavating. She'd hoped the flash from the camera would quite literally illuminate the issue, but it hadn't.

And now she had to figure out another option to dig deeper into the situation without actually going into the pit.

A rainstorm had come through the area while they'd enjoyed a particularly bland MRE lunch and now the sides of the pit were in danger of collapsing inward if they disturbed it too much.

"Well," she told herself, "Mother Nature's just trying to remind us-"

"Remind us of what, Miss Maitland?"

Summer turned her head and looked back over her shoulder at her boss, Elton West. She made a little gesture toward the pit and then the rest of their surroundings.

"She's trying to remind us that this is her home turf. We're the invasive species."

He peered over the edge of his glasses at her. "You're a forensic anthropologist, Miss Maitland. I expect better of you then to utter things that make you sound like one of those *natural scientists*."

"*Natural* scientists, sir? You make the scientific study sound dirty."

"Well," he quipped as he took a step toward her, craning his neck to look into the pit, "they do deal with dirt. Things that crawl in dirt. Spores, molds..."

"Humans are part of natural sciences. Biology is-"

"Humans," he shuddered as if an ice-cold wind had moved through his body, "are the least natural things on this planet. The things we'll do to each other," he sighed, "are an offense to nature. I'm still surprised the natural world hasn't erased us yet."

Summer wasn't sure if she should smile. "Elton? Are you okay?"

He blew out a breath. "Rainy days always make me a little melancholy."

She wanted to ask him when he wasn't a little melancholy but given the fact that they were almost three thousand miles from Hawaii, she was going to keep that little question to herself.

He gave a little groan and then a mirthless chuckle. "We're nearly three thousand miles from Hawaii. We've been dropped off on an island so small it could be considered a throw rug. And now you're telling me that you're not sure what we've found."

Before she could explain, he continued on.

"It's a human skeleton."

"Yes."

"US Army uniform?"

"Yes."

Elton's exhale was more than audible. "So before we end up dying of old age, can you please explain what the problem is?"

"It's just a weird feeling and-"

"Hands up!"

Summer startled and almost fell into the pit, but she managed to keep her balance as she turned her head.

Elton had his hands up, but his expression breathed fire. Two men held him at gunpoint and another held his gun leveled at her chest.

"Hands up!" The barrel of the gun jabbed at her before he swept it up into the air.

She understood what was happening all too well. The men were local and armed to the teeth.

Summer raised her hands above her head and did her best to breathe.

Two more men emerged from the thick jungle brush and kept their weapons pointed at Summer and her boss. The man who'd spoken to her moved closer, his gun held loosely across his chest.

Summer looked at the way he held the weapon and knew he was familiar enough with it that he was willing to use it.

So, she didn't have to worry about him fumbling with it and shooting by accident. No, this man and his friends knew what they were doing. If they felt like they needed to use their weapons, they would. And they'd hit what they were aiming at.

"You." He looked at her as if he was measuring her up against some kind of scale in his head. "Who are you?"

"Summer Maitland. I'm a scientist working with the Joint POW/MIA Accounting Command." She moved her hand carefully, unwilling to startle any of the men. Summer gestured to the pit beside her. "We were asked to come here and bring home any remains of American Servicemen."

The man questioning her moved closer, giving his men a command. She didn't understand the words he spoke, but she believed she understood the tone.

He'd given them an order.

What exactly? She didn't know, but there wasn't anything

she could do besides trying to get him to see that they weren't any kind of a danger to the men. Not a threat at all.

It was something she'd learned from her father who had been a Deputy Sheriff in her hometown. Men who displayed guns in this fashion were sometimes the most fearful men. They kept their guns close like security blankets.

Any challenge to their security or their power made them lash out at others. They wanted to be safe. In power. And they'd strike down anyone who threatened that fleeting feeling.

He stepped up to the edge of the pit and looked down into the wet muck.

Summer kept quiet, watching the man's face as he looked over the contents of the pit, starting and stopping on the part of the human skeleton that she'd only begun to unearth.

"American," he nodded.

She couldn't hold back the smile that answered his declaration. "Yes, American." She was fairly sure that she was correct, but she wasn't going to delve into the rest of her thoughts. They were starting to fall into place quickly, but she had a feeling that their survival was contingent on keeping these men from knowing what she suspected.

For a few moments, he was lost in thought, but when he turned and fixed a look on her face, she worried that he'd picked up on her anxiety.

Then again, being held at gunpoint was a pretty good excuse for being a little shaky.

It wasn't even the first time it had happened in her five years with JPAC, and it wouldn't be the last. Things happened when and where you didn't expect it. Misunderstandings, especially when you weren't on United States soil? So many things happen. The important thing was to remain calm. Well, as calm as one can with guns drawn and angry looks.

"Who?" The man in charge looked at Summer. His gaze was stern, almost suspicious. "Who told you to come here?"

Instinct turned her toward Elton. He was the one who had planned the trip, plugged in the GPS coordinates.

Elton's normally cool exterior was flushed. "It came through as an anonymous tip with a few items that an American soldier could have had in his possession. A set of coordinates for this island. And a hint that we would find a few sets of remains here."

Comments passed between the men and Summer was lost. She really didn't have a strong languages background. Sciences were her thing more than languages.

But she did understand expressions and knew when something had changed. When the man who had loosely held his gun across his body held it up and pointed it straight at her chest, she also saw the way his eyes went blank.

Empty.

In that moment, she wondered if this was going to be the end. These men didn't look like they wanted bargaining chips. They were more of the armed mercenaries determined to keep their secrets and money to themselves kind of men. They wouldn't want to draw the kind of attention that would bring the US Military down on their heads.

That left one more disturbing thought in Summer's head.

They also weren't going to want to leave behind witnesses.

Slowly, as if she was wiping her palms off on the legs of her pants, Summer started to reach for her key fob.

"Stop!"

Someone swung their rifle up and held it trained on her face. She couldn't quite see the man behind the weapon, but it didn't really matter much.

A few more excitable words and hand-gestures from their new friends and Summer knew things were about to change.

"Down!"

She met Elton's gaze with her own and gave him a nod. Compliance was the name of the game.

The last thing they wanted to do was to push the man's buttons. Keeping him as calm as possible put them in the best situation. Summer got down on one knee and as soon as she put the other knee down in the dirt, she heard someone behind her grumble.

A boot caught her in her lower back, and she tumbled forward. She barely had a moment's notice to squeeze her eyes and lips closed before she ended up face first in the mud.

It took everything she had to keep what was left of her cool. Summer focused her ears on the activity above her head as she reached down for her key fob. She felt the smooth face of the tracking beacon under her fingertips and turned it over until she felt the SEAL logo against her palm. Depressing the top of the fob into the metal disc, she twisted the logo until she felt it lock up. A single, solitary pulse vibrated against her palm.

~

Tex looked down at the phone on the table and picked it up, his eyes scanning over the auto-generated message.

His lips pressed into a thin line as he read over the information a second time to make sure he had a good understanding of the situation.

He forwarded the coordinates from the tracking device to a familiar number with an 808 Area Code and waited.

~

Everyone was busy cleaning up after dinner and Mustang had left his phone on the dinner table before he stepped into the kitchen with Elodie to wash dishes. Kai was manning the table, putting the leftovers into containers and Jag had just taken a small stack of platters to the kitchen for the wash, when the phone on the tabletop startled to life and buzzed furiously. Kai looked down at the phone on Aleck's dining table. "Mustang? You've got a message from someone named Tex!"

The SEAL Team leader was at the table in a second.

Hitting the button to dial, Mustang looked up at the assembled group and hit another button on the face of the phone. "I'm putting you on speaker."

Mustang laid the phone down in the center of the group and they all listened in.

"I just got a ping from the tracker I gave to Summer. You guys up for a trip to the Philippines to bring her home?"

Mustang shook his head. "You don't even have to ask. We're on our way back to base."

Movement in the room felt like a whirlwind and when it was over, Kai was standing there beside Elodie watching the door close softly behind the team.

"Does that happen a lot?"

Elodie looked up at Kai and shook her head. "There are times when things have happened quickly, but that fast? I don't think it's ever been like that. Then again, Scott's been a SEAL

longer than he's known me. I'm sure he'll let me know what he can when he comes back."

"Does that bother you?" Kai didn't like the confusion he saw in Elodie's eyes. "Not knowing what's going on?"

When she looked at him, he saw a gentle smile touch her lips. "I know how good Scott is at what he does. The others are too. And they have each other's backs. They'll come back as soon as they can and they'll do whatever it takes to make sure they all come back alive and in one piece."

He heard the words and saw the bright look in her eyes. He knew that she believed what she said. She didn't just love Mustang, she trusted him with her life. He knew the SEALs would do everything to come home just like she said, but he couldn't help worrying about his friends and knew that she must feel the same way.

Kai reached out and pulled Elodie into his embrace. She sighed and leaned into his hug. "Mahalo, Kai."

He grinned at her words and leaned his cheek against the top of her head in a comforting touch. "A'ole pilikia."

No worries...

CHAPTER 2

There were two guards on either side of the pit. It wasn't that deep to begin with, but it was still deep enough that any of the armed men would have no trouble killing either of them before they could climb out. *Shooting fish in a barrel* was the way her mind chose to label the situation, not that it made her feel any better.

Shifting her position on the ground, Summer got up on her knees and reached into her vest pocket.

Elton only caught on when he saw the flutter of purple before she quickly pulled the glove onto her hand.

A few excited comments and angry orders reached her ears, but she didn't stop.

Beside her, leaning against the muddy wall, Elton hissed out a few choice words of his own. "What the hell are you doing?"

"Investigating." She leaned forward and took in a long deep breath near the surface of the skull, wrinkling her nose. "Well, that's interesting."

"This isn't the time."

"Why not? What else do we have to do?" Summer didn't

bother turning to look at Elton. If she did, she'd have to ignore the irritation in his eyes and the pain she knew she'd see there. When Elton had been pushed in after her, he'd landed in a heap and had likely twisted something in his back.

She'd done all she could to settle him as comfortably as she could in the pit that was barely bigger than the size of a coffin, but there was no way she could just sit on her hands. At least she was keeping herself occupied and her mind off of when help would arrive.

What would happen after that? She had no idea. And she still had a job to do.

The angry voices settled down and when a few moments of silence passed by, Summer guessed they'd just become tired of staring at her. They'd already taken their phones and personal possessions, even her keychain with the tracker on it.

If they moved them off island or took the keychain somewhere else then she'd worry about it, until then she meant what she said. Summer leaned forward over the remains, gently tracing her fingers in the dirt around the remains.

"We don't have anything else to do right now," she spoke softly, but hoped that he heard the determination in her tone. "We can't expect anyone to come and help until tomorrow at the earliest, so I'm going to keep myself active or I'm going to lose my mind."

"Heaven help us if that happens." Elton grumbled under his breath.

She struggled to keep her mood even. Elton had a sarcastic tone most days, but she usually had an escape. He rarely came into the lab when she was there.

As much as she had to keep herself distracted, she was quickly realizing that she'd have to do the same for him. "Have you figured out anything about what they're saying?"

Elton shifted in the mud and moved closer to her. "Nothing is coming to me. I know enough Tagalog for basic greetings and a few phrases that were helpful when I was a child and my father was stationed here in the Philippines, but I'm not familiar with Hostage Negotiations 101."

"Might be a course to look into for fun."

"Ha! Fun." Elton cleared his throat and settled back against the muddy wall. "It was supposed to be a quick and easy look. Gathering information."

"We are. The remains are where they said they'd be, but there are things that are bothering me. Like how accurate the coordinates were. And this whole area. It seems too easy." Taking off her glove, Summer tucked it into a pocket of her field vest. If she had access to their supplies, she would have a covered trash can, but that would have to wait. Crawling across the small space, she sat beside Elton and closed her eyes, hoping she looked like she was almost too tired to stay awake.

"I think we're going to need to take a deeper look at your source. That uniform is real, but," she had to push forward before Elton could start arguing with her, "I doubt if that body belongs to the uniform. The skeleton is Mongoloid. The dog tags say otherwise."

Elton stiffened into silence beside her. "Are you sure?"

She heard enough surprise in his tone that she wasn't upset by his question. "There's always a chance that he was adopted or maybe he was from a mixed family, but from World War II? I don't think so."

More men entered the clearing above their heads and Summer struggled to keep her heart rate under control.

She focused on the job, the science. Those things kept her focus on things she had control over.

Looking up over their heads, she didn't hear any noise directly above them. She let out a soft breath. The men who had taken over their dig weren't exactly concerned with stealth. Leaning a fraction of an inch closer, she spoke under her breath. "And whoever he is," she swallowed at the lump in her throat, but couldn't quite move it, "he hasn't been dead for more than five years."

"Five?" Elton tried to turn in her direction but froze with a painful hiss of sound. "Part of me wants to ask how you know, but the rest of me?" He eased back against the muddy wall with a groan. "I'm afraid of what you'll say."

Summer smiled. "That's probably a good decision then." She didn't want to tell him that she'd gotten close enough to smell the skull. Elton wasn't someone who reveled in the hands-on stuff.

"I just wonder if someone wanted us here."

"You and me?" Elton scoffed. "What could we do?"

"Maybe not us specifically. Just someone to visit the site, stir up trouble."

"Well, we've got our share of trouble and then some," Elton agreed.

As the conversation in their camp dimmed down and Summer settled in to try to catch some sleep, she looked up at Elton with a curious smile. "I wondered why you approved this trip at the last minute and insisted on coming along."

Elton drew back, his chin pulling toward his throat. "You don't think I had anything to do with this, do you?"

She felt her brow furrowed at the idea. "No, not at all."

"Then why-"

"You prefer the administrative side of things for the most part. I'm more curious than anything. Trying to keep my mind active instead of freaking out."

"Oh," Elton's tone was melancholy, "it's nothing really interesting. More of a temporary insanity thing, I guess."

A lonely bird call sang out and Summer lifted her head and noticed how dark the sky had become.

Elton continued beside her. "I thought this would be one of those easy stopovers and then I might take a few days to… I don't know… see if I could see if anything jogged any of my childhood memories. See if anything is still familiar." His voice faded off. "See? Crazy."

"I don't know about crazy," her voice softened with her exhaustion. "It almost makes you seem… human."

She heard Elton's chuckle.

"Very funny, Maitland. Go to sleep."

She was already there.

When Elodie arrived at the Navy Lodge the next morning, Kai paid close attention to her mood. She greeted the night manager with her customary smile, but Kai had a feeling that even Jayden knew something was wrong though and waved him off to take his break a little early.

"Any news?"

Elodie shook her head as she opened a container and set it in front of him. "They're fine."

He gestured toward the staff refrigerator. "Something to drink?"

"Water, please."

By the time he'd picked up two bottles and turned back to the table, Elodie was sitting down, staring at the food in her dish.

"I could have sworn I made omelets this morning, but it looks like I made some kind of scramble."

Kai looked down into his bowl and took a deep breath. "Smells like heaven either way."

Her answering smile made him feel a lot better. "If you're trying to make me feel better, it's working."

He gave her a wink. "Between you and my mama, I have to keep working out or I'm going to look like a puffer fish."

Elodie's snort of laughter made him feel like he'd done something right.

They both took a few bites before Elodie spoke again. "I'm new to this whole Military wife thing," her voice was a little softer, "but it's easier when it's a mission they've been planning. I mean I still don't know what's going on when they leave, but it feels good knowing that they've trained for the specifics of the mission."

"And this one came out of the blue."

Elodie pushed her fork around the plate. Her gaze fixed on it for a moment. "Yeah. Someone's in trouble and Mustang's team is the closest to affect a rescue. That's as much as I could figure out before he left."

"Do you want to know more?"

"Of course!" She set her fork down and looked right at him. "Maybe not." She shook her head.

Kai wasn't used to seeing this kind of fear in Elodie. The last time he did, they were both in the crosshairs of a mob assassin. He'd really prefer to avoid that circumstance again.

Since he couldn't do anything about that, he had to try and focus her thoughts elsewhere.

"Scott," it was easier to call him by his given name when he wasn't around, "and the others are the best the Navy has to offer, right?"

"Absolutely!"

He heard the pride in her voice and took another bite.

"And they've trained together for hundreds of hours."

"Thousands," she almost growled out the fierce answer with pride.

"Okay, girl. You don't have to tear my head off. I'm on your side."

She took another bite and laughed just a little. "I know."

"And that's why you know that wherever they are, they're going to be okay."

"Because they have each other."

He saw the knowing smile on her face and nodded his head in a reply.

"They know how to think on their feet," she added.

"I bet they do," he agreed. "And I know one of them wants to get back here as soon as he can."

Kai saw her cheeks blush.

"He's going to come home to you, Elodie. None of them are going to take any unnecessary chances. They'll be home before you know it."

When Kai finished his meal first, he started to get up from the table, but felt her hand on his arm.

"Thank you," her smile was genuine and had lost the worry he'd read plainly on her face just a few minutes before. "Sorry I had to come and worry you through your meal break."

"It's no big deal." He grinned at her. "The food… *and* company are worth it. My mother and my tutu said to thank you for helping them fatten me up after the hospital."

Kai saw the momentary flash of worry cross her features, and he wanted to kick himself.

"Elodie, I'm sorry, I didn't mean anything-"

"Hey," she reached out and grasped his arm, making sure he was looking into her eyes, "you and me, we've been through hell together."

Kai nodded. "And we made it through alive."

He saw her bright-eyed smile deepen.

"We certainly did!"

Kai shared a laugh with her. "Things have to get easier from now on, right?"

Elodie gave him a nod in answer. "It has to! What else could go wrong?"

~

The sun was barely more than a haze in the sky when Summer finally gave up trying to sleep. All night long she was up and down, startled awake at dangerously close intervals. People arrived and left, angry conversations started and stopped, some with violent ends.

Thank heavens it had only been fist fights, but whatever happened it didn't make it easy to get any rest, let alone let down her guard at all.

Elton was suffering. And that added onto her worries. Especially when she contemplated how and when a rescue might happen. She knew she wouldn't be expected to get him out of the pit on her own, but she wasn't going to stand idly by either.

The sound of a boat engine starting jumped through her like an electric shock. She couldn't silence the gasp of air she drew in and her eyes darted to the top of the pit. When no one appeared, she shifted against the earthen wall behind her.

"I'm catching little bits of conversation."

The sound of Elton's voice turned her head. The early light of dawn made his face look even more drawn than it had when they'd been forced into the makeshift cell.

She wasn't going to say anything about it.

"Anything helpful?"

He started to shrug, but she could see the wince of pain on his face. "It seems like we might have been used."

She listened as Elton explained what he'd managed to piece together with the few words he remembered from his youth in the Philippines and filled in a bit with context and conjecture.

The picture he pieced together was more than a little bleak.

"So, someone wanted to get rid of some competition? Drug dealers?"

Elton shrugged one shoulder. "I'm not sure about the dealer aspect. Maybe grower?" He sighed softly. "I really need to go back and study Tagalog, I'm starting to feel like a real idiot about wanting to come along."

"I'd say you're doing pretty well. It's more information than we had a few hours ago." Summer tried to wave off his worry. "They had a plan at least."

Elton sighed. "There you go, trying to find something positive in all this."

She couldn't help but grit her teeth together. Her lifelong adage had always gotten her through tough moments. "Smile or cry, smile or cry."

He didn't comment on that and she was grateful. It was becoming harder and harder to keep positive in their situation and she didn't want to start crying.

"We'll find out more later," he began and gave her a look, "hoping that we'll have a later and get to finish our investigation."

"Anything about that boat?" Her positive outlook was slipping further and further away.

Elton groaned. "I think the boat that left has gone for more men."

Summer stiffened at the idea, her fingers digging into the moist earth beneath her. "Any idea how many are still here?"

Together, they collected their best guess.

Summer let out a steadying breath. Just shy of ten.

Ten.

She had no access to her phone and besides the beacon that she'd activated there wasn't a way to send any helpful information. She wasn't even sure she had any good information to give.

Summer dropped her head down to her knees and closed

her eyes. She wanted to scream! All of those positive thoughts she used as a shield?

They felt paper thin and as wet and muddy as they were, paper was worthless!

Science. She was a scientist! She found and identified remains.

She gave closure to families.

She gave American servicemen and women their rightful place at home.

But here she was frightened and fearful.

She was lying to her boss and herself by saying she was handling this whole ordeal, when in truth she was just moments away from losing her sanity.

Summer had a feeling she knew who they would send after them and while she knew that the team was crazy skilled and a kick ass group of warriors, the last thing she wanted them to do was to face the danger that they were literally going to wade straight into.

Did she want to be rescued?

Of course!

But she didn't want to know that someone might die to do it.

Tears formed in her eyes and her hands gripped tightly to her knees as she struggled to hold herself together.

Summer felt a hand on her back.

"One breath." She heard Elton trying to help her calm down. "One breath at a time."

She knew he was trying to be nice which was even more difficult for her to grasp. She almost started laughing when she realized that what she really wanted from him was his normal grouchy orders. 'Get yourself together, Maitland.' Something like that she could handle.

But Elton West being kind and nice? It just made everything seem so much more… surreal.

. . .

A wind seemed to pass right over them.

A whisper of sound with a tangible feel.

Summer didn't move.

She didn't make a sound.

Not even when someone jumped down beside her.

"Stay down."

Swallowing hard against the gasp that threatened to burst from her lips, Summer recognized Pid's voice. Pid. Which meant that they'd sent the SEAL team in to rescue them.

Thank God.

She turned to look at him. His gaze was focused on the top of the pit, his weapon at the ready.

Reaching out, she tugged on his sleeve, feeling stupid and childish.

She did it a second time. "Pid?"

He looked over at her and gave her a wink. "Just hold on. We'll have you out of here in a few minutes." Pid looked over her shoulder at Elton. "Sir."

Elton's voice replied in a subtle whisper. "We think there might be ten up there."

Summer nodded. "And a boat left earlier. We think-"

"We saw it too. Slate heard them talking before they left. Just stay still and we'll have you both out of here in no time."

A soft grunt sounded overhead, and Summer tensed, praying to anyone who would listen that Pid was right, and they were very nearly done with this whole horrible experience.

The seconds seemed to tick away as Summer huddled beside Pid, her heart in her throat. When he lifted his hand to his ear, listening intently, she swore she could hear her heart pounding in her chest like a drum.

"Got it."

Pid got to his feet and she reached for his arm to pull him back down beside her, but before she could make contact a familiar face leaned over to get a look at her.

"All right. Let's get you out of here and back home."

"Midas!"

Oh heavens. It was really sinking in!

Pid helped her to her feet and across the coffin sized pit. The instant she felt Midas' hand close around hers she let out a little sigh.

A moment later, Midas and Aleck were moving her off to the side as Jag took her place inside of the hole to help Elton out.

A quick comment from her had the men adjusting their plans to remove him. Elton grumbled at the situation in general as they quickly extricated him, but he managed a weak smile as they moved away.

Summer turned to look for the rest of the team and saw Mustang and Slate standing over a group of men kneeling in a line, their hands bound behind them. There were two off to the side, neither of them moved at all and she turned her eyes away. She might examine, identify, and reassemble human remains, but she didn't relish the idea of anyone losing their life because of her. Midas kept her moving with a gentle hand on her back.

"Don't think about it. Just keep moving. We're waiting for some counterparts from the Philippine Special Forces Regiment to show up."

She couldn't stop the fear from entering her eyes. "Are we in trouble?"

"No," Aleck gave her a smile, "it's just a professional courtesy thing, really. We had to let them know we were coming in."

Midas continued with the explanation. "Kind of like a

jurisdictional thing. We don't have to worry about an international incident. Kind of a win-win thing."

Summer felt a little woozy at the thought. "And what's their 'win' in this situation?"

"Drugs off the market. It's not your typical military action, but it's good."

She nodded. "Are we going to be able to finish excavating the site?"

She saw the look that passed between the two SEALs standing beside her. "Not right now. As soon as their airborne shows up, we hand these men over to them and then we get you two home."

Summer fought off her disappointment at his words.

She knew that's what he'd say, but it didn't take the sting out. There was more to learn from the site. More to discover. And yet there were men out there who were still involved in criminal activities. They needed to be removed before more work could be done. And that was if the Philippine government would welcome their assistance after she wrote up her report.

She just couldn't torture herself over things she had no control over.

Like that would stop her.

Aleck touched the tip of her nose. "Those are some pretty deep thoughts you've got going on in your head."

Wriggling her nose, Summer gave his hand a little swat like she did with one of her cousins. "I'm always stressing about something, but I see what y'all are saying. It's not like I don't have a ton of work waiting for me back at Pearl. I just… I just-"

"You're a good anthropologist, Doctor Maitland."

Summer barely resisted the urge to stick her tongue out at Midas. "Are you Lucy or Peppermint Patty?" She groaned. "Now I'm hungry."

The growl of her stomach disappeared under the sound of approaching boats.

"Please tell me that's-"

Midas grinned. "The cavalry. Let's go pack up your stuff so we can get out of here as soon as all the necessities are done, okay?"

Summer plastered a smile on her face and followed Midas, choosing to stay close to him as they packed up. Elton's injury needed to be seen to and she needed to cover and mark the site regardless of their ability to return. She just couldn't help the ache of leaving this mystery behind, but she had a feeling there was something even bigger waiting for her back in Hawaii.

CHAPTER 3

Summer looked around the pool area at Pearl Harbor Physical Therapy and tried to ignore the number of people in the immediate area. It wasn't that she had an issue with people per se, but since they'd returned from the Philippines, she'd been feeling a little... boxed in.

Ugh, just the idea had her a little on edge. There were nights she woke up in the dark and had to sweep a hand over her face, thinking that she still had damp earth on her skin.

They'd only spent a night under guard by the gunmen, but her sleep patterns hadn't gotten any better since they'd returned.

Staring down at the soda can she'd been turning around and around on the wrought iron surface of the table, Summer watched some of the condensation collect together and drip down the side of the aluminum.

She'd come with Elton for his PT appointment, not just as a support to him, but driving afterwards wasn't necessarily easy for him. The workouts that he did in the pool sometimes left him tired instead of energized and she was happy to help with the drive. It was also a reality check for her.

Seeing Elton healing was good for her.

At work she could concentrate on her work. At home? The walls felt like they were a little closer than they should be. The silence… deafening.

Even with the TV on all the time she still couldn't seem to relax.

"Summer?"

She heard her name, but it didn't fully register in her head. After all, who would she know there? Elton was still working with his therapist in the pool.

"Summer?"

A hand touched her shoulder and while she almost jumped out of her skin, she managed to knock her soda over on the table.

A helpful hand righted the can and swept a napkin over the tabletop. "Sorry… sorry. I didn't mean to scare you."

Summer relaxed as Elodie Webber dropped the napkin into a nearby trashcan. Shaking her head at her own ridiculous reaction, she gave Elodie a smile. "I'm sorry. I must have been distracted." Summer gestured to a chair. "Have a seat, please."

Elodie grinned at her and took the seat with a smile. "I heard you might be here, but I didn't expect to run into you right off the bat."

Summer admired Elodie's easy manner and wished that she hadn't acted like a complete idiot when she'd stopped to say hello. "I'd ask you how you knew, but I think the answer is obvious."

Leaning forward on the table, Elodie's smile was infectious. "I don't think it's any secret that the guys are a little protective."

"A little?" Summer couldn't hold back the little snort of laughter that burst out. "But they don't have to worry about me now. I go from work to home and I'm not scheduled for anything outside of the lab in the near future."

"Don't be surprised if you see someone stop in at work to check on you from time to time." Elodie's smile dimmed a little. "There can be danger anywhere you go."

Summer heard the truth in Elodie's words and her voice. There was a story there, but she wasn't sure if she should ask about it. She barely knew the woman. And even though she'd love being her friend, starting up that kind of conversation seemed more than daunting.

"Did Mustang tell you how we met?"

Elodie shook her head.

"The first time I met the guys was on a transport back from a dig site and everyone was trying to manage to get a look without actually *looking* at them. It's not every day you get to see a SEAL team. I admit I was more than a little starstruck when I saw them."

Elodie's laughter warmed her. "When I first met them, they literally saved my life. I can say I was a little star struck too."

"I'm not alone then." Summer tried to ignore how much truth had slipped out when she'd spoken.

"Hardly! I owe my life to them. All of them."

Summer sat awestruck as Elodie told her about her harrowing experience in the ocean, her own heart climbing high into her throat.

"I can't imagine that." Summer shuddered. "The most water I get into is the shallow end of a wading pool. I'm afraid that I'm going to end up in over my head if I go any deeper than that. I grew up in New England and the water up there," an unwanted shiver passed through her, "it's freezing. Not exactly fun for me."

Elodie's soft laughter made Summer smile too. "Do you

want to learn? If you want, you could ask one of the guys to help you out with that. You know, give you a few lessons."

Summer stared back at her. "Ask a SEAL to help me swim? That's like asking Simone Biles to teach me how to walk along a balance beam."

"They wouldn't look at it like that."

Summer agreed. They were too nice to say no if she asked them, but they had more important things to do. Like saving lives!

"I'm fine. It's not like I go to the beach at all."

"That's a shame, especially here."

She had to agree with Elodie. When she'd applied for the job at Pearl Harbor, she had to admit that the pictures she'd seen of the sunsets on the beach were part of the draw of moving to a tropical island, but being there on the sand and not getting in the water?

It felt more than a little silly. Like going to an art museum and just standing on the sidewalk outside and looking at the door.

Trying to get out of the conversation, Summer cleared her throat. "I can probably find a place nearby that gives lessons."

"How about here?"

Okay, so getting out of the conversation wasn't going to be as easy as she thought, and it seemed like Elodie wasn't the kind of person who would give up easily.

And Summer didn't have it in her to appear rude. She liked Elodie a lot. And when they'd returned from the Philippines, Elodie and the SEALs had invited her over for lunch. It felt good to spend time with them when she wasn't covered in muck or shaking with fear, and having Elodie there had been a wonderful bonus. A little extra estrogen made things a lot easier for her.

"Here?" Summer wasn't sure there was a way to get out of the conversation except to go through it.

"I'm sure there are all kinds of places that have lessons, but I'm talking about my friend Kai."

Summer didn't know what to say to that.

Leaning on her elbow, Elodie pointed at the pool. "He's why I'm here today. He's the one swimming laps along the edge."

Turning, Summer looked at the far edge of the pool. It took just a second to find the man swimming laps. How she hadn't noticed him before, she didn't know. He cut through the water like he was born to it. The arms that emerged from the water, stroke after stroke, were tanned and muscular. By the time he reached the end of the pool and turned to head back in the opposite direction, Summer was forced to pick up her warming soda to take a sip and try to hide the flush across her cheeks.

When she set the can down, she saw Elodie's sly smile. "Like what you see?"

Summer lowered her gaze to the table and indulged in a little laugh at herself. "If I do learn, I'm thinking I might join one of those kid classes at the Y or something. There's no way I'm getting in the water with a guy like that only to flounder around and end up sucking down half the water in the pool when I mess up."

"Well," Elodie met her eyes with a big grin on her face, "Kai used to lifeguard when he was in High School. I'm sure he could teach you just as well."

Opening her mouth to reply, Summer saw Elodie's knowing look and realized she was already losing the battle.

"Why don't you just meet him and see if you hit it off."

"You're talking about swimming lessons, right?"

There was a momentary pause before Elodie answered. "Of course! Oh good. Looks like he's done for the day."

Elodie didn't really need to point in his direction because Summer already knew where to look.

At the deep end of the pool, a swimmer emerged from the water. He braced his hands on the edge and a moment later he was standing there, water sluicing from his body like Aquaman. He just didn't have armor hiding the muscular perfection of his body.

Without thinking about it, Summer lifted her soda to her mouth and took another drink.

Of an empty can.

Setting it back down on the wrought iron tabletop, she tried to gather her frazzled thoughts together.

There were any number of normal, non-idiot things she could have said or done, but all that managed to come out of her mouth was a single breathy word.

"Wow."

"I know, right?" Elodie laughed softly from her seat across the table.

Summer turned to look at Elodie raising her eyebrow as her cheeks tingled with heat. "What?"

Elodie waved off the look with a wink. "I'm totally head over heels for Mustang, but I have eyes just like you. Kai is a handsome man."

Summer spoke before she could stop herself. "Very handsome."

"See?" Elodie lifted her hand into the air. "Kai! Over here."

As he turned and headed in their direction, Summer turned to fully face Elodie, her eyes widening across the small, circular table. "What are you doing?"

Elodie shrugged, but her eyes were dancing with humor. "Well, I am his ride today, so I need to let him know I'm waiting over here."

~

Even across the pool, Kai could see that Elodie was up to something. It wasn't just her smile, but the way she leaned against the table as he walked over. She kept looking at him like she was about to get him in a lot of trouble. That kind of bright smile meant she was going to enjoy every minute of it.

Lifting his towel, he used it to hide the surreptitious look he took at the other woman sitting at the table.

She looked like she might jump out of her chair if he spooked her. She held on to the edge of the table with one hand while the other had a near death grip on her soda can.

Kai laid his towel over his shoulder as he walked up to the table. He looked squarely at Elodie. "Hey, sis. Looks like you're having fun."

"Of course! I bumped into a new friend of mine."

New friend.

Leaning in, he kissed the top of Elodie's head. "Nice."

"I was thinking the two of you should meet." Elodie reached out a hand across the table toward her 'new friend.' "Talk about small worlds! This is Summer Maitland. She's waiting for a co-worker to finish with his PT and here I was waiting for you to finish your PT. Funny how we found each other."

Kai heard the distinctive note of a set-up in Elodie's voice, but it didn't bother him. Ever since she'd found happiness with Mustang, she'd been on a mission to find him 'someone nice.'

He knew a lot of nice. He wanted more than that, but he couldn't blame Elodie for trying. She was just too sweet for his own good.

He wasn't sure if Summer would take his hand with the way she was gripping onto the table and her drink, but his mother would have smacked his head if he didn't at least offer it.

"Summer Maitland?"

It took her a moment to react to his words.

Shifting on the chair she managed to loosen her fingers from the can and put it in his. "Summer," she agreed, "yes."

"Kai Akina. Nice to meet you."

The words were genuine on his end.

He liked what he saw when she met his eyes. He saw her looking back at him and he could see the spark of intelligence in her eyes. She didn't just look at things, she absorbed them.

She was pretty, there was no doubt about that. Even with the harsh white stucco wall behind her and the aging black wrought iron table and chairs around her, her skin was warm, a healthy glow if not a little light for someone who lived in Hawaii.

And her hair, a warm mahogany brown pulled back from her face in a ponytail, looked like silk, thick, with just a hint of a wave in its length. Heaven help him, he wanted to feel it in his hand.

Still, her eyes drew him the most.

Hazel, that's what people would call her eyes, but there was another hint of color around the edges. Amber, closer to gold.

Beyond that, he saw the person beyond her beauty.

Depth. Emotion. Intellect.

He could stand there all day and stare, but it wouldn't be enough.

Kai heard Elodie's soft laughter, and he turned to look at his friend. "What?"

She looked down at his hand and then back up. "Why don't you have a seat?" He saw her vague hand gesture toward the chair that was right in front of him, pushed up against the table. "Then maybe you'll let go of her hand?"

Then maybe I'll… he looked down and saw that he did still have a hold on Summer's hand.

"Sorry." Kai let go of her hand, probably not as quickly as he could have, but her skin was so very soft and her fingers where they brushed up against his, felt like heaven. "I didn't mean to-"

"It's okay." Her words tangled with his and he noticed the warm flush of color that touched her cheeks. "It's fine."

He gestured to the chair. "Do you mind-"

"Yes," the response was instant and then she rethought her words, "I mean no, I don't mind. Yes, please sit."

They both laughed at that and Kai pulled out the chair between the two women, managing not to wince too much when the iron legs squealed a little across the concrete.

He lifted the chair enough to stop the noise and then set it down with both hands to avoid any more ear-splitting, annoying sounds. Not exactly a great first-ish impression.

Setting himself down in the chair he managed it with just a twinge of pain in his back. It was something that had taken time and a lot of work to recover from his injury, and he was looking forward to the day when he didn't feel it at all. And then, maybe Elodie would stop fussing over him like she was about to do.

He met her nervous look with an overly emphatic smile. "I'm fine."

His words seemed to fluster her, and her brow furrowed just the littlest bit.

"Are you sure?"

Kai couldn't help but laugh. "I told you, I'm fine."

He looked over at Summer and smiled. "Will you tell her I'm fine?"

He saw the moment of shock on Summer's face, but it didn't last long.

"How would I know?" Her answer was straightforward, and her voice was stronger than it had been a few moments ago.

"Maybe the benefit of the doubt? Or perhaps you just think I'm too nice a guy to lie to my friend."

A drop of water picked that moment to slide down the side of his face from his hair and drip from his jaw to his chest. Sighing, he lifted the towel from his shoulder and wiped it off with a quick flick. He saw Summer lower her gaze at the same time and he wondered if it was just an instinct thing or maybe something more.

"Sometimes good friends lie to each other," she answered him. "They think that it's better to say something that isn't the truth if it makes things... okay for the other person. You could be saying that you're fine so she won't worry, or you could just be saying it because it's the truth.

"I just don't know you well enough to know which one it is."

As his cousin would say. 'Mic drop!'

He couldn't help but smile at her. "Well said."

"I mean-"

"No." He shook his head. "Don't take it back. A'ole pilikia, Summer. You should always say what you mean." *Around me*, he wanted to add. He wanted to hear everything she had to say.

Turning to look at Elodie, Kai saw the surprise on her face, but he also saw the smile tugging at the corners of her mouth. She was only too happy to watch him trip all over his feet with this woman.

"And to answer your question. I really am fine. Just a little tug here and there when I move, but nothing like it used to be. Relax." He felt a little tremor of a muscle in his leg, but that was only because he really didn't like to talk about his injury. It wasn't that he was upset about it, especially not with Elodie. She'd taken it all on her shoulders early on, but even though she assured him that she was mostly over whatever guilt she'd felt, he just didn't like to think about it no matter what.

Trying to look forward in his life was where he wanted his headspace to be. He wanted to move forward, not worry about the bullet he'd taken to his back and the damage it had done. Sometimes it was a random night that took him back to that day, pulling his mind back into the terrifying thought that his life was about to end.

Sometimes the feelings would just go away, disappearing like rain on a sunny day, but sometimes it took conscious thought to push them back. The random twitches he felt from time to time told him that somewhere in the shadows of his mind, those thoughts... those feelings were coming back.

He had to fight them back down.

Had to move forward in his life.

Kai picked a train of thought and grabbed onto it.

"Elodie said you're waiting for someone?"

Summer's smile held a little bit of mystery in it and a little hesitation. "He's kind of like my boss, really." Leaning on the arm of her chair she gestured back toward the pool. "Elton West. He's got his PT appointment today. If I don't drive him here, he tries to make up an excuse not to come and then he spends the rest of the day complaining about how he can't get any work done because he hurts."

Kai looked at Elodie. "You're lucky I'm so much easier to work with."

She gave him a pointed look. "You just like swimming, so it's not a fight."

He shrugged knowing that she was totally right, but he didn't want to confirm it right then and there. Instead, he looked at the man he'd seen earlier entering the pool and nodded. He was dressed from neck to knee in rash guards. Long sleeves on his top with a high neck. His pants fully covered to just below his knee. The outfit was better suited to the ocean than a pool. Currents instead of the relatively peaceful lull of a pool.

When he turned back to Summer, he doubled up his towel and set it down on the tabletop. As he looked up into her face, he saw her lift her chin and then her gaze up toward his face from his chest.

Hope warmed him and he felt his heart beat a little faster. Maybe she liked what she saw. He certainly did.

"Is your boss planning to do some body surfing later? Boogie boarding?"

Summer shrugged and tried to hide her smile. "He is a little overdressed, but that's Elton. I'm sure he went in and told them to suit him up head to toe. I'm not sure he really understood what they meant when they told him they were going to do aqua therapy for his back injury. I think I saw a few books on scuba diving on his desk the other week before he started.

"He likes to take things to the extreme, but that's what makes him the kind of administrator who does amazing work at the center."

"At the-"

"You two can talk about that later." Elodie interrupted his question but she didn't look the least bit apologetic about it. When Kai stared back at her with a pointed look she shrugged. "Her boss is about to get out of the pool and Summer has a question she wants to ask you."

Kai turned to look at Summer and saw the shock on her face that likely matched his own.

A question for him?

He was all for it.

Sitting back in his chair, he kept his focus on Summer. "Go ahead and ask."

For a moment he thought she'd come right out and ask it.

And then he saw her falter a little. The energy in her eyes shifted and dimmed just enough that he worried she'd give up before she even said a word.

Smiling at her, he leaned forward, bracing his forearms on his knees. Looking up at her face from that angle, he was taken by how the sunlight changed her eye color, making them more green than amber.

He was so tempted to tell her how beautiful she looked, but he had a feeling that might be coming on too strong. He didn't want her to think that.

Kai knew he'd have to say something before she left. He had to encourage her to ask him whatever it was that Elodie was hinting about. It couldn't be bad if she was trying to get Summer to ask him.

"I'm going to make you a bet," he gave Summer a smile he hoped would encourage her to speak. "I bet that if you ask me for something, the answer would be yes."

He startled her. That much was obvious. And the light that flared in her eyes seemed to have more than a touch of humor in it. For a moment, he considered that he might have gotten himself quite literally in trouble with the beautiful woman sitting beside him.

But he also knew that he wouldn't mind.

With all the work he'd done in healing and strengthening his muscles after suffering the bullet wound in his back, he was ready to do more than just go back to the usual things he did.

Before Summer could decide against asking, he added one more thought.

"As long as it's not illegal. My mother would kick my ass."

Elodie laughed out loud. "It's true," she gave him a wink, "she would."

"So," he gave Summer a hopeful grin, "what are we doing?"

He watched her draw in a breath. The subtle movement parted her lips and he found himself watching them a little too closely. A gentle bow on the top and a fuller bottom lip that he wanted to pull between his teeth. He was definitely in trouble with Summer Maitland.

"I'd like to..." One corner of her smile wobbled a little. "I mean, I was wondering..." She blew out a breath and pulled another one in and Kai was fascinated.

He loved the play of emotions across her features. She told whole stories with just the lift of her brow or the gentle furrow between them. He wanted to know more about her, so much more of what was going on behind those looks.

He just needed the opening to see her again.

Another breath and she drew her shoulders back and gave him a smile. "Just promise you won't laugh."

Laugh?

He did right then. A short exhale that held more than a ton of laughter in it. "Yeah, that wasn't about you, Summer. Sorry. I'm just starting to wonder if you're about to ask me to rob a bank with you or climb Stairway to Heaven. And we can't do either one of those. The first because I don't know how-"

"And your mother would kill you." The words seemed to burst out of Summer unexpectedly. And she blushed as she covered her mouth with her hand. "I mean-"

"It's true though," he smiled back at her, "she would. And the other is closed and I'm not taking you anywhere that dangerous."

She laughed again and he felt something swell in his chest. Whether it was just his lungs or his heart, he couldn't tell, but she made him smile and he could return the favor. He wanted more time with her.

"I was just wondering," she bit her teeth into her bottom

lip, and he swore his heart was beating loud enough for her to hear it, "if you'd be willing to teach me how to swim."

Before he could answer she blurted out another word.

"Better.

"Swim better."

She seemed determined to clarify it a few more times.

"I know the basics.

"I'm just not at all good at it.

"And I'm living on an island, so-"

"I'm done for today."

Kai turned in the direction of the voice and even though the man standing next to him had interrupted their conversation, he knew exactly who the man was.

Summer's boss was thin, with his arms and most of his legs covered in top-of-the-line rash guard swimwear, he stood proudly in his sandals and more than a liberal amount of sunscreen that was likely upwards of SPF 80, and the look on his face was no nonsense. "I'm going to the locker room to change and I'll be ready to go back to the office, Miss Maitland." He lowered his chin to give Kai a look. "That is if you're done with your conversation."

Standing up at the table, Kai held out his hand. "Kai Akina, sir. Good to meet you."

Shifting his towel to his left arm, the other man gave his hand a surprisingly hearty shake. "Elton West, Mister Akina. I trust that you'll be a gentleman, sir."

Kai had never quite met a man like Elton West before, but he kind of liked the not-so-subtle guard dog energy that rolled off of him. "Well, I'll try," he offered, "but I'm bound to mess up something, sometime."

Elton gave him a look from head to toe and back again. "Try harder, young man." Then he looked at Elodie. "Mrs. Webber. So lovely to see you again, but if you'll excuse me." He walked away from the table with his head held high and his pool towel hanging over his arm as if it was something fancy instead.

Kai saw Summer's mouth was as wide open as her eyes were.

"I've never seen him act like that before."

"He's just watching out for you." Kai's grin grew wider. "I guess he thinks I'm dangerous."

Something in her eyes caught his attention, but he wasn't sure exactly what it meant. He wasn't going to waste time wondering about it either.

"Do you still want me to teach you to swim? I'd love to." He held out his hand to her. "Can I have your phone number?"

Summer looked at his empty hand. "Do you want me to put it in your phone?"

"It's in my locker, but I'll remember it if you tell me what it is."

He saw her hesitate for a moment before she gave him her phone number.

And he repeated it right back to her a moment later.

Elodie gave him a curious, narrowed look. "You sure you're going to remember that?"

Kai pointed his thumb back over his shoulder. "The locker's only on the other side of the pool, but even if it was a long walk from here, I'd remember the number."

"Oh?" Elodie's laughter made her words brighter in tone. "Why's that?"

He focused his eyes on Summer again and felt his heart pounding loudly in his chest. "Because it's yours."

The color in Summer's skin rose and her hand lifted gently to rub at the nape of her neck. "Okay, then I'll uh… talk to you later?"

"Tonight." He turned slightly as she started to walk by

him, smiling at the heightened color that was spreading to her temples. "I'll call you tonight."

He swore he saw her look back at him as she turned to walk out of the gate and into the parking lot.

As soon as she was out of sight, Kai could feel Elodie poking him in his uninjured side.

"Look at you," Elodie gave him a big, girlish grin. "Getting her number as smooth as you please."

He draped an arm over her shoulders and laughed when she grabbed his towel and pushed it into his chest.

"Get dried off so we can go."

"Yes, ma'am." Kai danced back a step when she tried to land an elbow in his side, but he leaned closer a moment later and pressed a kiss to the top of her head. "You're the best wingman ever."

"Wing-woman," she gloated at him. "And don't you forget it."

CHAPTER 4

Summer had just dropped her keys in the little bowl by her front door when her phone chimed in her bag.

She didn't have a lot of people calling her or texting her. Her parents had their own chime. Her brother's was some kind of video game jingle. Even work had its own little blip of music.

Unless it was some random marketing company sending her a 2 for 1 coupon, there really was only one person who could be sending her a message.

Taking a long, slow breath, Summer ducked out of her messenger bag's strap and sat down on her futon, folding her legs under her. As she reached into her bag, the phone bumped up against her finger as the chime sounded again, vibrating the phone with a distinctive hum.

Leaning back against the pillows she swiped open the messenger app.

UNKNOWN:Are you home yet?

SUMMER: Just walked in the door.

UNKNOWN: Have time to talk?

UNKNOWN: About swimming.

UNKNOWN: And a bikini.

Summer laughed out loud.

SUMMER: Are you going to wear a one piece or two?

The three little dots that had already been dancing on her phone screen stopped and started again. And stopped.

UNKNOWN:

A picture popped up of Kai, his brow furrowed in confusion and the rest of his expression was as funny as it was handsome.

She shook her head. "How do you do that?"

Before she answered him, she used the photo to add him to her contacts knowing that she could probably get another one later, but there was just something so appealing about a guy as good looking as Kai who had no problem showing a lighter side of himself.

Guys that good looking usually wanted people to see the sexy, social media dating service side of themselves.

SUMMER: I thought you were telling me what you were going to wear. I'll probably borrow Elton's wet suit thingy and a snorkel.

KAI: Nothing that fancy. T-shirt and shorts are fine.

She started typing while she laughed.

SUMMER: Uh no. I need all the Lycra I can get. Or maybe something Victorian?

KAI:

She watched the dots start and stop two… three times and then it stopped.

"Great." Sighing, she laid her head back and looked up at the popcorn textured ceiling. "Socially Awkward Scientist – Zero points."

Summer set the phone down at her side and reached for the remote on her coffee table only to drop it back down when her phone rang.

Turning a little, she tucked one leg up on the futon and picked up her phone.

KAI CALLING

A phone call could be good.

A phone call could be bad.

Then again, doing nothing was probably worse. After all, he knows she's home. But, her mind argued, you could say you were in the bathroom.

Gross.

She scoffed at herself. She regularly handled the remains of dead people. A bathroom wasn't all that gross.

Except Kai had no idea what she did on a regular basis, did he?

What would he think of that?

Nothing if you don't answer the phone.

Before she could think better or worse of the idea, Summer picked up her phone and answered the call.

"Hey."

"I was worried it was something I said," he began, "or didn't say."

Her cheeks burned a little. Why? She didn't know.

Maybe it was the fact that his voice sounded so close. Like he was sitting right beside her. Swallowing, she tried to explain. "I thought it was me. You stopped typing and I realized that my comment was pretty lame."

His laughter made her smile as well. "It wasn't lame, just… thought provoking."

Before she could say anything, he continued.

"You said Victorian, and my mind gave me a couple of very interesting images. A corset was the first."

He wasn't laughing anymore, and she lifted her free hand to her cheek as she blushed.

"And the other?"

"Victoria's Secret."

She couldn't find a thing to say about that idea.

"I'm pretty far off on both of those ideas, right?"

Summer didn't know what to say.

"Aaaand that's me putting my foot in my mouth."

"No," she blurted out the denial. "I mean… Ugh. I'm no good at this."

"Good at… what?"

She leaned into the phone and looked at the floor. Talk about proving her own point without saying a word.

"You don't have to be good at anything, Summer. You just have to be you. I think you're pretty amazing already."

His words shocked her a little.

More than a little.

"You don't know me."

"I know enough," he sounded so sure.

"How-"

"I know."

She tucked her other leg up onto the futon, cuddling into herself. Worrying. Over what? Worrying that he didn't mean it? Or that she didn't deserve it? Or-

"What's got you so worried, Summer? I promise you, I'm a good teacher. I gave lessons all the time before my injury. I'm giving more now that I'm almost healed."

She heard the encouraging tone of his voice and wondered why she was making this difficult. Especially when he was making it so easy.

If she had been sitting there beside him, maybe she'd never say the words.

In fact, she knew she wouldn't say the words if he was there.

It was one thing to lay bare a rather embarrassing part of herself on the phone, it would be quite another to do it with his eyes on her. With her knowing that she could look into his eyes and he would see how odd she was inside.

"I trust you as a teacher." That was true. "That's not why this is a bad idea."

"It's not. It's not a bad idea. Look," she heard something in his voice that she couldn't identify, "forget the swimming for now. How about dinner?"

She opened her mouth to speak.

"Lunch?" He wasn't leaving her much space in between. "Breakfast? Coffee?"

"Hey!" Summer laughed and felt the tension in her shoulders ease. "Are you going to let me answer?"

"I wanted to make sure you had a bunch of choices, so you'd pick one."

"And I did."

Maybe it was wishful thinking, but she imagined a smile on his face.

And it looked good on him.

"Are you going to tell me which one we're going to start with?"

His words startled her enough that she had to go over them in her head a second time. "Start with?"

"Yeah."

The warmth and ease in his voice made everything seem so easy.

"It's better to think positive at times like this. Nothing wrong with getting to know each other before you... What's the phrase? Take the plunge? Maybe you just need to know a little more about me to know what I know about you."

Summer shook her head, trying to wrap her mind around what he was saying. "What?"

"There's something about you, Summer Maitland. Something that makes me want to get to know you. And I don't want to waste any time."

Time.

Wow.

That word hit her smack dab in her gut where it hurt.

That night, sitting in that muddy pit, trying to sleep and failing miserably because she was just too damn afraid.

And yet, he was right. She needed something more from him, but it wasn't that she didn't trust him to teach her. The last thing she wanted to do around Kai was put on anything that was skintight. No use frightening him away before he liked her, hopefully for more than just some physical attraction.

"I guess, dinner would be good. Right?"

She cringed. She really sounded decisive.

"I'll take it."

He didn't seem to mind how hesitant she sounded.

"What about tomorrow night?"

"Tomorrow night?" She pulled in a breath and shook her head. He certainly wasn't wasting any time.

"I don't know what your work schedule is like, but it's a good place to start."

"Yeah, I can meet you for dinner tomorrow night." It surprised her how easy it was to agree. "Where should I meet you?"

There was a little hesitation on his end. "You're not going to let me pick you up?"

And now a hesitation on her end too. "I'll need to change after work." It was true, but not the whole truth. She didn't want to say, 'I'll be up to my elbows in bones and DNA reports all day.' That would be a whole lot of creepy. Right?

"Where do you want to go? Someplace you want to try? A favorite place?"

"How about you pick somewhere near Pearl or Aiea? Your choice."

She heard him laugh, more of a chuckle really, and the sound warmed her through and through.

"You're going to let me choose? I like this." His voice had

been full of humor at first and then it changed. Deeper and softer, with a tone in it that sounded like he was sharing a secret with her. "I like you, Summer Maitland."

She drew in a breath and let it out as her heart seemed to swell inside her chest. "I like you too."

The silence that fell between them wasn't uncomfortable in the least. It felt like they were sharing that moment together.

"Tomorrow," he reminded her. "You let me know when you'll be done with work and I'll send you the details for dinner."

"Okay," she smiled and said her goodbyes. She was going to need to get some sleep. She was really looking forward to tomorrow.

The early morning wake up didn't bother Ajax. As the leader of his Delta Team stationed out of Schofield Barracks, Jackson Guard was always of a mind that he should be the first to show up, the first to wake up, and that meant putting up with a lot of his team's guff earlier than he'd like. There were other benefits to crawling out of the warmth of his sleeping bag earlier than the others. He liked to be the first one to get a cup of coffee. And he who brewed the coffee gets the biggest cup.

He had his gear packed up and in the truck before anyone else bothered to crawl out of their sleeping bags.

Shado scrubbed his hand over his face and gave him a dirty look. "What time is it?"

Ajax looked at his friend and shook his head. "You have a watch on your wrist."

"What?" Shado grumbled at him and pulled his arm from the warm confines and extended his arm in Ajax's direction with his middle finger on prominent display. "This wrist?"

"Will you two shut the hell up?"

Something sailed through the air and landed in the iron-rich red dirt a few inches in front of Shado's face, dimming the grin on his face.

Turning in the direction it came from, Ajax saw Baron drop his head onto his forearm. His gravelly voice was still audible even though it was directed into the hard-packed dirt under him. "Someone's going to have to wash that."

Shado scoffed at his words. "You mean you are going to have to wash that."

"Why?" Baron turned his head until he looked across the camp at Shado. "It's your socks."

Shado's rather colorful reply was muffled by laughter. Cullen Andrews crept out of his sleeping bag while Mace took a moment to stretch, giving them all a baleful look.

"There better be enough coffee for all of us."

"Ajax made it." Shado smiled as he grabbed up his socks and started to dust off the red dirt. "So, you probably have a chance to get some."

Cullen rubbed a hand over his dark blond hair and shook his head, letting a yawn stretch the muscles in his jaw. "Not if Baron gets to it before me."

The eldest of the group, Malcom 'Baron' Roth gave a slow, one-shoulder shrug. "Then don't be a lazy asshole, asshole."

Cullen grumbled under his breath but didn't say a thing. They all knew that Baron tended to let his bark do most of his speaking for him. If he hadn't gotten his name for the stiff-upper-lip calm that he maintained during the Delta's Q course, he might have been crowned 'Oscar' or 'Grouch' by the Deltas in his group. It was only his luck that he'd acquired his name before joining Ajax's team.

Pulling the ties on his sleeping bag, Mace slid a sideways look at Baron before meeting Ajax's curious stare. "Sometimes I think it would just be easier to leave him behind at times like this."

Ajax had to agree. "He'll just have to carry his weight when we get to the teaching aspect of our work later." Commander Chastain had asked them to run a CCD session for a platoon who had shown exemplary teamwork during a recent emergency situation and Ajax had asked his team to volunteer to make it into as fun of an event as possible, for the platoon as well as themselves.

But as it happened with many things, the actual execution was less fun than the idea of it had been.

"Remind me," Baron flopped over on his back and stared up at the lightening sky, "whose idea it was that we do this so early in the morning?"

Shado barely held in his laughter. "It was you." He touched the toe of his boot to Baron's side and danced away fast enough to avoid being pulled down to the ground.

"He was worried about getting another sunburn, but I don't see what the problem is, just take shelter under some of the bushes." Mace had no problem poking at his friend with his verbal barbs, it was the same with all of them.

"Where's the challenge in that?" Baron sat up and began to wiggle out of his sleeping bag. "Fine. Y'all are going to pick on me until I get up so I'm getting up."

"It doesn't matter what we do, man. You're always going to make yourself the easy target when you grump and growl at us."

Baron wasn't willing to give up the point. "Let's make it a contest between us too."

Ajax saw everyone perk up at the idea. His team was nothing if not competitive amongst themselves, it was how they kept in such great shape during PT sessions and out of them. "What do you have in mind?"

Baron cocked his head to the side. "You serious about this?"

"If you give us a good enough idea."

Standing up a little too fast, Baron grabbed onto Shado's shoulder and almost pulled him off of his feet. "Last one found picks PT location and activity."

The group had circled up and there were more than enough interested and yes, potentially even smiles that made their way around.

"Sure," Mace shrugged, "I know it won't be Baron winning. He'll probably give himself away when he starts snoring."

Cullen's laughter burst out and the others joined him, including Mace whose laughter wasn't as loud as his pointed look in Baron's direction.

Train, who had been silent until then piped up. "And first one found, does that last round here at the site to make sure we're all clean."

Ajax smiled and took another sip of his coffee. "Fine by me. We're a stone's throw from the new National Historic site and we're not going to make or leave a mess." The others nodded their agreement. "Make sure all of you have your places picked out and your supplies. Once the Commander calls and tells me they're fifteen minutes out, we'll all take our places. I intend to win."

Baron huffed out a breath. "You can't win, you're team leader."

Mace cuffed him on the shoulder. "He's participating just like the rest of us, you're just jealous cause he has a pretty reason to go home tonight."

Ajax nodded. He did. Everyone knew it.

Cullen jumped up to his feet and shook off his sleeping

bag. "That's because you have a fiancé who can't wait for you to come home."

Train's brow furrowed. "I thought she said she's filming today."

Ajax finished the last of his coffee. "You probably know her schedule better than I do. Yeah, she's filming today at Diamond Head Studios but just until mid-day. She'll probably beat me home." Ajax saw Train's expression turn a little glum. "When do you see Ku`uipo next?" His friend had fallen for a woman who lived most of the time on the island of Kauai and her job kept her there.

"Next weekend she's coming in to guest lecture at a few schools about their hospitality program at the hotel. When she's not working and I'm not working we'll… uh-"

Baron put his hand over his heart and sighed. "Out of the house! Great! Hallelujah."

Train gave his friend a glowering look. "Nice, man. Nice."

After Ajax and Hi`ilani had found their own apartment, Shado had moved into the house on base with Train and Baron, taking Jackson's room. Even with three bedrooms, the old bungalow style only included one bathroom and that didn't work for two bachelors and a couple.

Ajax circled his index finger in the air. "Wrap it up, guys. Get your gear packed-up and let's get ready for the exercise."

As Baron started to walk away, he grumbled at Ajax. "Did you have to call it that?"

Mace pushed a mug of coffee into Baron's hands. "Just get moving."

Baron called after him. "Awww, honey, you're so sweet."

As crazy as it sounded, Ajax wouldn't trade his band of misfit children for anything. They were his misfit children even when he wanted to kick a few of them in the-

"Ajax? We've got some uninvited guests."

He heard the edge in Cullen's voice and turned back around.

Much of the area where they were had been cleared at one time or another, left to grow back in for awhile before plants were cut back again. Preparations for the expanded area and scope of the National Historic Site had called for the place to be cleaned and marked for different reasons. The whole area was in a type of gulch with climbing hills and mountain walls all around, but the forests that came down to the site weren't just picturesque and lush, they were the home for wild animals.

Some of which had decided to make an appearance as dawn was approaching.

"Kind of cute." Shado pointed out the trio of baby pigs venturing out of the tree line. "You looking for a pet, Ajax?"

Ajax shook his head. "Not at the moment. Neither one of us is home enough for that, but a pig?"

"Boar." Baron interjected his comment.

"Why yes," Train gave his friend a wink, "you are a bore."

Baron didn't even bother to turn his head. "Wild boar."

It was true. A good ten feet away from the trio of babies was a full-grown adult boar complete with jutting bone-white tusks. They didn't look like much, but Ajax had seen pictures of the damage boars could do a human body if given the chance.

Mace was the closest one to the truck as far as Ajax could see in his peripheral vision. "Sir? We have arms in the truck. You want me to-"

"No live ammunition."

Shado nodded his agreement. "We don't have any idea what's in the woods."

Baron grumbled at him. "What are we going to do?"

The adult boar trotted further into the clearing, snuffling at the ground here and there.

"We have rubber bullets, Ajax." Cullen was on the other side of the truck. "I can load and be ready in minutes."

"Let's just watch for a minute. They might head back into the woods in a few."

The group stood quietly, letting the boars move around near the brush and overgrown weeds.

The three little ones seemed to give up on the sunlight and moved back into the subtle darkness at the edge of the trees.

The adult boar wasn't daunted in the least and moved forward, lowering its head behind a larger shrub near the tree line.

The men stayed still watching carefully as the bush shook a few times.

"What do you think he's doing back there?" Shado's voice was soft, and Ajax had to tilt his head to see that Shado had moved up beside him. The man had an uncanny way of moving silently. Stealth was just his way. "It sounds like he's digging at something back there."

"I'll get eyes on it."

Baron moved off to the side and Ajax waved him off.

Always on the edge of insubordination, Baron continued, moving off to the side. "Clear line of sight, Ajax."

"What's happening?"

"He's digging something up all right. Having to work hard at it too. Snout and hooves digging around in the dirt."

The bush shook again, almost jumping at one point.

Ajax saw Baron reach for his knife and felt his jaw tighten.

"You going to have me write you up today, man?"

"Like you would." Baron's tone wasn't his usual snark, it wasn't even ill tempered. It was slow, cautious, and level. "I've got to stop him, sir. I see a hand."

Everyone around the camp tensed as the words painted a new picture for them.

"Are you sure?"

"I'm sure." There it was, that cool, imperious tone that meant he was fixed on a target. "Ajax?"

"Drop him."

The movement of the knife through the air was just a glint of light out of the corner of Jackson's eye. The sound of the blade sinking into flesh was unmistakable.

The boar almost howled with pain, a short squeal that ended with a heavy thud that shook the bush again.

Cullen anticipated the order and came up on Ajax's left. Mace on the other. Both held their firearms at the ready, waiting for orders.

Ajax took point, moving forward toward the bush where the boar had fallen.

"Spread out. Be ready to fire."

He knew the rounds would do their fair share of damage to the boar if they were needed.

As they approached the bush, Ajax moved over to the side, knowing that Baron would cover him as needed.

The boar was unmoving as it lay in the dirt. Blood and iron-rich soil mingled together to create a darker clay, pooling under the boar's mouth like red saliva on its hide.

Ajax saw Baron's knife handle protruding from the boar's eye.

It was a damn good throw.

A clean kill.

That left Ajax with the ability to investigate what Baron had seen.

A hand.

Ajax said a prayer that the boar hadn't gored someone, leaving them injured. He still approached as carefully as he could. He'd never dealt with a boar before, and he trusted his men to watch his back in case more emerged from the woods.

He crouched down beside the bush and used his hand to push the lower branches away from the ground. Once he did that, Ajax realized that as much as he hoped that Baron had been wrong, the other Delta had been right.

The boar had bitten a hand and a wrist. The only good thing about it was that the person it belonged to didn't feel any pain. There was no chance that the body had any life left in it with large holes that had been torn into clothing and flesh. The one saving grace of the moment was that the face was still covered with soil.

He just didn't want to stare into lifeless eyes as he pulled his phone from his back pocket and dialed up his Commander. It picked up on the second ring. "Sir? We have a problem."

CHAPTER 5

Summer had a good start on the excavation before the coroner's van pulled up at the end of the dirt road. Taking a moment to stop, she removed her gloves and tossed them in the bucket she kept nearby. When she got back to the lab, she would check for anything she might have missed or any evidence that might have been stuck to the gloves.

When you're searching for clues at gravesites and more… impromptu resting sites, it's impossible to tell what would be helpful in the investigation.

As Summer made her way over to the van, she saw another vehicle pulling up behind it. The older gentlemen who stepped down from the passenger side of the van gave her a wave and a smile.

"Summer!"

"Doctor Chang. Thank you for coming so quickly."

He shook her hand and asked her a question in almost a whisper. "Should I worry about your armed guards?"

She shook her head and quickly introduced the Deltas. "They were the ones that found the remains."

The doctor looked impressed. "And took down a wild

boar?" Settling his glasses higher on his nose, he turned and gestured at the two people heading in their direction. "Have you met these detectives before?"

Summer looked at the two making their way over to the van and shook her head. "No, I haven't." She reached out her hand. "Summer Maitland. Nice to meet you."

The man reached her first. He held out his hand and gave her a solid shake. "Detective Clive Hernandez, Homicide."

He let go of her hand but didn't move aside.

Summer stepped to the side to greet the other detective, a woman.

She gave Summer a smile and a nod before they shook hands. "Olena Yasui, Homicide."

Between the two, Summer felt a bit of a connection to Olena. She had a pleasant expression and seemed to be a little more relaxed than her partner.

"I'll show all of you to the site, but I'm still not sure if this is my jurisdiction or yours, Herman. The remains are fairly desiccated but I'm not sure this falls under the HPD or our command. I managed to uncover enough to see that he's wearing a military uniform, but-"

The male detective, Clive, stepped in front of her and held up a hand. "You touched the body?"

Summer drew up short in surprise at the sudden movement, but it was only the first of a string.

Someone took her by the shoulders and pulled her back and someone else stepped in front of her.

By the time her mind caught up to her change in position, she recognized Cullen's short cropped blond hair. He was the only one on the team with his coloring, so she didn't have to see his face to know, but she heard his voice clearly enough. "You watch yourself, man."

"She touched the body!"

One of the hands on her shoulders released and tapped

on Cullen's arm, moving him just a hint. The voice behind her was a bit of a shock. Baron.

"The touching started with the big pig and I bet it wasn't the first thing to nose around so you might want to think about your tone, *Detective*."

Baron clipped the word into three distinct syllables even though his own tone was pretty light. He was still making his own thoughts very clear on the subject. A subject that Summer was pretty grateful for.

When Summer spoke, she addressed the female detective, sensing that she might actually consider her words instead of a knee-jerk reaction.

"This whole area is included in the Honouliuli Historic Site." She hoped she wouldn't have to explain the whole thing to the detectives, but there were times when what Summer considered something common knowledge only to be proved wrong. Considering that she spent most of her life mired in the past, she might be expecting a little too much.

The Coroner spoke first, looking between both detectives. "It's the site of the internment camp that they opened in Nineteen Forty-Three. We're standing on just a little part of the original acreage. Over a hundred and fifty acres of land, a few hundred tents and over a dozen guard towers."

Summer really couldn't imagine the size of it from where she stood. The brush and invasive plants had eaten up anything that might have been left behind when the camp closed up. Still, the military uniform on the body in the ground made her wonder if this was an authentic find or something else.

Detective Hernandez had folded his arms across his chest, pulling his dark HPD polo shirt across his arms. "You think the body they found might be from the war?"

Doctor Chang turned to look at Summer. "Well, that's up to Summer. She would have a better grasp on that than I would. She's been instrumental in identifying a number of MIA soldiers from around the Pacific." His smile was quickly becoming one of her favorite sights. "This is her area of expertise and me?" he looked at the Deltas standing protectively near her, "I'm not going to challenge these men."

Before Detective Hernandez could say a word, the other detective spoke up. "Thanks for inviting us in… is it Doctor Maitland?"

Summer appreciated the question, but she didn't stand on ceremony. Titles weren't thrown around all that much at the lab. Except when she called Elton 'Sir' to make him grimace and then smile. "Summer is fine. Detective Yasui?"

"Olena is fine."

From her side, Summer heard Cullen's voice grumble almost under his breath. "Beautiful."

"Olena," Summer gestured toward the site, "if you'd like to follow me, I can show you what I've uncovered so far. It's been a little slow with the damage done by the boar, I have to be careful to look out for small bits and pieces. You never know what's going to be helpful in making an identification."

As they moved through the brush, Summer saw Olena just behind her, easily working through the brush and ruts in the earth. Detective Hernandez was a few feet behind, picking his way through with a little more care.

Back at the coroner's van, she'd noticed that Detective Hernandez had nice leather shoes. Perfect for working in an office or on the street, but in the rich soil of the gulch, his smooth-soled leather shoes weren't going to make walking easy.

Olena spoke and Summer slowed down to make it easier to reply.

"Was there a lot of damage to the remains?"

Summer's shrug was even more hesitant than normal. "It's going to take a bit to figure out what damage was from animal predation and what comes from Mother Nature. The wear on the ground," she slowed as they walked around to the far side of the large bush that had shielded the remains from view, "is uneven. What's visible of the remains makes the interment look as if it was rushed? The hole's too shallow to hide it for any real period of time. One big season of rain or a large tropical storm and it might have been uncovered just like that. I'm not sure what we're looking at right now."

She heard someone cough or clear their throat and Summer suspected that it was the other detective, but she wasn't sure. When she looked at Olena she saw the other woman's narrowed glare and a tight muscle in her jaw. It must be Detective Hernandez.

"I'm not a fan of making random guesses when I've had less than a few hours of time working on the site. Sure, I can guess, but without uncovering more of the remains and seeing the head and the rest of the limbs I could make a comment that might send you off on a wild goose chase."

"And just how long," the detective made it clear in his tone that he'd already waited long enough, "would that kind of an investigation take?"

Summer had to think about it. Without reservation, she turned to look at the coroner. Doctor Chang had been one of the first people she'd met when she'd moved to the islands, outside of the people on base. He'd always been as encouraging as he was validating. He treated her like his equal without question and she adored him because of that.

"I can call in a few more staffers from the lab and they can help me uncover more of the remains. I would hope to give you a strong recommendation by the evening if that's the case."

Doctor Chang reached out a hand toward her. "I might be able to speed things along if you don't mind me giving you some help."

At her hesitation, he laughed. "Don't let me hear you making any jokes about this old man getting down and dirty. I did a summer at an archaeology site in Colorado. I think I could be pretty handy with a brush and a trowel."

Summer couldn't help but laugh. "That would be great. It would save us time too." She paused for a moment, curious. "You don't have something waiting for you back at the office?"

The coroner and Olena exchanged a look before he answered. "Not at the moment. We're… waiting for something, but we're stuck for now."

There was a story there, but Summer didn't want to waste time standing around. They could talk and work at the same time.

As they walked up to the remains, Olena winced a little. "It's a little…"

"Gross."

Summer turned and saw that Cullen was only a few steps away from them. And when he saw her looking at him, he shrugged. "Someone's got to watch your backs for more pigs."

"Then maybe," Ajax's voice held more than a note of laughter in it, "you should face the woods?"

Cullen's shrug only served to emphasize the muscles under his army green T-shirt. "I guess that would be helpful."

Baron shrugged. "I'm the one who dropped the pig."

Shado clapped a hand down on his shoulder. "Takes one to know one, man." He hopped back before Baron could grab him. "You walked right into that one."

The mood darkened when Detective Hernandez blew out a breath and looked back over his shoulder. "Until we have a definitive answer about who we have here, I've got other cases to work on." He looked at Olena. "You coming?"

She didn't hesitate. "I'll stay. I think we might have something here. I can bag and tag at the very least." Olena looked back at Summer. "If you need or want any help."

"Absolutely." Summer hadn't thought of it in the way that Olena had. "You have experience collecting evidence and that would be a huge help. I can focus on other things."

Grinning back at Summer, Olena reached into the pocket of her slacks and pulled out a hair tie. "I'll go back to the car and grab my kit."

Summer didn't miss the glare in Detective Hernandez's eye, but if Olena wasn't going to say anything she wouldn't either.

As the Detectives walked back to their vehicle, Summer could see the tension between them. The way that Detective Hernandez leaned closer as he spoke, or rather, as he lectured, didn't escape her notice and it didn't escape anyone else paying attention.

And Cullen?

He was paying attention.

When he took a step in their direction, Summer saw Ajax reach out.

"Give her some space."

Cullen's face spoke volumes, but he didn't push past his team leader.

Summer turned and reached for a new pair of gloves from her own kit. When Cullen looked in her direction she smiled. "He's right, you know."

She didn't miss Ajax's grin as she explained her words to Cullen.

"I mean, you didn't ask me, but I don't think either one of them would have wanted you to step in. There's an odd power structure between men and women in the same jobs. She doesn't need you to step in and tip the scales for her."

Summer pulled on her gloves and got down onto the padded mat she'd left in place at the site. Doctor Chang joined her as his assistant and driver went back to the van for some supplies of their own. They weren't going to help with the evidence collection, but they would be great help in discovering the cause of death and looking for hints about the person themselves.

It might sound a little ghoulish, but the more time you spend around corpses and cadavers the more you learned to glean from them.

Doctor Chang leaned in to examine the remains and nodded. "This is going to be interesting whether it's one of yours or one of mine."

Summer nodded in agreement. "At least here, I'm not worried about being thrown in with the body."

Biting into her bottom lip, she ducked her head and looked down at her gloved hands. She hadn't meant to mention anything about her last assignment that was still stuck in some red tape, but she'd opened her mouth and out it came.

Chuckling to herself, Summer realized that she'd make a horrible criminal, likely to spill her guts if she was questioned.

When she started to explain the work she'd already done, she met the doctor's curious gaze and saw the way that Mace had leaned in closer, but instead of looking at the remains he was watching her carefully.

They may not have asked her about her off-handed comment, yet, but she knew the time would come. She just didn't know when. Working with so many amazing people was one of the side benefits of her job, but she knew where her main focus was. The remains still partially covered in earth before her had a name and hopefully a family looking for them. Every identification she made felt like she was reuniting a family. It didn't mean she was filling the gap they'd left when they went missing, but maybe it will make a difference to bring them home.

With the additional help she knew she'd make a lot of progress quickly. The others in the lab were already actively working on other remains and until she knew more it didn't make sense to call them in.

She made a mental note to send Kai a message if it looked like she was going to be in the field for more than a few hours. It wasn't a matter of wanting to beg off of dinner, but she knew this might end up being a long and exhausting day.

Opening the door to his apartment, Frank Ritter had to brace himself. He'd forgotten to stop by the store again for oil or WD40 to fix the nerve-rattling screech of the rusted hinges on the door.

He would have called the maintenance man if he wasn't already a nosy asshole who liked to stick his nose in where it didn't belong. It wasn't that Frank gave him the time of day, but his granddad liked to jaw a little too much for their own good.

Grinding his back teeth together, Frank pushed the door open and stepped inside, closing it as quickly as he could to minimize the noise.

If he was lucky, his granddad had fallen asleep and was out cold.

"Boy? That you?"

Frank shut his eyes and shook his head. "Yeah, it's me."

Forcing a smile onto his face he walked into the main room of the tiny studio apartment they were sharing. "Hey, Pops."

The old man sitting in the lounger glared at him. "Don't

'Hey, Pops,' me! Where the hell have you been! I'm hungry and you didn't leave any damn food in here!"

Frank let out a breath. "I made you breakfast before I left. There's sandwich stuff in the icebox. Chips in the cupboard." As he said the words, he walked into the tiny kitchen area and stared at the mess he saw on the counter. An open bag of chips sat on the counter, likely stale if his granddad had left it open. Beside it was an open bag of bread, a few pieces flopped out onto the lip of the bag and the scarred countertop. The package of cold cuts open beside it still looked full.

Touching it with his hand told him how screwed he was. It was warm to the touch and likely on its way to being rancid.

Scrubbing his hand over his face, Frank enjoyed the scratch of his growing beard. The pain was better than the anger that rose up in him.

"Looks like you started to make yourself a sandwich, Pops. Did you forget it?" He saw the way the old man leaned forward, squinting at the TV even though his glasses were on top of his head. "Pops? You listening to-"

"Shut the hell up and make us something to eat."

Dropping the shopping bag down on the counter, Frank tossed the cold cuts in the trash and the couple of slices of bread that seemed almost stale. Regretting it the moment he was done. He could have toasted the damn things, but that didn't matter. He wasn't about to go around digging in the trash even though they were really hurting for money.

Opening the bag, he took out the groceries he'd managed to buy and set them up on the counter. He didn't have the time or energy to go out and pick up more cold cuts. He'd have to make do with the can of corned beef and the onion he'd picked up, maybe mix in some pasta. It didn't make a lick of sense, but it would be cheap and make more than a meal if he was lucky. He needed something to take for lunch the next day.

"You puttin' something together in there?"

"Yeah... yeah. I'm working on it."

"Hmph." The old man certainly was on a tear. "I don't hear nothin' and I don't smell nothin' besides my upper lip. Don't tell me you're as worthless as your mother, Thom."

Frank felt his back teeth grind together. Thom was his father. Apparently, his granddad had slipped back again. "I'm working on it, Pops. I just got home."

"Not my problem."

Grumbling under his breath, Frank let himself speak freely. "Nothing ever is, old man. Nothing ever is."

He started to cook up their meal, letting his ears focus on the TV on the other side of the tiny space.

The news was on. The anchor wearing a fancy Aloha shirt like they always did. It wasn't long before the pasta was boiling and he'd cooked up the onions, readying himself to dump the opened can of corned beef into the pan. He almost missed it, his mind set on producing something he could eat that wouldn't suck all that much for the sake of his stomach and his ears if his granddad started complaining again.

But something in the newscast caught his attention. Turning his head a moment later.

"...and while we weren't allowed to observe the work going on at the Historic Site, we were told by an assistant from the coroner's office that there were human remains found there. The mystery revolving around the sudden discovery is whether or not the remains are from World War II or a more recent death."

The other anchor sat back and nodded thoughtfully like he gave a shit. "I'm sure we'll hear a lot more about this as things develop. Surely something this mysterious will garner a lot of attention in the community."

The first man tapped his hands on the desktop, turning the focus back to himself. "There hasn't been much said about the progression of work at the site. We can't ignore the idea that whoever they found there could add to the long and sad history of the events after the attack on Pearl Harbor."

Frank caught sight of his granddad as he stood from the lounger, his eyes almost sparkling with glee.

"Sounds like we made the news, son."

Nodding his head, Frank tried to ignore the way his heart pounded in his chest, but he couldn't. Not when his forehead prickled with sweat, and his hands started to shake.

If it was the man they'd put out there, then things would have to move faster. His granddad's step stumbled as he lurched toward the tiny table they had near the kitchen. The old man caught himself on the table with his hand and all but fell onto a chair.

"See, son? You can manage to get a few things done with my help. Get the chow on the table and we'll talk when we're finished eating. We've got a few more folks on my list and then we'll be done."

Frank looked down in time to see the contents of the pan smoldering, about to catch fire. "Fuck." He turned off the burner and put the pan aside. He was really getting fed up with the whole plan, but he understood his granddad's anger. How he'd been betrayed by the military he'd served. Frank had grown up listening to his stories, feeling the anger and rage in the older man.

He didn't really relish the things they'd done.

The things they were going to do.

But he wanted to give his granddad peace before he died.

That time was coming soon. The disease in his head and the one in his liver set the clock ticking faster than it should have.

They'd finish his list and then he'd put his granddad to rest and move the hell back to civilization.

"Son? Where the hell's my supper?"

"Coming, Pops. It's coming."

Summer put her car in park and sat still, letting herself breathe for a few moments before trying to get out. Her arms and legs ached, and she could feel the beginnings of a sunburn on her skin.

She'd been careful with sun exposure, but she'd probably sweated off some of the SPF and hadn't put any back on after a hasty meal that a couple of the soldiers brought to them from Times Supermarket's Deli.

Scarfing down the food was as satisfying as it was desperate. Beside her, she'd seen the Delta Team with their own meals and the odd additions of Doctor Chang, his assistant, and Detective Yasui. It was a world away from eating at the lab where people rarely ate at the same time and maybe it was just the fluorescent lights that made it hard to talk about much of anything or be at all social.

Sitting in the shade of some trees, she'd managed to enjoy herself a little and get to know the others more than she ever had.

Her phone on the center console lit up with a reminder for dinner.

It was a pain, really. She thought she'd cleared out all the memos for that.

She'd messaged Kai a few hours before letting him know that she was called to an unexpected assignment for work.

Summer hadn't mentioned her work when they'd met, and she was almost sure that Elodie hadn't either. And Kai? He hadn't asked.

She hoped he didn't think she was just trying to brush him off, but she really wasn't in any shape to go out to dinner.

Spending hours on her knees. Digging her toes into the hard packed dirt to lean over the remains had left aches in her feet, calves, and thighs.

Even sitting there in her car with the air conditioning on she felt like she was baking in an oven.

A quick look in the rearview mirror told her she was right. She was pink in a way that wasn't a blush, not that she did much of that. She had dirt on her skin, the iron-rich, orange-red soil left light streaks on her face even after she'd gone over and over her face with wet-wipes.

She looked pretty gross.

And she felt that way too.

Looking down at the phone in her hand, Summer unlocked it and opened her phone app. As much as she wasn't a 'talk on the phone' person, she really didn't want Kai to think she didn't want to see him.

If anything, spending the day in the dirt uncovering remains had reminded her again that life came and went.

Seeing Kai again?

She didn't want to miss out on that.

The phone picked up on the first ring.

"Summer?"

She smiled, enjoying the warmth she heard in his voice. "Yeah. Is this a good time?"

His laughter made her heart pound harder in her chest.

"Talking to you? Anytime. Are you home?"

Summer nodded and then followed it up with a verbal answer. One of the last texts he'd sent her after she'd all but broken their date had been to let him know she reached home safely. "I might not make it out of the car, but you'd be surprised how comfortable it can be to nap in here."

"I don't think that would be safe, would it?"

She closed her eyes and smiled. The sound of concern in his voice was like music to her ears. It was nice to have people who cared about her. "No. And I'm not serious about staying here, but my legs are aching and getting out of my car sounds like way too much activity for me."

He laughed again. "Sounds like me after my first few PT sessions. I didn't want to move for days."

Summer hesitated for a moment and then just opened her mouth to apologize. "Kai, I really am sorry about tonight. I was called out of the office and we were swamped all day. I hope you were serious about that rain check."

Then she had to wait.

And hope.

"I'm not giving up on dinner."

Her shoulders sagged with relief. His answer gave her a burst of energy and she turned off her car and picked up her purse from the passenger seat. "Great. I mean, thanks."

"Nothing to thank me for, Summer. I should say the same to you. It's not every day a beautiful woman agrees to have dinner with me."

She laughed and found it made the walk toward her apartment building more bearable. A little less painful. "I bet you have a lot of beautiful women," she grinned at the echoes of his compliment, "agreeing to have dinner with you."

He hummed in agreement. "My mother, my tutu, Elodie, and a whole bunch of cousins."

Summer reached the front door of the building and opened it with her key. As the door was closing behind her, she had a moment of regret. Sure, she was exhausted and likely crusted with dirt, but she wanted to see him.

She wanted to sit across a table and look at him. Listen to him. Laugh… with him.

Living in Hawaii was great but meeting Kai and discovering all of the feelings he was stirring up inside of her had changed things. It made her smile more. It made laughing easier.

And it seemed to make the world around her brighter, just because of him.

She'd likely be horrible company if she did go out to dinner with him, but she was selfish enough to admit that she wanted to see him.

And be seen by him.

Pulling herself together, she stepped up to the bank of elevators and pushed the UP button.

"Kai?"

"Yeah?"

"I was wondering..."

She paused as the doors opened up and she stepped inside hoping it didn't cut off the call.

"Summer? Are you still there?"

The doors closed and she looked at her phone. It didn't cut out. Little miracles.

"Yeah, I am. I was wondering if you ate already."

"Me?" She heard his warm laughter. "No. Not yet."

She opened her mouth to invite him over and stopped. The noise in the background of the call was crazy. It sounded like he was in a football stadium.

Or a bar.

Summer knew she couldn't blame him. She'd already told him she wasn't going to have dinner with him.

"Hey," she could hear him, just barely over the ambient noise, "give me a second, okay?"

"Sure." She hoped her voice didn't sound as disappointed as she felt.

The elevator stopped and she saw her floor number lit up on the console. She stepped outside as soon as the doors opened and walked across the hall to her door. Habit had her inside in a moment.

The noise seemed to fade away and almost completely disappeared.

"Sorry about that, I had to step outside."

She turned her head and stared at the wall fighting the conflicting emotions inside her. "I didn't mean to bother you."

"Hey, stop that." She swore she could hear him smile. "You're not bothering me at all. In fact, I was just about to call you."

"Me? What for? Why would you call me?"

"Well, we were supposed to have dinner tonight and I know you were working late so we couldn't go out like we planned."

"I really am sorry-"

"I'm not complaining, Summer. When I read your texts it sounded like you were exhausted. And now that I've heard your voice, I can hear it too. Worn out. I don't want to bother *you*." She could hear him smiling as he used her words with a gentle soothing warmth in his tone, and she leaned closer to the phone to listen to him, "But I was hoping you'd let me drop off dinner for you."

"You want to bring me dinner?"

"Sure. I'm guessing you're hungry."

She wanted to beg off. Nerves had suddenly shaken her, but her stomach grumbled in her belly calling her on her own lie. Nudging her to tell the truth. "I am."

"You don't have to invite me in or anything. Just tell me where to find you so I can drop this off."

"This?" Summer rolled her eyes at herself. "What is it?"

His laughter was infectious. "You said I could pick the place. And this is where I would have picked. So as long as you're not a Vegetarian or Vegan, I've got you covered." She heard the ambient noise return, building in volume. "The order is ready and as soon as I grab it, I'm getting in my car. All I need now is your address."

Summer didn't want to argue with him.

She couldn't really.

It wasn't just that she was hungry, she wanted to see him.

What kind of company she'd be when he showed up she didn't know, but she was just selfish enough to want him there at least for a few minutes.

Living, breathing, full of energy. She wanted to be near that.

Near him.

She lowered her chin to her chest and rubbed at her temples with her fingers.

What she didn't want to do is ruin his dinner and the rest of his night if she managed to infect him with her feelings.

"Summer?" His voice was almost a whisper. Tender and gentle. "Are you okay?"

"It's okay."

"No, Summer. You. Are *you* okay?"

She had to blink away the tears that gathered in her eyes. Yeah, Kai didn't need this. Her mood would just drive him away and she didn't want to do that, not when she'd just met him.

Summer couldn't help feeling like she'd really messed things up before anything ever really started.

Drawing in a breath, she knew she had to put off seeing him until… later.

Composing herself as well as her words, she forced a smile on her face in hopes that it would make her sound confident, sure of herself.

"Summer? Talk to me."

Yes. She said in her head. *I'm fine. Just not tonight.*

Simple.

Say it!

"I might not be great company."

She hadn't planned to say anything like that, but there it was, out there.

The background music and crowd sounds faded away on the phone and she imagined that he was standing outside, the phone to his ear, thinking about her like she was thinking about him.

What was he going to say?

"I'd be happy just dropping this off to you. I don't want to worry about you going hungry tonight because you're upset. You probably don't feel like cooking. If you don't want me to stay-"

"I didn't say that." She bit down onto her bottom lip and mentally shook herself. Struggling to figure out why her mouth wasn't getting with the program and knowing that deep down she was only saying what she really wanted to say. Deep down inside where she normally kept things locked away something had cracked open. Maybe it was just something that happened over the years. Or maybe it was something that had started the moment she met him.

No matter what. No matter when.

The crack was there.

And the words coming out were the truth which was even more terrifying than the easy lie she told herself on a regular basis. That she was fine just the way things were. Something that had been eating away at her since the Philippines.

"If you don't mind me being a little..." She didn't know how to say it.

"You don't have to be anything or anyone but you, Summer. Like I said, I can just drop this off. Let me do something nice for you. Maybe it'll make your day a little bit better. At the least you won't feel sick later. It won't keep you up.

"And we can talk about dinner another night."

"I bet you didn't think I'd be such a drama queen, huh?"

"Drama?" He laughed and she surprised herself by joining in. "This isn't drama, Summer. It's just real life. You're having an off day and I just want to make it a little better. You don't even have to see me."

"I want to."

Once the words were out, she felt so much better. The weight that had been hung around her shoulders was just gone. Was it so easy?

Open your mouth and say what you mean?

"I'm glad, Summer. So happy to hear you say that, but if you change your mind just say so. I'm a big boy. I won't take it personally. I just want to make sure you eat so you can get some rest. If you want to tell me what happened? Great. I'm a good listener.

"If you want to sit in silence, then I'm good with that too. What I want from you is time. A few minutes or an hour. It's all good because it's more than I had before. I don't want to scare you off, Summer. I don't want to wear out my welcome. I just want to get to know you."

She nodded, keeping that to herself in silence.

"Okay," she couldn't stop from smiling, "let me give you my address."

CHAPTER 6

Kai didn't know exactly what to expect when he arrived at Summer's apartment, but there was one thing he was sure of, he couldn't wait to see her.

It had been a gamble to head over to Dixie Grill before calling her, but she'd beaten him to it.

Sure, it could have ended badly but he had to think positively. That had gotten him this far.

Summer.

The name fit her.

Warm. Brilliant.

Especially her smile. He hadn't seen it all that much yet, but he wanted to change that.

It had been the driving need, well one of two, that had led him to order food for her just in case.

Yes, he wanted to see her, but he also wanted to make her day better. He'd easily read between the lines of her texts. He bet she was a lot like the women in his family. They kept going and going and going, taking care of their family, and excelling at their jobs. He'd grown up around so many amazing women that he probably was a better judge of women than men.

Proven painfully so by the way he'd let himself be conned into changing the route of the private charter fishing boat to make the customer happy, only to have that customer shoot him in the back and try to kill Elodie.

They'd survived that and he was almost back to full strength physically.

Inside his heart and mind though? He wasn't quite sure he had rid himself of the pain and suffering he'd gone through.

Shaking himself free of those darker thoughts he focused on what was in front of him.

Namely the door of Summer's apartment.

1101.

Breathe, man. Breathe.

Reaching out his arm, he knocked on the door.

"Summer?"

It took less than a minute for the door to open and when it did, he couldn't help but smile.

"Beautiful."

Her cheeks flushed with color and it made her almost red near her temples and at the edge of her forehead. "Thanks."

"You look like you got a lot of sun today."

Her eyes rolled a little. "A lot! Come on in." She stepped back and he moved into her apartment. She swept out her hand. "What do you think?"

He knew she was asking his opinion of her apartment, but he couldn't seem to look away from her.

Summer shrugged a little and crossed one arm across her chest to tug at her sleeve. "I'm sorry, I just pulled on something comfortable. I know it's not-"

"Don't apologize." He stepped in closer and let his eyes

roam over her face and the barely noticeable sprinkle of freckles across her nose and cheeks. "I think you look great."

The look on her face was searching, hopeful. "What? This old thing?"

"Yeah. Just like that." He gestured toward the kitchen and she nodded, following him. "I've been looking forward to seeing you again."

"Good," she countered, "because I was feeling guilty."

Kai set the bag down on the table and removed the to-go boxes and set them aside, shaking his head. "Guilty about what?"

He tried not to look right at her. The last thing he wanted her to see was how much he wanted an answer.

"I knew I wasn't going to be great company tonight. I probably won't even move after we sit down. It's just that I wanted to see you tonight."

Kai paused and looked over at her, lowering his hands to his sides. He wanted to reach out to her, but it wasn't the time. This wasn't the time to rush things.

Not when she was tired.

And hungry.

This was the time to take care of her and spend time getting to know her.

The rest?

The rest would happen. He wanted it. And he knew it.

But first things first.

"I'm really happy you changed your mind."

She leaned in and he could see her drawing in a long breath, ending with a smile. "Me too. It smells so good."

"I thought you'd like it. Elodie and Mustang took me there after one of my PT appointments and I almost inhaled the food on my plate."

"Then I really do need to eat some of this." Summer's

laughter felt like sunlight against his skin. She gestured at the covered plates on the tabletop. "Which one is mine?"

He saw the glint in her eyes, and he couldn't help himself. "You can eat it all of you want."

Summer leaned her elbows on the table. "Don't tease me, you might end up hungry."

Kai heard the warning in her voice and it only made him smile even more. "I could deal with that."

She licked her lips, and he drew in a deeper breath.

"Let's open everything up and I can tell you what you have to choose from."

He reached for a plate closer to her and she reached out, touching the back of his hand.

"Wait."

Something in the back of his head told him to relax. She might be changing her mind, but he didn't know what exactly that meant.

"Can we," she turned her head and looked over at the soft cushions on her couch, "maybe sit over there?"

"Whatever you want." It was an easy answer and the truth. Maybe he'd watched the Princess Bride a few too many times with his mother, but while he wasn't quoting Wesley exactly, he felt like he understood the feeling behind the words.

If she wanted to sit on the couch. Fine.

He just wanted this.

Time.

Together.

When he picked up the plates and stacked them up, she moved over to the refrigerator.

"What do you want to drink?"

He reached the sofa and set the plates down. "Water's great. Whatever you have."

"You're making this too easy."

He heard the humor in her voice, but he also heard some history in it as well.

"There are so many hard things we have to deal with in our lives. Why worry about the little things."

Summer handed him a glass of water and set one down on the coffee table as she curled up on the sofa. "I can't wait to see what you ordered. It all smells so good."

Yeah, he puffed up a little at that. He wanted to please her. He wanted to make her happy. It was a little crazy really.

He'd dated women in the past and it was fun. And once, he'd even thought he was in love, but there was always a distance he'd felt that he couldn't understand.

From the moment that he'd met Summer, touched her hand, he'd felt connected. Felt there was something moving between them.

He just didn't want to let that energy go.

Picking up the first plate, he opened the top of the clamshell container and set it down between them as he explained what he'd ordered. "I picked up some of everything from the smoker. And a few of their sides, fries, fried pickles, cornbread."

"Cornbread?" She sat up and craned her neck to look in the box with the sides. "Are those pieces of corn in there?"

He saw the light in her eyes, and he shook with silent laughter. "Yeah. It was the first time I'd had it that way and it was great."

She looked up at him with a curious side-eye. "You like cornbread?"

Kai shrugged. "What's not to like? It's like cake."

That had her laughing in earnest. "Yes!"

She reached out her hand and stopped with a grimace. "Sorry."

"What for?"

She turned her hand over. “Bare hands?”

Kai shrugged. “Not a problem for me. Locals? We eat a lot of things with our hands.”

Sitting up a little she gave him a narrow-eyed look. “So, you don’t mind…”

“I’ll grab the forks and stuff they put in the bag after I wash my hands.” He got up from the sofa and looked around. “Bathroom?”

Summer got up and reached for his hand.

He gave it to her without question and felt his heart jump in his chest.

She led him into the bedroom and into the connected bathroom, only releasing his hand when she turned on the water and started washing her hands. She stepped off to the side as she worked the soap on her hands.

It didn’t help that the lights around the mirror made her look like she was glowing.

Kai stepped in beside her and washed his hands with the two of them standing together. It was an oddly intimate moment, and he couldn’t help but lean a little closer, brushing his arm against hers.

When he reached under the water to rinse off, the water sprayed a little, like a ricochet from one hand and off the other, sending droplets of water at both of them.

“Hey!” She laughed and turned toward him. The water had left a splatter design across the front of her grey T-shirt.

Kai felt horrible, but he couldn’t stop the laugh that burst from his lips. The movement sent another spray of water from the faucet and this one hit him, leaving another arc of splatter on his T-shirt. Looking down he shook his head. “Talk about a complete fail.”

“I don’t know.” Summer shut off the water and handed him a towel from the bar on the wall. “It’s water so it’s not going to ruin anything. And you look good in water.”

His laughing mood shifted, warmed. She was just joking with him, but he couldn't help the way her words affected him. Water had always been a big part of his life. His tutu had named him well.

Summer hung up her towel and he reached across to hang his back up beside hers. The odd movement pulled the pendant of his necklace free from the neck of his shirt, letting it swing forward.

She caught it in her fingers and tilted her head to look at it.

"I didn't see this before."

He smiled, enjoying how close she was. "I don't wear it in the pool."

She nodded slowly as her eyes continued to roam over the pendant. "An octopus?"

"He'e," he agreed. "My tutu kane, my grandfather, made it for me."

She nodded again, rubbing the pad of her thumb across the bone carving. "Is there a story behind it?"

He lowered his chin and met her eyes when she looked up at him. "It's my aumakua."

Kai saw her confusion. He'd expected it, in a way.

"The closest I can come to explaining it in English is a kind of ancestor spirit."

He swore he could see her mind working through his words and the fact that she was really trying to understand him really meant a lot.

Leaning into her, his hand settled on her hip and he felt her warmth through the thin fabric of her shorts. Everything about her drew him in.

"Is it something about the animal or..."

Summer looked up at him and he saw her lips part.

Kai saw the way her breath slowed, and her eyes darkened.

He couldn't help the smile that curled the corners of his mouth at the gentle sound of her sigh.

"I was always moving in different directions as a kid. My grandfather took me down to the beach to swim. We swam out near the reef and he took me down to the sand and rocks. We were almost to the bottom when I saw it. An octopus moving around the rocks, his arms reaching out, moving things, searching.

"My grandfather held out his hand, his fingers spread wide. He pointed at all of the fingers and then he touched the back of his hand. When I saw that I looked back at the octopus still searching across the ocean floor. All those arms but one head controlling them. That's what I'd been missing. Instead of being all over the place I could have focus. I could use my mind to control all of that energy."

"So now, everything works… together."

He nodded, unable to move his lips without leaning in for a kiss.

He wanted to, but he wasn't about to kiss Summer for the first time standing in her bathroom. No, there was going to be a time to taste her lips, but this was not it.

Leaning in closer, he touched his lips to her forehead and felt her breath on his neck. "Come on." He found her hand with his and led her back into the living room. "Let's get you fed and off your feet."

He saw color rising in her cheeks and a brightness in her eyes as she walked along beside him.

"Don't be surprised," she warned him, "if I fall asleep face first in one of the plates."

They laughed together as she sat down, but he didn't miss the fact that she held on a little longer as he walked past to sit down on the other side of the sofa.

. . .

A jingle on his phone roused him from sleep.

Kai reached out and picked up the phone from the table, swiping his finger over the notification alert.

NALANI: Hey bro – You OK – I don't see your car

He smiled at his sister's message.

KAI:I'm good. Go to sleep.

There was a pause and he figured that she'd done just that. He lifted his arm to set it back down on the table and stopped when it vibrated in his hand. Kai read the message on the screen and laughed silently.

Summer stirred and he rubbed his hand down her back, soothing her. He felt her draw in a deep breath and she rubbed her hand up his chest, bunching up the cotton of his T-shirt.

She shifted against him and managed to slip her foot between his as she settled back into sleep.

Kai took a long moment to enjoy the feeling of her against him and turned back to the screen to read the message again.

NALANI:Be good

Grinning like an idiot, he answered back.

KAI:Always. Night.

Turning off his phone he set it back down on the table.

The television was still on, so he reached back and picked up one of her throw pillows and pulled it under his head, leaving him the ability to see her better.

He'd be happy even without the light.

Just having her sleeping peacefully against him was incredible.

They'd had a great time with dinner, sometimes reaching for the same thing at the same time. Any hesitation she had about using her fingers was gone by the time she pulled the last fried pickle out from his grip.

She'd told him about her first experience with Hawaiian food when she'd moved to the islands. Stumbling through the words to order and ending up with something she couldn't even recognize. He'd loved every minute of her stories, but she'd shied away from talking about her work.

It didn't bother him so much as it made him curious. The fact that she knew the SEALS so well told him she was at least connected to the military, but he didn't get the feeling that she was a soldier. Not that he knew a lot about the military at all. He knew the basics.

You didn't grow up in Hawaii and not know at least a few things. Especially on the island of Oahu. The bases and installations were all across the island. And the history of World War II wasn't as far in the past for island residents.

A number of the most popular hikes on the island had history with the war. Pillboxes. Bunkers. Even the hike up through Diamond Head Crater ended up in a structure used by the military in the past.

Local storage companies had leased out old tunnels that the military had dug into the mountains. Even the interstate highways on the island were created to link the major bases back and forth.

He just couldn't figure out why she didn't tell him what she did for work.

Unless...

Looking down at the woman whose cheek was resting on his chest, he wrapped his arm around her, and hugged her closer.

It didn't really matter to him if she didn't want to talk about her work. That was just a part of who she was, and this wasn't about learning everything there was to know about each other right off the bat.

He wanted to spend time with her, learn about her, but he

wasn't in any kind of a rush. If it took him years to find out everything there was inside of her head and heart, he'd consider himself lucky to have that time with her.

Her hand moved and he felt her fingertips stroke his chest. Gentle, rambling movements. Almost tickling him, but soft enough that he could hold back the laughter.

Her sleepy sigh tugged at his heart and he folded their fingers together settling her down once more.

She'd barely made it through dinner and once he'd put the plates and napkins in the trash, he'd sat down beside her just to say goodnight.

But her eyes were almost closed, her dark lashes fluttering against her cheeks.

He couldn't walk away right then. He didn't want to startle her.

Who could blame him for wanting to wait a little while?

With the TV still broadcasting another episode of whatever barbeque competition show she'd found on streaming, he settled in beside her.

The back of the sofa was high enough that it wouldn't hurt her neck to rest right there since she'd wiggled down into the plush cushions while they'd eaten. He lifted his arm to place it on the back of the sofa, tucking his leg up between them on the seat cushions.

There was no doubt about it. Summer was the most beautiful woman he'd ever seen. Every curve of her face, even the rounded edge of her ear that peeked out between the waves of her hair, every inch of skin that he could see was beautiful.

And yet, what drew him the most was the intangible parts of her. The expressions on her face. The fluctuation of her voice and the warm tones that remained even when she was laughing. The spark in her eyes that told him she saw things in the world that he would never be able to understand.

She could be with anyone at that moment. She could be the life of the party in any room.

But she'd accepted his invitation to dinner.

She'd invited him over.

Him.

Because she wanted to spend time with him.

How was it possible to feel humbled and proud at the same time?

Maybe that's just who she was.

The woman who made everything possible.

The woman who inspired him to move forward with her in mind.

To focus on the future and everything that he could have… with her.

Kai had been lost in his thoughts, mesmerized by her peaceful beauty, until he felt her shift and lay her head on his hand against the back of the sofa.

If she stayed there for long, she'd end up with a sore neck in the morning.

That's when he knew he had to wake her and get her in bed.

Alone.

And then he'd leave.

He'd leave much happier than he had been earlier, full of hope, and feeling a kind of peace that he hadn't felt for a long time.

Reaching out his free hand, he trailed the backs of his fingers across her cheek. "Summer?"

She didn't move much. Just a twitch of movement around her eye, high on her cheek.

"Summer?" He brushed her hair back behind her ear. "Time to go to sleep."

Her shoulders rose and fell. "I am."

"Yes, you are, ku`ulei." Sighing, he brushed the pad of his

thumb along the high arch of her cheek. He really hated to disturb her, but if she fell off of her couch, he'd feel all kinds of guilt. "Time to go to bed."

Kai leaned forward and reached for her, second guessing at the last minute that he might not be able to pick her up from that angle, but it was too late to change his position.

Shifting back, Summer moved with him, and somehow, he tumbled back with her body stretching over his.

The movement had knocked the breath out of him a bit, but he settled back against the cushions and gently gripped her hip to keep her steady on top.

Was it a surprise how easily they fit together?

Absolutely.

The best kind of surprise.

"Summer? We should get you in bed and I'll go home, okay?"

Kai reached down to grab a hold of the sofa frame to give him leverage to sit up, but Summer grabbed a hold of his T-shirt and shook her head, rubbing her nose and lips against his chest.

"Stop moving."

He heard her grumble and had to smile. "It can't be comfortable for you, ku`ulei."

She tilted her head back and her eyes looked almost amber in the flickering light of the TV. "It's nice. Stop. Moving." Her eyes closed and she was fast asleep.

Remembering every moment of the night over again in his mind made his heart throb in his chest. They hadn't said much in the way of feelings and he hadn't even kissed her, but there was something so achingly perfect about holding Summer as she slept, he knew he wasn't going to be able to wait long to see her again.

He needed this woman in his life like his next breath.

Kai could only hope that she liked him enough to give him another date and more after that.

Their hands still woven together, he lifted his head from the pillow and placed a kiss on the crown of hers and wished her sweet dreams. “Mana’o nahenahe, ku`ulei.”

He already had his.

CHAPTER 7

The State Coroner's Office was down by the docks. Just a stone's throw from the old Dole Cannery in Iwilei. The drive into town didn't take all that long considering that the morning rush was over. Pulling in through the open gate, Summer looked for the open visitor space that Doctor Chang had left for her. A dark, tinted window SUV was parked beside it.

"Fancy." She smiled to herself as she got out of her car and caught herself humming a little as she shut her door and set the lock.

She'd only made it a few steps when she heard a friendly voice.

"Summer, wait!"

Summer stopped behind her car and saw Olena climb out of the SUV. Unsure of exactly how to greet the detective that she'd just met the day before, she opted for a little wave. Sure, they'd gotten literally down and dirty in red dirt, but that wasn't exactly a usual occurrence for Summer.

She doubted that Olena understood her predicament, but she took care of it, nonetheless.

"Long time no see!" The detective shifted a thick folder from one arm to the other. "What has it been? Twelve hours?"

The two shared a laugh and Summer gave her a one shoulder shrug. "At least that long. What's changed since then?"

Olena's expression sobered. "A whole lot of nothing." She gestured to the door. "Why don't we go inside and see what the doctor has for us?"

"Sounds good to me." Summer stepped up to the door first and pulled it open for the detective. Together, they walked toward the autopsy room, Olena carrying on most of the conversation as they went.

"You look like you got some sleep last night."

Summer shrugged, feeling like if she opened her mouth she might overshare.

Slowing down her steps, Olena gave her a searching look. "Okay, there's definitely a story there. Spill, Summer."

Summer hesitated, teetering on the edge of wanting to tell her and also worrying that she might seem a little 'off' thinking about things like romance and a hot guy before they meet the coroner to talk about what was possibly a murder victim.

Olena stepped back and leaned against the wall. "Look, it's probably none of my business, but there's something different about you today. At least what I can see. And if I'm overstepping by asking about it," she held up a hand in surrender, "no worries. I'm just happy to see that you're smiling like that. All that heat and dirt yesterday? Yuck."

Agreeing, Summer couldn't help but add, "In my line of work we're either out in the field and getting grimy or we're in the lab and everything is so sterile. There's really no middle ground."

"Yeah, I don't envy you the dirt part, but the lab? I'm sure you have excellent air conditioning."

It took a moment for Summer to see her point. Nodding, she smiled a little more. "Yeah. We do."

Olena's answering smile was contagious. "Maybe I should have gone into… what's your field again?"

"Forensic Anthropology, but not like BONES on TV. I don't have a hot FBI partner to whip out a gun to protect me. I don't kick criminal butt. I do identify remains for the military."

"That's still pretty kick ass."

"Thanks."

Olena was quickly becoming someone that Summer would like to be friends with. As a detective Olena was already one of the coolest people she knew, but she was really different from the people she worked with. Friendlier to say the least. Maybe it was working with human remains all the time, but the people she worked closest with had always felt a little closed off.

Not that Summer considered herself socially adept in any way. She'd spent most of her 'free time' in college working in labs and whatever side jobs she could find to help pay for her tuition. It just didn't seem like her coworkers were curious about her life outside the lab.

And finally, she might actually have one.

"That's it," Olena nodded slowly, "that's the smile I'm talking about. Look, you don't have to tell me if you don't want to, but whatever it is that put that smile on your face, keep it going."

It was one moment of indecision.

The bite of her teeth into her bottom lip.

Then Summer couldn't hold it back anymore.

"I had a date last night."

"Date? Wow," Olena gave her wink, "you know how to pack a ton into a day!"

"It wasn't like I went out or anything. I was exhausted after the dig and planned to just stay in, but he brought food over."

"Good food?"

Summer was taken aback by the question, but she answered it smiling. "Very." She let out a sweet sigh. "It's the best first date I've ever had."

"Hold up." Olena held out a hand. "He came over with dinner for a first date?"

Nodding, Summer felt all the sweet emotions flooding back again. "And it might have ended badly when I fell asleep and drooled on him."

The look in Olena's eyes was priceless. "Drool. How romantic."

"Crazy, right? Still, when he woke me up for work this morning, he hugged me goodbye and kissed me on my cheek. Lingering, you know?"

Summer lifted her hand and touched the spot where his lips had caressed her skin.

"It's all kind of crazy, but…"

"But the best kind of crazy, right?"

The two women shared a smile.

"The absolute best."

A door down the hall opened up and Doctor Chang leaned out and gave the two a stern fatherly look. "Ladies, come on in when you can."

Summer gave him a wave as they started walking. "Yes, sir."

The room was cold when they entered and Summer saw Olena tense a little at first. As they followed the doctor to his workstation, Olena leaned in. "Now I remember what kind of air conditioning you have. Let me rethink how awesome I think your job is."

"It's true, Detective Yasui. We're just a degree or two above a polar bear sanctuary, but we make do."

The computer screens above his desk already had images on them and Doctor Chang started to point out his findings. "I didn't locate any bullets or metal in the body, but that was just a fallback test because of the missing flesh that we couldn't locate."

Summer listened carefully, going over the x-rays and images that he showed on the screens.

"I didn't find entry wounds of any kind on the remains."

"So, are you thinking it was some kind of non-violent death?"

The doctor looked at Olena and shook his head, his mood somber. "I wish I could say that, but this man was strangled. Some kind of ligature was used, but with the damage to the flesh it might take me awhile to figure out exactly what it was."

"And DNA?" Summer leaned in to look at one of the x-rays. "Were you able to get a good sample."

He nodded. "Yes, I think we'll be able to find out quite a bit of information when the results come back."

Olena shook her head and gave Summer a look out of the corner of her eye. "This is where it would be helpful if you were BONES. We'd have that DNA report in like five seconds."

"On TV, yeah."

The doctor continued on. "Once the report comes back, I'll send a copy to you, Summer."

She agreed. "I'll check it against our database." Summer looked over at the table with the clothes that the doctor had removed from the body. "Has anyone gone over his clothes?

If not, do you think HPD would mind if I took it back to my lab and compared the uniform to what we have? I also have access to the local military museums."

Doctor Chang looked relieved, but he turned to Olena first. "Detective?"

She nodded. "If Clive was here, he'd probably tell you no. In fact," she nodded her head, "I'm sure he would, but for the time being, this case is mine." She turned to Summer and gave her a kind of helpless shrug. "I know it goes without saying, but just keep in mind the normal documentation that we'll need for chain of custody and evidence and I'm more than happy to sign this all over to you."

"Thanks." Summer looked at the condition of the clothing on the table and couldn't help the feeling that crawled up her spine. "I know what this looks like, but I can't help but think there's something else going on here."

Leaning his hip against one of the tables, the doctor agreed with her. "There's something we're not seeing."

Olena was leaning over the autopsy table, her eyes focused on the man's neck. "Is there any way to get a better idea of what was used to strangle him?"

The doctor moved to stand beside her. "Yes. Now that we've collected samples from his remains, I can try to hydrate the flesh and get a better idea of what was used."

The door opened and one of his assistants called the doctor away.

Summer watched Olena as she examined the body, leaning in as close as she could. "What are you thinking?"

"Clive thinks it's some kind of protest. You know, the kind that has a bone to pick with the government. Or in this case, with the National Historic Site."

"I can see that" Summer agreed. "There are a lot of people who would rather forget that particular part of history. It wasn't a shining moment for America."

Olena's expression seemed tighter than it had before. "Most people think of Internment Camps and think of the ones on the continent. It might have been easier to distance themselves from it. The camps were often a long train ride away from where they had lived. Here?" Olena's head shook back and forth as if she was trying to erase the very thoughts in her head. "Here, it wasn't done to all of the Japanese. They were picked out for specific reasons. It was harder for the military to use the excuse that it was for their safety.

"They took teachers, priests, community leaders and those that had any means of leaving the islands or communicating long distances."

Summer felt a pain settle in her chest at the very thought. "Teachers?"

Olena nodded. "My grandfather was put in the Sand Island Camp and then moved to the Honouliuli Camp later on."

"Was he a teacher?" She'd heard the rough scratch of emotion in the detective's voice.

"He was an electrician. He worked at a radio station doing maintenance. When they took him, he was at work. Led off in front of his coworkers. Questioned at length. They thought he might have been communicating with the Japanese Navy using the radio equipment.

"Even though Hawaii was still a territory, my grandfather considered America his country."

"Did he talk to you about it? Your grandfather?"

For a long moment, Olena didn't even move. When she lifted her head, Summer saw tears gathering in her eyes.

"He died when I was little. Grandma didn't say anything either. She'd get quiet sometimes. Anniversaries of Pearl Harbor. Grandpa's birthday. It was my uncle who told me about it. He was the oldest of the kids. He was the one who had to make money and try to help the family while grandpa was in the camps. Grandma still had to raise five kids while he was locked away. Pregnant with the sixth. Uncle Hira was the one who rode his bike down to the camp to tell his father about the birth.

"There wasn't much that he had to say that held anything positive in it about his family's experience, but the only time I saw him shed a tear was when he talked about grandpa on the day of his release. He said that his father didn't utter a word that day. From the moment he walked out of the gates, through the ride to their rented home. He didn't even want to go inside. He sat down on the steps and cried. Silent tears rolling down his cheeks. They'd lost their house because they couldn't pay for it. Six children and two adults squeezed into a cottage one third the size of their home.

"He just sat there and cried."

Summer reached out and put her hand on Olena's shoulder. She had no words to say to the other woman. She couldn't imagine what she could say that would make a difference.

Drawing in a breath, Olena continued, her voice rough with emotion.

"Uncle Hira said that the next morning, they woke up and grandpa was in the kitchen going through his tools, cleaning everything and putting it all in place. The whole family hung back watching him, wondering how he was feeling. When he was packed up, he locked the box and looked up at his family. He told them, 'Ganbatte!' Which they'd heard from him so many times before. The most literal translation I can think of is 'try hard.' People use it to encourage each other to reach a goal. Something more than wishing someone luck because it means they should work for it.

"He never told my uncle or any of the other children what happened to him in the camps. If they tried to ask, he'd wave off the question and tell them to go to work. Do something."

Summer didn't know if Olena would think it was weird, but she needed to do something at that moment. Stepping closer, she pulled the detective into a hug. "I don't know if it helps to tell you that I'm sorry all of that happened. I can't imagine how it must have been for any of them going through all of that in the middle of a war."

Olena hugged her back and then slowly stepped away, wiping at her eyes. "Many of those who went through it are gone, but their families still feel connected to it. The stories haunt them, like shadows in the back of their minds. Mine too."

"So, you think this might be someone's way of bringing that time back, at least in memory. Dumping someone's body at the site, dressed in a military uniform from the period, is their way of drawing attention to it?"

Olena was hesitant to answer. "It seems like it would be a moot point, wouldn't it? They're already working on making the site into a museum. Teaching future generations about what happened during the war. Planting a body there would draw negative attention to it, but I'm not sure what they'd hope to accomplish beyond that."

"Crazy," Olena offered, "but then again, people who commit murder are already… a little off, you know?"

Summer gave her a lopsided smile. "I wouldn't know since I'm not about to kill anyone. And I'm not planning to in the future either."

"Good." Olena let out a big breath. "I'd hate to have to arrest you. I'd rather just keep this totally friendly, okay?"

Another weight lifted from Summer's shoulders. "Friends. Of course."

~

The streets in Chinatown made his skin crawl. Frank had gotten up at the crack of dawn to make his granddad breakfast and make sure he took all of his medications. Without a moment to himself he had gone to work making early deliveries of bread from a bakery to a bunch of restaurants.

It was only after he was done with that and had returned the truck that he hopped a bus into Chinatown. Finding a seat by himself was never easy and sometimes he just had to get up and stand in the aisle to avoid touching other people and having them touch him.

He had to find another one.

He was working off of a list and if he was honest about it, he was just about done with it. He'd whittled down the list to three, but he was fed up with the whole idea. He was doing it to help his granddad. He wanted to make him happy. Get him justice for what he'd gone through for just doing his damn job.

But Frank knew that every time he found one and crossed it off the list, things changed inside of him. Doing… these things. It was almost too easy.

He was revolted by the very idea of it, but it also made him feel like there was magic pumping through his veins.

He just wished he didn't have to go and pick out the ones. If his granddad could get out more. He'd let him pick. The rest of it was the part that he was beginning to enjoy. Walking up and down the streets in this dirty part of town?

It made his skin crawl.

The food. The hanging ducks and chickens displayed in the windows. The stores with glass jars full of dried animals and herbs. How could that be decent let alone legal?

The drunks asleep in alleys, the homeless panhandling at the corners.

Even with a police office smack dab in the middle of the area, they couldn't clean up the streets!

Frank crossed Hotel Street to get away from one of them, easily making his way since only buses were allowed on the road. He saw a sign for a pastry shop and stepped inside. He'd made his granddad something to eat, but he'd forgotten to take care of his own hunger.

It wasn't until he was standing in line with people filing in after him, that he realized the length of the line in front of him. A few minutes later, he was still standing in the same place.

He grumbled under his breath. "Can't they hurry it up?"

Frank heard someone behind him laugh and he turned, ready to tell them a thing or two. The young woman behind him gave him an easy smile.

"It won't take long. They're fast." She leaned to the side, looking up to the front of the line. "Looks like someone's buying pastries for the office. Just wait," she looked back up at him, "you'll see."

Nodding slowly, he turned back around.

He heard her voice again but didn't look back.

"You should check out the menu board and figure out what you want. When you get to the front, you can just give them your order. Save some time."

She sounded like she was trying to be helpful, but you could never tell with people. They always had their own agendas.

Her suggestion seemed harmless and probably made sense, so he looked up above the heads in front of him.

At first the words seemed smudged to him, but with the heat in the small bakery he was sure he just needed to blink and clear his vision.

It didn't help.

The person at the front finally picked up their bags and shuffled away from the counter. Frank took another step closer and peered up at the menu board with a frown.

There weren't words up there. Just a bunch of scratchy letters that made no sense.

But they had prices up there. They could manage numbers well enough.

The woman behind him stuck her nose in again. "Have an idea of what you want to order?"

"How the hell am I supposed to decide," he groused, "that's gibberish up there."

The woman didn't have anything smart to say to that.

Oh, she was happy enough to butt in when she wanted to be helpful.

The person in front of him took another step forward, but he wasn't so sure. Turning on his heel he leaned down and gave the woman a hard look. "You read that stuff?"

Startled, she shrugged her shoulders. "Sure. They have the full menu up there."

Frustration.

That's what he felt.

It pinched at the back of his neck and made his mouth dry like the desert.

"You're joking with me, right?" He pointed back at the wall, but his eyes were fixed on her. "You tell me you can read that shit?"

Frank saw her eyes dart back over his shoulder and even as her face paled visibly, she still managed to make him feel like a fool.

"Sure. If you need help," she offered him a smile, but she might as well have slapped him across the face, "I'll be happy to read it for you."

He shook his head.

And shook it again.

The pressure inside it was building, making it hard to think. "I don't need your help."

"Uh… okay." She took a step backwards and that's when

he realized he'd taken a step closer to her. "Look, mister. I don't want to get in an argument."

"Then tell me why you're like this." The back of his neck felt like it was burning. "Tell me why you like them."

"Them?"

Before she could take another step back, he reached out and grabbed her arm. "Yeah. Them." He pulled her closer and turned to look at the wall again. He pointed at the white menu board up above the counter, ignoring the shock written on the features of the people before him in line. "You mean to tell me you can read that Japanese shit?"

"Ja-Japanese?"

The confusion in her tone turned his head. What game was she trying to play?

He narrowed his eyes at her. "Tell me the truth. You can actually read those scratches?"

"Those scratches..." She spoke the words so slowly, he wondered if she was losing her mind. "That's Chinese," she protested, "it's not..."

He let go of her arm as if she'd burned him.

And maybe she had.

As he stepped away someone in the room laughed.

They laughed at him.

Laughed.

He turned to look for him and saw a whole bunch of stupid people staring back, laughing.

His hands flexed at his sides and he felt the knife tucked away in his jeans pocket.

They wouldn't laugh so hard if they saw that.

They'd think twice about making fun of him if they saw the blade.

And when they felt it cut in deep, they'd understand the mistake they made.

Not now.

He heard his granddad's voice in his ear.

Not now, Thom. Recon. Stealth. Don't draw attention.

"But it's her fault," he answered back and saw the faces turn down with anger. "She's the one."

Someone stepped from around the back of the counter. "Sir, we're going to have to ask you to leave."

"Don't," he warned him, "don't talk to me like that."

"Look, buddy. Get out of here."

Frank didn't see who spoke that time, but he sounded close.

He sounded mad.

Well, he wasn't the only one.

"It's you too, huh?" He took a step toward the door. He could hear the people and noise from the street behind him and saw people move out of line to look at him.

Ten.

Eleven.

Twelve.

More than that.

They were looking at him with anger and shock.

He felt the same way, but they didn't seem to know who was at fault.

They were glaring at him!

"Mister?" Another person in line was staring at him. "Get out."

He reached for the knife and felt a sting in his ear and heard the hiss of his granddad's voice. *Boy, don't you sass me.*

Frank covered his ear with his hand, rubbing at the sting of pain that always happened when he messed up.

Leave, he told himself. Go.

The guy up at the front picked up a phone from the counter. "I'm calling the police if you don't-"

He didn't hear a word after that.

Frank darted out the door and blended into the crowd of

people on the sidewalk. Their sheer numbers giving him a way to hide.

He'd messed up.

He hadn't followed orders. His granddad would know.

One look from the old man and he'd know.

Frank stepped into an alley. Just a narrow space really. He pushed himself in between the bricks and stucco, dragging in breath after breath.

He'd fix it.

He had to.

He needed to prove to his granddad that someone in the family had the guts to do what needed to be done.

CHAPTER 8

Wednesday night dinner at his mother's home was just as hectic and loud as it always was, but Kai found himself being a little more introspective than normal. Okay, honestly, he didn't normally have much time to think when he was with his family. There was just too much happening to let his mind drift away. His sisters gave as well as they got, if not better, and he had to be on the lookout for their jokes and jibes.

Nalani and Uluwehi hadn't stopped talking about plans for Sunday dinner at their cousins' house since they'd walked in the door and he was happy to let them lose themselves in conversation. His own thoughts were miles away, on the other side of a mountain.

He'd spoken with Summer on the phone after she finished work for the day. She was tired, but not as exhausted as she'd been the night before. She was still shying away from talking about work, but he wasn't going to push. It was enough that he could hear her blush and smile in her voice.

He was glad she wasn't all that embarrassed about how

she'd woken up in his arms. The fact that she'd fallen into such a deep sleep against him made him happy. They may not have had much time together, just a few hours of *conscious* time and more time asleep, but she felt comfortable around him.

She trusted him enough on some level to relax into his embrace.

He would do whatever it took to keep that connection with her. Keep it, and deepen it, because he wanted many more nights like that. Years and years would be just fine too.

He just had to keep building on what they'd started.

And he was planning to ask her to see him on Sunday. She might not be ready to get into the water as a swimmer, but he was hoping he could convince her to spend a little time with him. It was just as important that she feel comfortable in the water and he could do that for her.

"Kai?"

He stood at the stove, working a wooden spoon through the thick beef stew on the stovetop. Watching as the chunks of potato and carrots turned up and then slipped under the hearty tomato stew. Looking into it he couldn't see any of the celery that he'd put in it and wondered if he should have added more.

"Kai!"

"Hey, lolo! Pay attention!"

Huffing out a breath he turned and looked over at the two women sitting at the dinner table. "What?"

His sisters laughed and Nalani spoke first. "Are you going deaf, or are you trying to ignore us?"

He shrugged at them and almost fought off a smile. "I'd love to ignore you both, but it won't do me any good, yeah?"

Uluwehi winked at him. "You know better than that."

Kai wondered how much trouble he was in with the two of them. "So, what do you want?"

His sisters shared a look before Uluwehi answered him. "We want to know where you were last night?"

Nalani was quiet, but her wide eyes spoke volumes. He wondered if she'd shared his text messages with their sister. Or if they'd just talked about it on the phone.

"I was out with a friend."

As soon as he spoke the last word, he knew he'd made a mistake. But really, there wasn't much he could have said that would have kept them quiet. It would have been hard enough just talking to one of them, but his sisters together? Things could get out of hand… fast.

Uluwehi leaned forward, bracing her arms on the table. "You spent the night with a friend?"

"We had dinner and it was late."

"Dinner?" Nalani hadn't sounded so excited in a long time.

Kai wondered if he was going to get out of this interrogation with his sanity intact.

"And then she invited you back to her apartment?"

Before he could figure out how to disappear into thin air like Houdini, he heard the screen door swing open.

"Who invited you back to her apartment?"

His sisters went wide-eyed and pointed at him with glee. Nalani laughed and told him in a sing-song tone, "You're gonna be in trouble."

"Kulikuli," his mother scolded Nalani. "Maha'oi!"

She set her purse down on the kitchen counter and a shopping bag beside it. Taking hold of Kai's arm, she leaned in and pressed a kiss to his cheek. "Aloha ahiahi, boy. Are the girls picking on you?"

He leaned into her and returned the kiss, resting his forehead against hers for a moment. "It's okay."

His mother slid a sideways glance at her daughters sitting

at the table. "And why is he the only one helping with dinner?"

Nalani turned a pouting look at him. "He said he'd do it."

Kai nodded. "I did. They're working on plans for Sunday."

His mother nodded and gave him a gentle pat on his shoulder before she moved back to pick up the shopping bag she'd set down. "It'll be a big party. Hi`ilani's been so busy with the TV show, it's been a few weeks since she came."

Uluwehi nodded. "I bet more of the cousins are goin' come to see if she brings that guy."

Kai looked at his sister, confused. "Which guy? Her fiancé?"

"No," she gave him a pointed stare, "the actor."

His mother caught on before he did. "Cort Caldwell."

He couldn't stop the grimace that settled on his features. "I hope not."

Uluwehi leaned into her sister. "I just wanna see her boyfriend. If he comes and you know he will, I bet he brings his hot friends."

They both laughed and kept talking about the party. Kai used the distraction to talk to his mother. Turning down the burner on top of the stove, he lowered his voice to talk. "I'm thinking of inviting someone on Sunday."

His mother was one of the smartest women he knew. With one pointed look she told him she was onto him. "You're always welcome to invite your friends, baby. You know that."

He looked at her and saw the glimmer in her eyes. "I want to bring her, but I don't want them to give her a hard time."

"They're your sisters." She sighed and touched his cheek with her palm. "So, you can try to tell them to be good."

"Oh, I can tell them," he assured her, "but I just don't know if they'll listen. The last thing I want is to have my family frighten her when we've barely had our first date."

He could almost see the wheels turning in her head.

"A first date where she invited you back to her apartment?"

"More like I invited myself."

That earned him a look that could strip paint from the walls.

His mother leaned in closer and told him in all seriousness. "You behaved, right?"

"Yes, mom." He loved this woman so much. "I was going to meet her out at dinner, but she had a long day at work. She cancelled and went back to her place to rest, but I didn't want her to be hungry. I stopped by Dixie's and picked up dinner for both of us."

His mother smiled and nodded. "I bet she was happy to have you stop by."

He laughed, his shoulders shaking. "I got a bunch of sides and barbeque, so yeah."

She gave him a pointed look, one of her eyebrows rising up. "I bet she was happier to see you."

Of course, she said that. She was his mother. He was the youngest. The only boy.

"I was happy to see her."

His mother opened the bag of Ani's Sweet Bread and waved a hand toward the fridge. Still smiling he opened the door and reached in for the butter she had on one of the shelves. Kai handed it to her while she pulled a bread knife from the block.

"So that's where you were all night, hmm?"

He nodded and then answered her in words. "We ate in her apartment, sitting on the sofa, the TV on. We talked... a lot.

"I probably could have left when the plates went into the trash-"

"You could have," she agreed, "but you stayed. You wanted to be there with her."

Kai nodded and felt heat rise in his cheeks and across the back of his neck. "I still want to be there."

Her eyes were bright as she looked up at him. "How did you meet her, baby?"

"After my PT session. Summer was sitting with Elodie."

"Summer?" His mother nodded slowly. "Summer. Pretty name."

His heart was pounding in his chest. Just thinking of her. Just saying her name. "Beautiful, mom. She's just beautiful."

She touched her hand to his chest, the bread and butter forgotten on the cutting board.

"She's so smart and funny but I don't think she'd believe it if I told her. I know it's crazy. I meet her one day. Have dinner with her the next. And then she's falling asleep in my arms."

When he looked down at his mom to see how she was taking his admission, he saw that her eyes were a little misty with tears.

"I'm crazy, right? Feeling like this?"

"Like what, baby?" She blinked and looked up at him with a curious smile. "What does it feel like?"

He opened his mouth to explain, and words failed him. He wanted to say something that explained just how happy he was with Summer, but he went a little soft in the head trying to put it in words.

"Good."

It wasn't exactly the sweetest thing to say but it was true.

"Being near her makes me feel stronger. Gentler." Finding words to explain was harder than just feeling it inside of him. "Better."

He saw her lip quiver.

"Mom? You okay?"

She touched her hands to the sides of his face, holding him still and warming him with her love. "I'm wonderful. I can see the difference in you."

He dropped his chin down to his chest and gave her a smile that said he wasn't sure he believed her. "Really? What does it look like?"

She tightened her hold on him and gave him that look that told him to shush and listen. "It looks good on you, son. It looks like you've got hope. A light in your eyes. And I can't wait to meet your Summer."

Kai reached up a hand and covered her hand with his. "I'll ask her tomorrow."

"Oh?" His mother sounded a little too excited at the moment. "Are you going over to her apartment again?"

He hesitated. "That's probably not a good idea."

The look she gave him made him a little nervous, as if he was one wrong word away from getting a pinch on his arm.

"I want to do this right." He assured her. "This isn't just about how she makes me feel," he touched his free hand to his chest, "it's about how I want to get to know her and make sure she knows that I've never felt like this before. About anyone."

She searched his eyes for a moment longer and nodded. Stepping back to get a better look at him. "Then you're doing the right thing, son. You're a good man."

"A good man who's letting us starve!" Nalani gave him her best eye roll. "Isn't the stew done yet?"

His mother sassed her daughter right back. "Have you two set the table yet?"

Kai turned back to the stove before he laughed, but it didn't do him any good since his sisters could see his shoulders shaking.

"Enough laughing, bruddah." Uluwehi yanked open the utensil draw near his hip. "We're hungry."

As she turned to head back to the table he reached out and wrapped her in his arms for a big hug. As he pecked a kiss on her cheek, she made a mock gagging sound. "Let go! I'm starving!"

The whole family started laughing as they sat down to dinner.

~

Summer spent the morning looking at military uniforms from different eras, looking for a match to the outfit that the body had been dressed in. The more she looked, the more frustrated she became.

Tags that had been in the garments at one time had been removed. It hadn't been done with a gentle hand either.

Someone had messed with the uniform trying to hide where it came from. Or maybe they'd done it for another reason that they'd figure out later, but she really didn't like the ramifications of their actions.

There was a point to these actions.

There was a plan.

And everything about those plans scared her.

What happened to the victim had been planned.

It wasn't something that happened accidentally. It wasn't a spur of the moment thing, a crime of passion.

This was intentional.

What part of their plan included a uniform that likely belonged to the military? Was it in protest? Was it in anger? Betrayal?

Maybe plain old murderous intent?

Senseless death.

When the alarm on her phone sounded, she was all too happy to put away her research and make the short trip to

Elton's office. Knocking on the door she was rewarded with Elton's almost cheerful voice.

"I'll be out in a minute. I just need to finish with something quick."

Summer looked down at the screen on her phone. "It better be quick," she reminded him, "if we don't get there a few minutes ahead, you have to use the outdoor shower before getting in the pool."

Elton's answer was a rather colorful if not anatomically questionable grumble.

"Okay then. I'm going to use the restroom and I'll meet you out in the parking lot."

"That would be too much information, Summer!"

Laughing to herself she walked down the hall toward the women's restroom. "Summer," she mumbled under her breath with a smile. "He finally calls me by my first name."

By the time that they arrived at Elton's Physical Therapy appointment, Kai was already in the water and heaven help her. When Elodie had pointed him out the first time, Summer couldn't help but notice how… fit he was. Learning that he'd been shot and nearly bled to death on a boat had made it even more amazing to see how well he was doing.

Now that she knew who he was, and having the downtime as she waited for Elton's PT appointment to finish, she could sit back and enjoy how amazing Kai was. From one side of the pool to the other, his strong form cut through the water as if he'd been doing it all of his life.

Smiling, she mentally shook herself. He probably had. What is it that Elodie had said to her the other night when she'd called to remind Summer to actually take Kai up on swimming lessons? Oh. Yeah. Kai meant water in the Hawaiian language. Elodie had even told her Kai's full name, but Summer hadn't been able to wrap her mind around it. Instead of a name, it sounded like a line in a poem. Like lyrics in a song.

Delving into anthropology she'd studied a number of cultures, looking into more of the physical aspect of their cultures. With forensic anthropology she'd studied the many differences and similarities of the sexes and races. Language wasn't her specialty. Something her linguist friends had no qualms about pointing out regularly, but because it was his name, she wanted to know more.

She wanted to hear him say it and tell her about its meaning.

She loved hearing him talk about anything, but having him explain the origin and meaning of his name?

Summer couldn't wait to hear it.

It felt like an oddly intimate thing to her. Maybe it would be the same for him. That's why she wasn't going to ask him about it. She'd just let it happen when he wanted to talk about it.

And that was the crazy thing about it.

She had a feeling that was where they were headed.

Something intimate.

Heat rose in her cheeks and she cast a bit of a guilty look around to see if anyone was looking at her. If anyone was going to wonder what she was thinking.

Thankfully, no one was.

And Summer could sit back and enjoy the sun on her face.

"I like that smile."

A hand settled on her shoulder before she could sit up in shock.

"It's just me, relax." Elodie gave her a little pat and took the seat opposite at the table. "How are you?"

"Good." Summer almost laughed. She was better than

good, but she was so used to giving the innocuous answer it had just popped right out. "It's nice to see you again."

"Same here." Elodie set her bag down on the table and leaned forward. "I was hoping to get a chance to see you today."

Movement at the end of the pool turned Summer's attention for a moment and she saw Kai touch the far wall and then turn to head back in the opposite direction. She'd lost count of how many laps he'd done.

Summer dragged her attention back to Elodie, but she knew that her smile had deepened a bit. "I wasn't sure if you were coming. Kai said he drove himself."

"Oh," Elodie leaned on one arm of the chair, "so you two have been talking."

Worried that she might turn a bright red from embarrassment before she'd burn from the sun, Summer lowered her gaze to her hands folded in her lap before she looked back up to meet Elodie's eyes. "I think you know we have. Kai said he talked to you about me."

There might have been a moment of hesitation on Elodie's part before she spoke again.

A teeny tiny one, but a moment.

"And now I get to talk to you about him."

Summer shied away from the idea. "There isn't all that much to say. Except," she dove back in before Elodie could ask her something, "that I think he's amazing. You'd think a guy who's that fit and muscular would make a girl feel intimidated, but every minute I've spent with him, in person, on the phone... I just feel comfortable."

There was a quizzical look on Elodie's face and Summer began to rethink her words.

"What did I say?" She waited for an answer, but Elodie didn't really offer one. "Did I say something bad?"

Elodie seemed to gather her thoughts, but the oddly

pained expression on her face made Summer think she'd completely messed things up. "Comfortable?"

"See?" Summer sagged back in the chair. "I knew I'd say the wrong thing. There's a big reason why anthropology fits me so well."

"Oh? Why's that?"

"Well, when I'm looking at a site and interpreting information, I don't have to do it in a set amount of time. Those games on TV with all the trivia? Spitting out the right answer in two point five seconds? I'm horrible at it.

"I mean, I know the correct answer. A lot. But I second guess myself. No, that's not the word I'm looking for. What I... what it... I like to consider my words. I like to think through a question more than once. Some of my teachers thought it meant I was challenged or slow. They put me in a study hall during every open period thinking it would help me get over my issues if I just had more study time."

"But that's not what it was." Elodie nodded and gave her an empathetic look that Summer treasured.

"No. I just wanted to consider the question and the answer. I knew what I wanted to say, I just wanted to think it over one more time before I put down the answer or said it out loud."

She watched as Elodie seemed to think through her words. A moment later Summer heard her words and knew that she had been listening. Knew that she was understood.

"I bet you didn't use a lot of erasers."

"Every year my parents bought me new ones for school even though I had barely touched the ones from the year prior. I graduated high school with a pencil box full of them."

The two laughed together before Elodie asked her another question. "Do you still have the box of erasers in a closet?"

Summer didn't have to think over that answer. The

memory was still fresh in her head. "No." She leaned a little closer and almost whispered the words. "I left them in the study hall."

Elodie reached across the table and took her hand. Summer felt the gentle squeeze as if it was almost a hug. "How did they not see how bright you were?"

Summer pondered her answer. "I'm not sure that's what they thought. They did test me for a number of learning disabilities, but they could never seem to find one."

"I guess, they just didn't understand that what you needed was just time."

"It's probably why- No, I'm sure that's why I don't usually hang out with people or do social things. In groups I feel like I have a time limit just like a game show.

"Someone sits down to talk, or if they walk up to me at an event and start talking to me, they end up asking questions at some point. And I'm not saying they shouldn't. I'm not even saying I don't like it."

Summer took in a slow breath and Elodie nodded slowly as she kept eye-contact, as if Elodie was saying Summer could relax and take her time.

Because of that, the tension that Summer carried around with her a lot eased in her shoulders and her posture.

"I just feel like I'm disappointing people when they ask a question. Like I'm saying I didn't pay attention to them. Or maybe that I'm not interested in conversation. It's a lot of pressure and I know most of it is me putting it on my own shoulders, but sadly, it's still there."

"And Kai doesn't produce that kind of… anxiety in you?"

Summer shook her head and felt her heart pound in her chest. "Not anxiety, no. When I'm with him I feel calm, but also not calm." She winced and sighed. "There's that way with words that I have."

Elodie gave her hand another squeeze. "You never have to

worry about that with me or the SEALs. They all care about you. Mustang was so relieved that they were able to get you and your boss out of the Philippines in one piece."

It was easy to agree with her. "I owe them a lot. What's this," she wondered aloud, "the second time they had to pull me out of a mess?"

Elodie waved off her worry as she sat back in her chair. "It's their job. Are you ready to go for three?"

Something turned in Summer's belly. "No thanks. It's supposed to be all good things come in threes and being held by gunpoint is so not my thing."

"Did they set a time for you to go back and finish?"

Summer cast a glance at the pool, and she saw Elton taking a slow run in the water that was almost up to his shoulders. The strength in his back was returning faster than his doctors had anticipated.

"The Philippine Army is doing a little… snake removal first. After they know it's safe, they'll have us come back in."

Elodie grinned. "Safety, safety, safety."

"Don't I know it." Summer sighed as Kai finished another lap in the pool and stopped. "I'm in no hurry to go thousands of miles away for as long as I can help it."

Kai walked through the water and met his therapist at the side of the pool. She sat down on the edge and spoke with him. The two going back and forth for a little bit.

Summer leaned her arm on the table and looked at Elodie. "Do you think everything's okay?"

It only took a second for Summer to see for herself.

Kai broke into a big grin as he raised his arms in the air like a victory.

His therapist laughed out loud as Kai almost launched himself out of the pool, landing on the edge in a crouch before he stood up tall, proud, and so deliciously good looking that Summer worried that she might be drooling over him again.

Embracing his therapist, Kai turned them almost in a circle and Summer could hear her loud exclamation. "Ho'o-maika'i!"

He released her from his embrace, and she handed him his towel.

Wrapping it around his waist, he tucked the end in and turned to look in their direction.

"Well?" Elodie's question spoke for both of them. "Are you done?"

Kai's grin only got bigger as he lifted his eyebrows and lifted his hand and flashed a shaka sign to them. "All pau!"

Summer got to her feet with a joyful shout. "Awesome!"

Kai started forward and she expected him to go to Elodie for a hug first and turned her head toward Elodie.

A moment later, Summer was lifted off her feet and turned around in a circle. It was dizzying and it was full of joy.

By the time Kai set her down on her feet, she was a little unsteady, but it didn't matter. He had his arm wrapped around her, holding her steady. Elodie came to them and gave Kai a one-armed hug and a kiss on his cheek before she stepped back.

"You look like you feel good."

Summer didn't miss it when he hugged her a little closer to his side.

"I feel like a king!"

"You look even better." Elodie gave him another quick hug and then surprisingly, she hugged Summer. "I'll see you soon and we'll talk then. You two..." she looked between them with a big smile on her face, "you two just have fun, okay?"

As soon as Elodie picked up her bag and turned to leave,

Kai turned and wrapped both arms around her, a huge smile on his face. "Did I scare you?"

She sighed and enjoyed the feel of his embrace. "I just feel a little dizzy."

Summer saw the look of concern that fell over his features.

She felt the way he lifted one hand and touched the side of her face and looked into her eyes.

"You want to sit down?"

"No." She shook her head. "You're the one who makes me a little dizzy. You're so warm, gentle and still so strong. I watched you swim, moving through the water like you were born in it.

"All of that power. And still you seemed to be okay with sitting on the couch with me the other night, doing nothing."

He lowered his hand from her cheek and rubbed his hands slowly up and down her arms, sending the most delightful chills through her body. "I was happy because it was you, Summer. Spending time with you? I can't explain what happened when we met, but I feel this connection to you."

She lifted her hand between them and touched his bare chest above his heart. Summer felt the warmth of his skin, but she felt heat- No, she felt a kind of electricity that passed from his skin to hers.

It was breathtaking.

And when she looked up, the intensity in his eyes sent all the blood in her body rushing around to some very interesting places.

"I think I know what you mean." She could barely hear her own words. "I think I feel that too."

The smile he gave her then made her toes tingle.

"Then I think," his deep, indrawn breath pressed his chest against her fingers, and she swallowed hard to hide the giddy sigh that was trying to escape from her throat, "we should celebrate."

Summer nodded slowly.

And then shook her head. "I can't… not tonight. I have to go back to work and then I need to go to a museum downtown to look through their collection tonight."

That obstacle didn't seem to get him down at all.

"Sunday." He grinned at her. "I want the whole day."

She stared at him wide-eyed in shock. "The whole day?"

Nodding, he explained. "As much of it as you'll give me."

"What… what do you have in mind?"

"I want to take you to the beach."

Summer felt the color draining from her face. "The beach? That sounds good."

He gave her a reassuring smile. "Don't worry. I just want you to come into the water with me. We'll walk a little, talk a little. Get your feet and maybe your knees wet. We'll take it from there."

Her expression softened. That almost sounded great.

Except for the *into the water part.*

"Okay," she grinned at him. "I think I can handle that.

"Awesome." He leaned in a little closer. "And, since I just finished my physical therapy, we're having a party at my cousin's house. I'm hoping you'll come with me."

She blinked at him, but hesitated to answer.

"Summer?"

He caught her attention with just that, saying her name.

"A party?"

With her vision filled with his face it took her a moment to process the question he'd asked.

Before she could answer, he spoke again.

"It's just food, music, and a bunch of people having a good time. If you don't want to go, no pilikia. No trouble or worries."

"It's not that I don't want to go, per se. I'm just not sure if they'd want someone there who barely knows you. The last thing I want to do is make things awkward." She smiled as she said the words. She wanted him to know that she was okay if he decided to take back the invitation. "We can celebrate together at the beach."

He leaned closer and she saw a drop of water from his hair drip down onto his lower lip. Kai licked it away and she took in a soft gasp of air. "Any time that you'll give me, Summer… I want it. I want you to come to the party and meet my crazy family. Elodie and the SEALs will be there."

"Oh… okay." She blinked up at him, feeling the heat of his skin permeating every inch of her body. "I think I'd like that," she swallowed and smiled up at him, "I'd like that a lot."

"Yeah?" His voice was so soft she wasn't even sure she heard him over the ambient noise around the pool.

"Yeah." That and so much more. She mimicked his earlier gesture, the tip of her tongue tracing over her bottom lip. Summer saw him look down at her lips before he raised his gaze back to hers.

"Summer…"

His lips were so close to hers she swore she felt the vibration of sound that was her name.

"Ku`ulei."

She opened her mouth to ask him what that meant, but a moment later, she forgot that and everything else in her head.

His lips touched hers. A gentle, chaste kiss.

Her heart, heaven help it, didn't know or care how chaste it was. Her heart stopped all together and then jumped in her chest.

Kai pulled away just enough that sunlight fell against her cheek.

Summer's eyes fluttered open, and her lips curved into a smile. "Wow."

"Exactly." His smile lit her up from the inside.

And then he kissed her again.

Only this time, it wasn't so chaste. He brushed his lips across hers, their bottom lips creating the most amazing friction that she felt suddenly dizzy.

Her breath tried to escape her lips, but he covered her mouth with his and drank it in.

Could there be anything more perfect in the world?

"Summer!"

Elton's rather panicked voice turned her head.

Kai's too.

"Summer? Do you have any sunscreen in your bag? I forgot mine and my nose," she watched him almost slap a hand over his face, "my nose is burning!"

"I'll check, sir!"

The older man sighed in abject relief. "Oh, thank heavens."

Kai took her hand and walked her to the table where she'd left her things. "I've got to head in to work. Can I call you later about Sunday? So we can plan things? And maybe find a time to see each other before then?"

"Absolutely."

She felt the sun at that moment, but unlike Elton, it didn't burn. Her sun gathered her close and kissed her forehead, leaning against her for a long moment before he stepped back.

"Later," he gave her a little wave. "A hui hou kakou, Summer. Until we meet again."

CHAPTER 9

By the time Sunday rolled around, Summer was ready to get outdoors.

The more she worked on the mystery of their unidentified remains, the more she felt like she was going further and further down the rabbit hole. At least she wasn't alone.

Detective Olena Yasui had been to see her a few times. So much so that Summer got her a temporary pass to get onto the Joint Pearl Harbor Hickam base. By the time Friday rolled around, Olena made another visit to the lab to go over the information that both of them had discovered.

They had made some relative progress in the investigation, but they'd also come up against a bunch of walls. The DNA test was a bust. Their first search into DNA started with AFRSSIR, The Armed Forces database of DNA collected for identifying remains. That, they'd both decided, would have been too easy. There was also a chance the remains might be that of a veteran who hadn't been reported missing yet, but didn't have his DNA on file because of the era. But the likelihood was that he wasn't a veteran. Elton and the other Administrators of the laboratory asked her to continue working on the case, just in case, but also because he'd been found on what had been a military site back in the day. If it turned out that the killing was politically motivated or focused on veterans, they needed someone inside the investigation.

So even though that meant that the remains would stay in the State Morgue as a John Doe for the foreseeable future, Summer was staying on as a consultant in the local investigation.

"And CODIS?" Summer asked only to cross her T's and dot her I's, knowing if something had come through Olena would have called her.

"Sadly, nothing." Olena shook her head before Summer could ask the next question. "And no missing person reports fit him either. Some in general, yes, but all of those that could have fit had identifying marks that sadly..."

"Our John Doe doesn't." A somber silence descended between them before Summer spoke again. "I took the information off of the tag at the Police Museum and sent a message to the company."

That got Olena's attention, turning the detective's head.

"Did you hear back from them?"

Summer hedged a little and turned so she could lean her hip against the table. "Good and bad."

Taking out a glove from her lab coat, Summer pinched it around the shoulder of the shirt and turned it so that Olena could see it. "Luckily, the Police Museum had a shirt almost identical to this one on display."

Olena winced a little and folded her arms across her chest. "I admit, the last time I went through the museum was on a tour while I was in the Academy. I don't remember something like this."

"I can see that. A lot of museums have collections that are huge. Most of their collections are in storage and climate-controlled environments. They switch out displays from time to time to give the visitors a better idea of what they have. They may not have had the exhibit up when you were there, but it saved me a lot of time to have it out and available to see when I arrived. They had to find someone to open it for me, but the wait wasn't long at all."

Summer pointed out the stitching along the shoulder and collar. "Shirts, and more specifically uniform shirts, are made the same way. Stitchers that work on them end up almost hypnotized. The long lines of stitches are kind of mind numbing, especially when you're tasked with being fast and accurate.

"That means that they won't have artistic embellishments or individual characteristics. Some shops even have a kind of conveyor belt like system where each stitcher only does one part of a garment. It helps the bottom line and the speed if a stitcher, quite literally, sews the same line over and over. Even the stitch length is something that can tell us if the shirts match. The color of the thread in between layers can be a good way to match them as well."

Olena dropped her chin down and looked at the shirt in Summer's hands. Nodding slowly, she looked back up. "Because it's kind of insulated, right?"

Summer grinned. "Yes. This is the closest I ever got to learning how to sew," she explained, "but my grandmother was an amazing seamstress. She did this thing called French seams, which meant that the excess end of fabric that's not shown on the outside of a garment is folded over on itself in a certain way making the 'raw' edges invisible."

Olena chuckled a little. "I don't think I've ever seen one of those. Most of what I wear comes out of catalogues for work. I doubt I own anything like that."

"I know what you mean. I buy a lot of my stuff for comfort and ease of care. No handmade stuff for me. You should check in a family closet like your mom's, or an aunt's or a grandmother's. Chances are they have something with a French seam. The first time I saw the difference in color on the thread was when my mom accidentally tore a hole in the side seam of her blouse." Summer lifted one arm and used her opposite hand to trace along the seam that went from her underarm to her waist. "Before my grandmother could repair that seam, the rest of the French seam had to be taken apart."

Smiling, Summer shook her head. "My grandmother didn't like to seam rip, so she gave me the seam ripper and sat me down. After explaining what she wanted me to do, she put the fear of God into me. 'Heaven help us if you tear the fabric, Summer.' I think I might have bitten through my lip if I wasn't so scared that blood would drip on it. But once I'd pulled out the first line of stitches and I could see the thread that had been sandwiched in between the layers, I could see the slight difference in thread color."

Olena nodded. "Sun and the detergent from washing it would have lightened the thread."

"They let me take the shirt off of the mannequin, but I couldn't cut through the seam. Not that I was planning to, it would be like having my grandmother staring over my shoulder. I didn't need that fear weighing on me.

"Don't get me wrong. She loved me and I totally loved her, but she was from an era where women were accomplished and poised and I liked dirt and rocks and the best her friends could say was that I would be a pretty girl if I tried, or that I was a little shy."

The look in Olena's eyes said that she understood. "For me and my cousins, it was like it was ingrained in our DNA: be respectful, be quiet, and be studious. And excel everywhere you could." Her shoulders shook with silent laughter. "I was always a tomboy. I had three brothers growing up and

I wanted to be outside with them. I think my mom ended up settling for me getting good grades and being active in sports."

"At least you had sports." Summer's laugh was almost a snort. "I think that might have made me a little less nerdy if I'd done something sporty. What did you play?"

Olena grinned and Summer couldn't ignore how beautiful the detective was when she was thinking of things other than solving a homicide.

"A little of everything, except for basketball. I broke a bunch of fingers in PE with that. My favorites were Air Rifle, Cross Country and Volleyball."

"Favorites?" Summer tried not to gape at the other woman. "I almost cracked my tailbone bowling." She paused for a moment, thinking back to what little she knew about life on Oahu outside the base. "When you say volleyball, did you play at the University of Hawaii? I've heard volleyball is big here on the island."

The way Olena beamed at the question, Summer relaxed a little. One on one conversations in her life could get a little stilted if she wasn't careful.

"Yeah, I played volleyball here. UH Wahine Volleyball is big in the state. Probably even bigger than UH Football. The unofficial official sticking point is that Wahine Volleyball is basically the only sports program at the University that makes money. And Volleyball got me a scholarship to UH. My mom and dad were at every game with family members all cheering."

Summer's laughter was more like a hiccup. "Would you believe they don't cheer for scientists when we work?"

Olena laughed along with her. "That's so hard to believe. Maybe it's because you don't get sweaty enough."

"Eww. Thanks, I think."

"When this is all over and volleyball season starts, I'll take you to a game with me. I think you'll like it."

Her first instinct was to beg off. People jumping up and down, yelling and screaming, even if it was in support of student athletes, that was a bit of a worry. Sighing, Summer went back to her earlier point. "I turned their shirt over and over, looking for some trace of thread that had worked its way free somewhere on the garment and found one in the left sleeve down by the cuff. Everything was as good of a match as I could make without taking their exhibit with me."

"If it's needed, we can get the HPD Brass to loan it out as evidence for testing."

"Thanks! That's what I was hoping you'd say." Summer set the shirt down and picked up a paper printout of the email she'd received from the uniform company. "They said based on the comparative similarities as I described them that it's more than likely one of their shirts. The problem is-"

"How many were sent to Hawaii?"

Summer drew in a fortifying breath. "A ton. And even more went to the Continental U.S. And goodness knows there were enough troops back and forth, but there's also the fact that the local police at the time used the same kind of shirts."

Olena's brow furrowed in confusion. "We wear blue now."

"Yes, exactly, but back then police and military had similar uniforms."

The furrow only deepened. "So, someone could argue that this was about the police as well?"

The two thought over it for a minute, but Olena was the first to speak. "But if the killer dressed him up to make a point, he wouldn't take the body to a military location if it was about the police."

"True," Summer nodded, "but we have to consider that

the killer might have purchased the shirt and the rest of the clothes he dressed the victim in from a thrift store, or a retired police officer, or-"

"There's also the possibility that he killed someone who served as a police officer from that era." Olena took out her phone and sent out a quick text message, explaining it to Summer as she typed. "I'm asking them to dig up records of officers who worked in that time. Asking for anyone who retired, was fired, or quit the job."

Summer agreed. "I'm sure the list can be weeded through quick enough. The curator at the Police Museum said he'll find out the specific dates when that uniform shirt was used. That will help narrow things down even more."

The room went silent, and Summer turned to look at Olena. The detective was looking at her as if she was trying to figure something out about her.

"Detective?"

Olena grinned. "What?"

"Why are you looking at me like that?"

"Why not? But seriously, I like the way your mind thinks. You could be a good detective, you know? Have you ever thought about joining the Honolulu Police Department?"

Summer warmed to the praise, but she quickly felt the awkward rush of fear that coursed through her veins. "Remember? I almost broke my butt bowling?"

Olena winced and nodded. "Yeah. Uh, maybe you're better off here."

The sigh that passed Summer's lips was one of relief. "Thank you."

"Still," Olena continued, "I think after this is over, we're going to have to stay friends. I may just have to show you how to bowl without falling on your butt."

"Oh joy," Summer grumbled, remembering the ghost of the pain that had lanced through her body, but she was also hoping that Olena was right and that they'd stay friends after the case.

Friends.

Summer was making more and more of them these days and if felt good.

Really good.

When Kai pulled up outside of Summer's apartment building, easing his car into the now familiar visitor spot, he took a quick look at his face in the rearview mirror.

Just the sight of it brought back a memory from that morning when his two sisters let themselves into his house and scared the crap out of him in the bathroom.

Being the loving and maniacal sisters that they were, they made fun of him shaving before he went to the beach. Nalani had also pointed out that he'd taken out almost half a dozen swim trunks and laid them on his bed before he decided which one he was going to wear.

"Who is she?" Nalani always seemed to know him a little two well.

He'd told them both a little about his plans for the day and not all that much about Summer except that she was someone he liked, a lot, and threatened them as only a loving brother could, that they had to act like adults when they meet her at the party. And when they stood there a little off kilter at the pointed tone in his voice, he let out a pent-up breath and reminded them to, "No make A, yeah?"

Nalani laughed and Uluwehi just gave him a monumental stink eye.

"Don't worry, Kai. We won't make asses of ourselves."

Uluwehi grumbled under her breath that, "I'm not

making any promises." But she hugged him on the way out of the door as his sisters laughed between themselves.

He'd just have to hope that they'd take pity, not on him, but on Summer. The last thing he wanted to do was have her feel uncomfortable around his family.

All of his family.

But there really wasn't a way to sugar coat it. Sometimes, unlike the swimming lessons he was going to surreptitiously give her, you had to jump off into the deep end.

And this family dinner?

Well, it was as deep as you could get.

He knew he could depend on his mother and her friends to help out, but his sisters? They were more like the wacky sidekicks in a Disney film. Sometimes nice, sometimes awkwardly breaking into song, and sometimes you wanted to punt them off into the next scene. Still, they were his family. And he loved them.

Most of the time.

Okay then, time to go.

Stepping out of his car, he made his way to the front doors of the apartment building and smiled as Summer waved at him from the lobby.

Before he could reach for the door, she pushed it open and held out her hand to him.

Her open gesture hit him like a ton of bricks.

He took the hand she offered and instead of turning to walk back to his car, he stood there and used her hand to draw her closer.

And then a little closer.

When she was almost toe to toe with him, he gave her a big smile. "Mahalo, Summer."

She drew back a little, her expression plainly telling him that she was confused. "You're thanking me? For what?"

It's like she had no idea how amazing she was.

"For coming today. For meeting me downstairs even though I would have been happy to wait. And," he lifted their joined hands, "for reaching out to me and holding my hand."

Kai lifted their hands a little higher and turned them. When he leaned down, he brushed his lips against the backs of her fingers and then again on the back of her hand.

"I've been missing you."

The look in her eyes told him she felt the same way and he knew he had to get them moving to the car before he decided he was going to kiss her right then and there. It would be amazing. There was no mistake about that, but he wanted to find the perfect moment for a repeat of that first kiss, and he had a feeling he knew exactly where it was going to happen.

He just had to get there first.

"I'm," she balked before they even started to move, "I'm a little worried about today."

You and me both, Ku`ulei. But probably for different reasons.

"I'm okay with going to the beach. I have on SPF higher than Einstein's IQ, but I just need to know if this is okay." She stepped back and he looked at her outfit: khaki shorts and a loose long sleeve cover-up that looked like an old baseball jersey.

"Yeah, fine, but if you don't have your swimsuit on underneath you might want to put it on before we go. There's a bathroom there, but it would be easier if you could just take off the shirt and… what's wrong?"

The smile she offered him was a little hesitant.

"I've got my swimsuit on underneath, but I'm hoping we can just get into the water and maybe… go up to our knees?"

He narrowed his gaze at her, trying to see exactly what was bothering her.

He just couldn't seem to find it.

"How about this," Kai smiled at her, hoping it would ease some of her anxiety, "I'm going to make a promise that if you don't want to do something, then we won't. If you want to spend the morning sitting on the sand, that's good. If you want to spend it sitting in the car, I'm fine with that too."

He turned her hand in his until her palm was flat against his chest.

Kai knew just how fast it was beating because around Summer, his heart always seemed to be in a race toward something. Likely the future… with her.

"You just tell me no. And it'll be no. This is supposed to be fun for both of us, okay?"

She nodded and together they started walking to his car.

It was hard enough to let go of her hand to close her door, but as soon as they were on the open road, he reached over and picked up her hand again, threading their fingers together. It felt right. Natural.

It felt like Summer.

And that was all he needed.

By the time he pulled into the parking lot at Waimanalo Beach Park, Kai was more nervous than excited. There was this little niggling feeling that no matter what he did to help her relax, she just wasn't going to want to go into the water.

It wasn't a deal-breaker in a relationship as far as he was concerned, but being in the water was a large part of his life.

And because of that, he wanted to share it with Summer.

He found a spot near the end of the parking lot and smiled at the familiar bumper stickers he saw on the cars and trucks nearby.

KEEP WAIMANALO COUNTRY

Half a dozen logo stickers for surf and clothing shops and more quippy phrases.

WHA? YOU IN ONE HURRY? TRY GO EARLY

DA KINE

HI LIFE

And a bumper sticker that put it all into perspective for him.

HANG LOOSE!

The sticker had a shaka sign behind the word and it reminded him to sit back, relax, and take a breath.

He let go of Summer's hand and put the car into park before he looked over at her in the passenger seat. "Ready?"

Summer drew in a breath like she was preparing to jump off a cliff. "Yes."

"I'll get everything out of the back."

Kai opened his door and got out, making his way around to the trunk and opening it up with a smile. He picked up the insulated cooler bag with the food in it and a couple of big beach towels. There was going to be a lot of shade available so he wouldn't worry too much about her burning, but he'd be more than happy to keep an eye on her.

All of her.

Just in case.

"Hey."

He turned and saw her standing beside him. "Hey." He couldn't help smiling at her. "You look so good."

"In a ratty old top and shorts? Awesome."

Kai shook his head. "Fight it all you want, but I think you're beautiful. No amount of second guessing me or making jokes about yourself is going to convince me to join in."

He knew she wasn't fishing for compliments.

No, the look on her face said she just didn't believe it.

Crazy? But true.

He was just glad he'd met her when he did. He'd just keep telling her the truth and maybe one day, she'd believe it. Even then, he'd tell her again and again how beautiful she was to him, because it was the truth.

She held out her hands, reaching for the armload of things he was holding. "I can help."

Nodding, he put one of the towels into her arms and then she surprised him by taking the second.

"Anything else?"

"No." He straightened up and closed the trunk. "Let's go find a place to eat."

They stepped up onto the grass surrounding the parking lot and Kai kept his focus on the beach. Waimanalo Beach was a long, nearly pristine stretch of sand that faded into water so blue it looked like turquoise, shining in the sun. The trees in between the two were mostly ironwoods and provided a thick canopy covering their heads.

As they walked, people started calling out to him.

"Hui!"

He turned and lifted a hand in greeting.

Another voice from the sand. "Eh, bruddah! 'Sup!"

And another. "Chee-hoo! Howzit, boy!"

Laughing, Kai greeted them back in turn. By the time they reached the edge of the trees and stepped out onto the sand, very nearly alone, there had been nearly a dozen people who had called out to them.

Summer turned her head and looked at him wide-eyed. "Who are all of those people?"

"Friends. Old classmates. People from the neighborhood. Everyone around here knows everyone else at least enough to say hello when we pass by each other."

"That's a lot of people."

Kai stopped on the sand, just outside of the tree line, but

still in an area where the trees would give them cover for a while. "It's just the way we live here. Faces become familiar, they remain familiar, like a big… huge, extended family. They might not even know my name. I don't always know theirs."

"It's a lot."

"It's Hawaii." He set down the insulated cooler and reached out a hand for a towel and she gave one to him. Flicking it out, he set it down on the sand and smiled when she did the same with the other, laying them side by side. "You'll get used to it," he explained, "until it's just the way things are for you too."

She sat down on one of the towels and reached down to her sneakers. In moments she'd toed both of them off. "Yuck. Sand in between my toes."

He shrugged a little. "It's not a bad feeling. Now that your shoes are off, I think it won't be so gross."

"I hope so."

"I packed a lunch for us. You just have to let me know when you're hungry." He reached over and slid the bag closer. "Fruit. Sandwiches. Chips. There'll be plenty to eat at dinner tonight, but this should be more than enough to keep us going until then."

He unzippered the top and moved a few things around, reaching for a drink at the bottom. "Do you want a water or a juice?"

Kai stilled his hand and waited for an answer. It didn't come. "Summer?"

When she didn't answer, he turned his head to look at her and found her sitting with her eyes fixed on the ocean.

"Summer?"

When she just sat there, her attention on the ocean, he started to worry a little.

Closing the cooler, he turned and reached out to her. Kai

set his hand on her upper arm and felt her warmth through her long-sleeved top. She crossed her other arm over and set her hand on his, giving it a soft squeeze.

"Are you okay?"

He watched her draw in a long, deep breath and then she turned to look at him and he was dazzled by the look on her face.

She was glowing.

Almost incandescent.

"It's silly, right?"

He was a little lost. "I don't know what 'it' is. But if you say so. Yes."

She squeezed his hand again. "I'm just talking about me being weirded out by this. I'm looking out there and the water looks like a painting. Sure, I can see the water coming in and rushing onto the sand, but there's nothing scary out there coming to get me.

"I know I'm not helpless. I mean, I can doggy paddle and maybe crawl in the water. And if you're there, I know I'll be safe, but I'm sitting here freaking myself out for nothing. It's crazy right?"

Kai moved closer until their legs touched and he wrapped his other arm around her back. "You're allowed to be worried and scared. That's not something you can just stop because you say so. The first time I tried to get back on the boat where I was shot," he drew in a breath as the old rush of nausea pushed up into his throat, "I almost fell to my knees. I heard a car backfire in the parking lot, and I thought I was back in that moment." He used his hand to rub her arm gently. "I'm not sure if your fear comes from an accident or something else, but whatever it is, we can take it slow. Nothing has to be done in a day. And nothing has to be done today. If we end up sitting here until we go to dinner, I'm happy. Holding you? I'm good. More than good."

"It's not like I almost drowned or anything like that. It was just control. I don't remember exactly when it happened, just that it happened. I was in the water and I think I was having fun. Splashing around? I remember laughter and people smiling. And then it's like the water pulled me away. Up and down, turning in circles. I'm not even sure the memory is accurate, but it's what I see and feel when I get near water, even in a pool.

"I felt like I was out of control. Alone. Scared silly. After that I just stayed away from water that had a life of its own." She winced a little. "That's not completely accurate. Pools do it too. I think it boils down to when I can't feel the ground under my feet. Like if I take a step, I won't be able to have that solid feeling beneath me."

"Then we'll stay here. We don't have to go anywhere near the water if you-"

"That's the thing though. I want to."

She pulled her legs under her and stood. Kai followed suit, keeping close, but not trying to hold her and move her off balance.

Summer turned to look back at the water like she'd done before and drew in another deep breath. "I want to go out there. I bet the water will feel amazing against my legs. And the sand scratching between my toes? It will probably feel like heaven under my feet."

She turned to look at him and he felt all the air in his lungs rush out of him at the beautiful look of determination in her eyes.

"I just need to know if you'll be with me."

She reached out her hand to him, barely lifting it between them because they were still fairly close to each other.

Without hesitation, he took hold of her hand and gave it a gentle squeeze. "Always, Summer. If you want me there, then there I'll be."

She grinned at him. "Okay. Then let's go and walk through the water."

He nodded, unable to keep his eyes off her beautiful face. "Let's walk."

~

It felt like heaven.

The water at the edge of the sand lapped over her feet, washing in and back out into the ocean. Kai was right. Every step brought sand squishing up between her toes. Somehow it was different. When her feet had been dry, and the sand had found its way inside her shoes felt like sandpaper. Which made a whole lot of ridiculous sense, but having sandpaper in your shoes?

She almost shuddered thinking about it again.

Mixed in with the saltwater rushing up on the sand, it felt almost like velvet. Not the super slick polyester fabric that crushes with just a touch. It felt like the one made with natural fibers that had a real heft and substance.

Walking on velvet with her hand in his.

It was, in a word, sensual.

With all of the clinical, evidentiary work that she did, taking things apart and analyzing the tiniest pieces of it, feeling the sand under her feet in that way gave her control. Helped her feel a real connection to the earth.

And Kai.

Holding his hand.

Feeling his fingers sliding between hers.

The gentle brush of his fingertips.

It was heaven on Waimanalo Beach.

. . .

Turning her head, she saw Kai looking at her with a smile, as if he was entertained by watching her.

Once that thought was in her head, she liked the idea of it.

A lot.

"You know," she slid a sideways glance over at him and saw him turn to listen as she spoke, "if you asked me to come back here again, I think I'd like it."

"Yeah?" The look on his face warmed her like the sun. "I'd like to bring you here again too."

A wave coursed over her feet and rose up to her lower calves. She tensed a little, but she held onto his hand and he held on tight. Instead of the fear she expected to rise in her throat, she felt exhilaration instead. "Until then," she gave him a soft smile, "maybe we can walk in a little deeper?"

"Absolutely." Kai walked alongside, putting himself further in the water. It wouldn't do much if the wave that coursed over the sand pushed on them with a lot of force, but his hold on her hand? She knew he'd hold onto her.

He'd keep her safe.

And the deeper they went as they walked, taking paths that went farther and farther out, the water began to crest and rise to just above her knees.

Her heart was pounding like a racehorse, her skin dotted with sweat as the sun poured over both of them.

She didn't understand it. Watching Kai swim at the pool. Seeing how swiftly he moved through the water. The powerful sweep of his arms, the froth that bubbled in the wake of his feet spoke volumes about his skill and strength in the water. To feel him at her side, holding her hand, measuring his steps to hers, spoke volumes about Kai as a person.

And he was with her.

The more time she spent with him the more it felt normal, better than normal.

She felt like things were changing inside of her.

And all if it for the better.

Waiting had never been Frank's strong suit.

Patience wasn't something he'd been born with.

When he'd gone to live with his granddad after his parents died in a storm, it was something that had been beaten into him.

Pain.

Blood.

Terror.

Those he understood.

Those he lived with.

And even when his granddad had grown too weak, and Frank had grown strong the dynamics didn't change.

He respected his granddad. Honored him in the way a parent should be honored.

Frank listened.

He followed.

He didn't fucking talk back.

He did what he was told.

And that meant waiting.

That meant getting dirty and grimy and waiting behind a shit ton of boxes in an alley.

The worst part was trying to ignore the bugs and four legged fiends creeping around. He hated it, but he did it because Pops had a few more things that needed doing.

And Frank, well, he was the only one who was good enough to do what it took.

Night had fallen about an hour before Frank took his first

look out from behind his barricade. Where he'd hidden himself, he couldn't see cars going by and there really wasn't much foot traffic to speak of. He'd planned well.

He sat back behind the boxes and touched the back of his head against the brick wall. He'd get a little sleep without worrying that he'd be interrupted. Those few hours he needed.

That sleep would give him the focus and the strength to take another one.

A slow smile peeled across his lips.

He was getting good at it.

When he'd taken the first, he'd made mistakes. He'd almost let the man pull free and escape. Frank had felt real panic in those moments. Panic that had turned into elation when he'd gone down for the last time. His mouth gaping open. The spray of blood from his lips like one of those cheap battery-powered fountains they sold the tourists in Chinatown. That first kill still felt like it was on his hands.

He could still smell the coppery scent of blood in his nose.

Just a few hours to let people get good and drunk. Drunks didn't care if they heard a fight. They didn't make good witnesses.

And the man who worked in the electronics store? He'd be in the back room until at least ten. Frank would time it perfectly. He'd wait and take him down in the next alley on the way to his car.

Another alley filled with boxes and rats.

A fitting end.

Yes. They were getting closer and closer to the end.

And then Frank could get the hell off this stupid island.

CHAPTER 10

As soon as they arrived at the party, Kai noticed one very disturbing fact, the normally large gathering resembled an event on the scale of the 50th State Fair. The immediately surrounding streets had been cordoned off with sawhorses with reflective tape and there was a big banner above the garage at the main house that said HO'OMAIKA'I KAI.

"Wow," beside him, Summer looked up at the banner with wide, expressive eyes. "It's like you're a celebrity."

"I think that was my sisters. I hope that's all they did." Grinning at her, Kai tilted his head toward the house. "Let's go see who's in the kitchen."

Before they got to the door, it swung open and two little girls launched from the step toward him.

"Kai! Kai!"

The two slowed as they reached him and instead of bowling over Summer, one of them hugged her and the other, him. It took him a minute to remember which was which, they both seemed to be growing like weeds. He touched his hand to the head of the little girl choking off his air with her strangle hold on his waist. "Summer, this is

Kailani Ahfong. And that little opihi holding onto you is Leilani."

Leilani giggled. "We're sisters!"

Summer brushed the little girl's bangs back from her face. "Really? Sisters?"

Kailani puffed up a little. "I'm older by two whole years!"

Her sister shook her head so much that the flower she had tucked above her ear fell to the ground. "Tutu Leo said it's eighteen months!"

The little girls leaned in toward each other and Kai wondered if they were going to start an argument right there.

Reaching his hands out, he put one hand on each head and tilted them back so they were looking at him. "No fighting."

It was Leilani who looked the most put out. "But I like fighting. Papa said I'm good at it."

"Well," Kai grinned at the two, "be good at it later. I want to take Summer inside to meet everyone."

They looked absolutely crestfallen at the idea, but they didn't argue with him.

Before they could run away, Summer picked up the flower that had fallen from above Leilani's ear. Crouching down beside the little girl, she tucked it in. Leilani leaned in and gave her a big hug around Summer's neck. "Mahalo, Summer."

When the girls left, they ran around the corner of the house. Kai shook his head. "Auwe. I wish I had that kind of energy."

Summer grinned at him. "I know what you mean. That's intense."

He lifted a hand and placed it over his belly. "I think I'm going to have bruises tomorrow."

Leaning in, Summer rolled her eyes. "I doubt that, silly."

"Silly?"

They both turned to see someone standing in the doorway. Kai heard Summer's soft intake of breath.

"Come on in Kai and bring Summer inside. Your mother's waiting for you to introduce her."

With his hand on Summer's lower back, they made their way up the stairs. He could hear Summer whispering under her breath. "That's Haunani Chun from the Honolulu P.I. TV show." She shook herself. "I mean that's the actress who plays her. How do you know her?"

Kai lifted a hand in greeting. "Hey, Cuz!"

"Aloha, Kolohe." She gave him a big hug, whispering into his ear. "It's about damn time."

Then she stood back and looked at Summer. "Aloha, Summer. I'm so glad you came!" Hi`ilani gave Summer a big, welcoming hug and when the two leaned away from each other Kai noticed that Hi`ilani had taken Summer's hand in her own. "Come on in. I'll introduce you."

By the time he realized what was going on, the screen door slammed shut with him on the outside. "Hey! Wait for me!"

Inside the kitchen it was a little bit of chaos mixed in with smiling faces and sweet laughter. Kai watched as Hi`ilani introduced Summer to the other ladies. Her Tutu Leo, a few more cousins that had come over from the Leeward side for the party, some other women from the neighborhood and finally, his mother who had watched the whole event from the adjoining living room.

Kai made sure to be there when Summer came face to face with his mother. And amazingly enough, Hi`ilani let him do the introductions on his own.

"Mom, this is Summer Maitland. She's friends with Elodie and her husband, Scott." He gave her a hopeful look before he turned to Summer. He searched her face hoping that she was okay with the crazy pace of all the introductions.

Thankfully, he didn't see any hesitation at all. "Summer, this is my mother, Nanea Akina."

Summer's smile was full, and she reached out her hand in greeting. "It's really nice to meet you, M-"

His mother pulled her into a hug. "Aloha no, Summer. You are truly welcome here." His mother met his gaze with her own over Summer's shoulder, and he could see the warmth shining within. "Come, I have something I made for you."

Kai watched as his mother lifted a lei from a side table and held it in both hands. Moving back to Summer she smiled at the younger woman with great Aloha.

"Having you come today is perfect timing. When I went out to pick flowers this morning, I found that my puakenikeni trees had blossomed overnight." Nanea turned the lei slowly in her hands as she spoke. "These flowers start like this, a pale pale yellow, almost white. The next stage is a buttery yellow. And finally, the blossoms will turn a rich yellow-orange color. Back in the day when cruise ships kept the harbors really busy and Matson was more than just a fleet of container ships, they had luxurious cruise ships. Puakenikeni was given the name 'ten penny flower' because that's what people paid for it in that era. Now, with all of the big houses and developments it's harder to find plants that bloom enough for leis, so I'm so happy there were enough to make this."

His mother gently lowered the lei and set it softly on Summer's shoulders.

"I hope you'll enjoy the lei and wear it tonight."

Summer lifted a hand and her fingertips played over the delicate curves on the edge of the petals. "It's so beautiful. Thank you."

Kai saw the look that his mother cast in his direction and he was surprised to see the glossy look of tears on her lashes.

"Now you two," his mother waved them toward the door, "go outside and meet people. We'll have the food out in no time."

~

Summer sat on the grass, leaning back against Kai's chest. She wasn't sure she could move for the foreseeable future. Not only was her stomach full, but she could feel Kai's warmth against her back and along her sides where his legs touched hers.

She couldn't help but sink into him. He didn't seem to mind. Instead, he wrapped an arm around her waist and held her gently against him, his breath sometimes brushing against her ear.

A quick look off to the right told her that the SEALs were about to leave. They had a mission briefing in the morning and they'd already said their goodbyes to Kai. They'd included her in it as well and she had to admit it was kind of surreal to be passed down the line of big, muscular men, getting a hug from each one.

Now, she lifted her hand to wave to Elodie who blew her a kiss before stepping into her husband's side, leaning into his one-armed embrace.

There had been a time, a very recent time, when Summer ached a little inside at the sight of love like the kind that Mustang and Elodie shared.

It felt like something she could see. Something she could understand.

But not something she could have.

Shifting a little, she set her arm over Kai's where it lay over her stomach.

"Summer?"

She turned her head and smiled at Hi`ilani. It was strange to be on a first name basis with someone she'd seen on her TV. She'd even binge watched Honolulu P.I. with a bottle of wine one weekend.

"The girls and I were wondering if you'd like to go with us to a Karaoke bar one night."

"Karaoke?" She'd sounded out the word. "It sounds familiar?"

The girls laughed at her confusion, but Summer could tell they weren't laughing 'at' her.

Nalani, one of Kai's sisters, sounded it out a different way. The one that Summer recognized immediately. Like 'Care-ee-oh-kee'.

"Oh! Yeah. I'd like to but I'm… I'm really bad at it."

Uluwehi was the first one to pipe up. "Me too! But it really doesn't matter after my second tequila shot. Come on, say you'll come with us, yeah?"

"Yeah," Summer nodded. "Sure. As long as I'm not working late, that'll be great!

"Oh?" Nalani leaned in a little. "Where do you work?"

Summer hesitated a little. "Pearl Harbor Base." When she saw that wasn't enough of an answer, she tried to pick something that was real but innocuous. "I work in one of the science labs on the base. Basic boring stuff."

Summer turned to look at Hi`ilani and saw the other woman's bland expression. Something in the way she looked at Summer said Hi`ilani didn't buy what she was selling.

Maybe Hi`ilani was just a really shrewd judge of character?

"Ooooh, here come the other hotties." Nalani playfully fanned herself as Hi`ilani got up. A moment later she was enveloped in the arms of a very hot guy.

A very hot guy who Summer surprisingly knew.

"Ajax?"

Someone called to her and she turned her head. "Hey, Summer! It's you!" Shado gave a wink as he moved closer. When he sank down to one knee, he looked behind her. "Hey, bro. You gonna punch me out if I give her a hug?"

Summer felt Kai's laughter against her back.

"You're supposed to ask the lady, first."

Summer got up onto her feet and stepped into Shado's arms for a hug. "It's good to see you again."

Shado stepped back and gave her a smile. "Less heat. Fewer dead bodies on the ground."

He'd spoken softly enough, but Summer still tensed up. She hadn't said anything to Kai about her work beyond the fact that it was on the base. Nothing would kill a romance faster than talk about dead bodies. Before she could turn and see if Kai had heard anything, Mace shoved Shado aside and pulled her into a hug. "Leave it to the scrawny one to almost ruin a party. I'll duct tape his mouth if you want me to."

Summer had to choke back her laughter. "No, leave him alone," she leaned in with smile, "for now."

Mace gave her another quick hug and when he released her, he pointed a finger at Shado. "You better play nice, bro."

Summer saw Baron and Cullen heading her way, but she saw Kai step up beside her and shake hands with Mace.

She couldn't help the rise of color in her cheeks as she saw the two men introducing themselves.

She touched Kai's arm with her hand. "I'm sorry I didn't-"

Kai surprised her when he leaned in and touched his lips to her cheek. "A`ole pilikia, ku`ulei. I can introduce myself."

Summer saw Mace nod at the comment. He gave her a wink before he moved away, and Cullen filled his spot. After she greeted Cullen and then Baron who surprised her with a warm greeting, she realized that she'd lost track of Kai in the shuffle.

Ajax stepped into her view and she relaxed a little more. "Hey. I bet this is a little overwhelming, right?"

Summer couldn't do more than nod.

He hugged Hi`ilani closer to his side as if he couldn't get her close enough. "The first time I came here with Hi`ilani I thought it was some kind of street fair or wedding reception in someone's yard."

Her shoulders sagged a bit in relief. "Oh good. I thought the same thing. When Kai said it was just a family get together-"

"You thought, maybe ten or twelve people at the most."

"Exactly."

The couple shared a sweet look before Ajax spoke again. "Don't worry too much, it gets easier. I promise."

"Just thinking that it's a normal family gathering but it looks like a once in a decade reunion... it's kind of daunting."

"It's kind of like joining the Army. Ow."

Summer saw the pointed look on Hi`ilani's face, but she also saw the loving look that Ajax gave her. The man was in deep.

"Hey," Ajax rubbed his side, "you said it too."

"Just don't scare Summer away. Kai would never forgive you."

"Kailani? Your sister?"

Summer felt a little rush of relief that she wasn't the only confused one in the group.

Turning her head, she saw Kai just behind her. Before she could think better of it, she touched Kai's arm.

Touching Kai was a gentle compulsion at that point.

He turned and didn't seem all that surprised to see Ajax.

The two men greeted each other with an embrace.

When Ajax turned back to her, he had a big smile on his face. "This Kai?"

"This?" She looked between the two men. "How many Kais are there?"

Ajax deferred to Kai, letting him think through the answer.

"Uh, let me think. Offhand… in this group?" Kai's gaze flickered up into the night sky for a moment. When he looked back at her, his expression was a study in sincerity. "Ten? Maybe twelve?"

Summer was starting to understand. "That's why you thought Kai was Hi`ilani's sister Kailani? Is Kai a pretty common name? Like David or John?"

Again, Ajax turned to Kai for the answer even though Summer suspected he could probably give the answer as well.

"It's not quite the same," his face held a thoughtful expression to it, "Kai is a nickname of sorts."

"It means water, right?" Summer prayed that she was right. She hoped it wasn't one of those words with a bunch of meanings.

Kai's smile warmed her like the sun. "Exactly. Kai is water, but a lot of Hawaiian first names are more of a statement than just a thought or a single word. If you want, I'll explain more later, but I have a feeling if we keep Jack from making his way over to my cousin, he might chew a hand off to escape captivity."

Summer winced at the idea. "Then maybe we should release him."

Ajax leaned in and kissed her on the cheek. "I'll be around, probably until the end of the party. Not sure about the other guys, but if you need us, just let us know, okay?"

He walked away and Summer waved at the other Deltas. She felt like she'd dodged a bullet of sorts. Yes, they were off base and this had nothing to do with the military or the Army specifically, but she wasn't sure how long it would be that she could avoid talking about her job if she kept running into people who knew what she did.

What she did wasn't anything that was of National Security importance, so she didn't have to keep things a secret. Civilians visited the building for The Defense POW/MIA Accounting Agency. She knew that before anything else happened, she was going to have to take a risk and tell Kai that her average everyday job dealt with human remains.

Chances are that Kai could handle that. However, there were people in her life who hadn't been able to deal with it. Morbid. Disgusting. She could still hear their words echoing in her head.

Still, it was better to do it now before she fell all the way in love with him.

It wouldn't hurt all that much.

Right.

It was going to hurt.

Badly.

But sooner, rather than later she would have to tell him.

Just not in front of a ton of people. Back at her apartment.

Yes, that's what she was going to do.

Summer felt Kai's hand tugging on hers.

"The kids are about to dance, want to sit with me and watch?"

The words brought her out of her odd reverie.

"Which kids?"

He pointed over at the side of the house and she saw the two girls she'd met when she'd first arrived. Hi`ilani's sisters.

They'd changed out of their T-shirts and shorts and were now dressed in adorable little puffy tops gathered by elastic just under their arms. Their skirts ended just above their knees with what looked like pantaloons under it giving the skirt some flair. With their hair down around their shoulders instead of pulled back in ponytails, they looked completely different.

Sitting off to the side were nearly a dozen musicians. Guitars, ukuleles, a stand-up bass, and something that was laid across a table before another musician. She'd ask Kai about it later, but at that moment, the girls commanded everyone's attention.

Settling himself beside her on the cool blanket of grass, Kai leaned in and murmured to her. "We call this kanikapila. People dance. People sing. Kind of a like a jam session. Everyone joins in with whatever they'd like to do."

Summer nodded and enjoyed his warmth. The night was dark enough that even with the inherent humidity in the air, there was still a bit of chill that moved across her skin.

The musicians began to play, and Summer let the music wash over her. The little girls began to move in unison. The lyrics of the song were a mix of Hawaiian and English so Summer could enjoy every minute of the dance.

The girls were under ten but they both moved with a skill and assurance that Summer knew she didn't possess. They were amazing to watch. Their feet tracing patterns in the grass while their hands moved through the night, telling their own story.

It was hard to imagine that the silly little girls who had wrapped their arms around her just a few hours ago were gliding through the song as if they were years older.

When they finished, Summer started to clap along with everyone else, blinking back a few tears that she couldn't quite explain. Looking at Kai, she saw the look in his eyes as he watched her. Warm and full of emotion. Just the way he looked at her made her warm all over, aching to be in his arms and have those eyes on hers all night long.

"Summer?"

She heard the hesitation in his voice and she smiled even more. What would he have to be worried about?

"Kai! Come on!"

"Yeah, come dance with us!"

Summer caught one of the girls around her waist as she stumbled and caught her knees in her skirts. "Careful."

The little girl turned and looked at her. "Tell him, Summer!"

"Yeah," her sister jumped onto the same idea. "Tell Kai to come dance with us!"

She didn't know what to do except look at Kai and ask him in all earnestness. "Do you dance?"

The girls laughed out loud. "Of course he does! Come on, cuz!"

Summer couldn't help getting wrapped up in the little girls' enthusiasm. "Yeah, come on, Kai. Dance!"

He seemed shocked for a moment, but it didn't take long before he got up on his feet, tugging the hem of his shirt down before the girls each took a hand and led him out onto the grass.

Kai's spot beside her wasn't empty for long. Hi`ilani sat down beside her with a gentle laugh. "I had a feeling the girls were going to drag him up there. They love dancing with Kai."

Summer grinned. "I have to admit, I'm excited about it myself. I've seen some hula but not very many men were on stage."

"Well, this is going to make his mother really happy too. Her mother was a kumu hula. A hula teacher," Hi`ilani clarified. "But Kai usually shies away from this."

"Oh?" Summer looked at the lovely woman sitting beside her. "Is it because of your sisters?"

Hi`ilani shook her head. "Probably not. He's pretty

immune to their begging by now, but you? I think he might be trying to impress you."

Now that, Summer didn't really expect.

Guys that she knew didn't really like to dance with a partner, let alone as a kind of performer.

She really was looking forward to this.

The three were talking to the musicians and Summer could tell that there was a bit of a debate going on. The girls were talking one at a time and Kai was shaking his head. "I wonder," she said aloud, "what they're suggesting."

Hi`ilani winced. "I have no idea, but they're bound to happen on something he likes."

"At the risk of sounding a little nosy," Summer began, "how are you and Kai cousins? Is it through your mother's side?"

"It's through my Waimanalo side," Hi`ilani grinned. "Kai is what you'd call our calabash cousin. It's not about blood or genealogy. It's all about the heart."

"All about Aloha?" Summer wondered. "Is that what you mean?"

"Exactly. Calabash is a kind of wooden bowl that food can be served in. So, calabash family are people who you'd share a meal with. Good friends, long time neighbors, people as close as family." Hi`ilani continued. "Kai's family has lived near ours for a couple of generations. We share birthdays and other celebrations. If my dad wasn't here to walk me down the aisle at my wedding, I'd probably ask Kai. Our family only has girls in this generation. Something my father groans about constantly. He would have brought out his rifle to threaten Jack for our first date if Jack didn't already have him outgunned. Instead, they talked about weapons and both dismantled and reassembled my dad's rifle before we left for our date."

"That sounds like fun?"

Hi`ilani shrugged. "Jack and I have had our ups and downs, but we've finally decided that what we have isn't just worth fighting for. It's all about the love we share and neither one of us is letting go ever again."

The musicians started in and the pace of the music was almost double the rhythm of the first song. It was interesting to see the differences in the dance steps. Both the little girls and Kai did the same steps as far as she could tell, but the girls had more sway in their hips and their hands were full of grace. Kai's movements mimicked the girls' but the way he carried himself… the only word that she could think of was masculine. The lyrics were lost to her as she tried to see the dance as a whole, but then Kai stopped in place and circled his hips around.

Goodness.

Summer's face was on fire.

Oh, there was nothing specifically naughty about the movement and the expression on his face was a bright, almost flirty smile.

The lyrics repeated and she felt herself still and hold her breath, watching that same circular swivel of his hips.

A couple of voices called out from the crowd and an ear-splitting whistle turned Kai's head. He gave them a little lift of his chin and a wink.

The song continued and Summer had to admit that the world around her faded into the background. The more the crowd called out and the little girls beside him giggled, Kai added a little flair into his dance and Summer wondered if her face was as red as it was hot.

Heaven help her.

She'd never been so turned on by a guy before.

It wasn't just the sexy swivel of his hips, but it was the way he carried himself. Tall. Talented. This wasn't just a guy getting up and fooling around to the music. Kai had skill.

And he also had her full attention.

Summer was grateful for the distance between them because if he was close enough for her to touch, she would probably have grabbed him by the shirt and kissed him.

Was it silly?

Absolutely.

But was it true?

Yes. She wanted to kiss him again.

She wanted to see if the heat and warmth she'd felt from their earlier kiss would be even more now. Would those embers fan into flames?

By the time the dance stopped, and Kai and the girls finished their movements in a similar pose, the crowd was roaring with applause and quite a few catcalls and whistles for Kai.

The little girls beamed up at him and Kai made them both laugh when he swept them up in his arms, one on each hip.

Kai walked straight toward her and Summer felt as if her mouth had gone dry. Her hands were almost numb, and the rest of her trembled with some kind of unnamed emotion.

He was already the most handsome man she'd ever met. The way he spoke to her and listened? He was a treasure! And the way he looked, holding two children in his arms, walking toward her with a purpose?

It put all kinds of thoughts into her head.

And a few thoughts in other places.

By the time he reached her, she was dizzy with the need to touch him and lean into his embrace.

Summer plucked at her shirt, trying to get some air and calm down her pulse which was pounding at a dizzying speed.

He put the girls down at his feet and Hi`ilani ushered her sisters away, leaving Summer as alone with Kai as they could be in the middle of a gathering that large.

"Hey," Kai set his hands on her upper arms and gently smoothed his palms up and down. "How are you doing? You look a little… tired?"

She latched onto the idea with relief flooding through her body.

"Yeah, it was all that sun. I should probably go home."

Summer took a step to the side and Kai took a step in the same direction.

"I'll go with you."

She waved him off. "You should stay. It's your party. Everyone's so happy that you're fully recovered. Stay."

"Summer."

She stopped when she heard the tone of his voice. "What?"

He gave her a little wink. "I drove you here."

Oh.

Yeah.

"I remember that now."

"Let's take a little walk down by the beach." His tone was softer… sweeter. "The wind off of the ocean will help with the heat."

"Yeah?"

She knew that even if he told her it was an abject lie, she was still going to go with him. Being alone with Kai Akina sounded just like heaven. And who didn't want to go to heaven?

"All right," she leaned into him, "let's go."

CHAPTER 11

The wind off of the ocean didn't do a thing to ease the heat that was prickling against her skin. Instead, the rush of air that swept past them as they walked only made it harder for her to think. It made it so much easier to feel.

And she wanted to feel his lips on hers again.

The question was, did he?

Summer felt his hand tug on hers and she turned to look at him.

"Hey."

She parroted him on a soft sigh. "Hey."

Kai tilted his head and looked at her in the silver spill of moonlight. "You look like you're a million miles away."

Smiling, she tightened her hold on his hand. "I'm right here."

"Want to tell me what you're thinking about?"

"Not really," she murmured, almost under her breath. "But I'm going to ask you a question."

"Ask."

She loved the look in his eyes. She could feel his concern with just the sweeping caress of his gaze, and it gave her strength to believe his answer was going to be what she wanted to hear. "The other day at the pool, you kissed me."

Kai smiled. "I kissed you a few times."

He certainly did.

"I was just wondering, if you planned on doing it again?"

"Yes." His expression changed. He was still smiling but he also looked relieved as well. "I was planning on a lot of kisses."

"Tonight?" She almost took the question back. She didn't want to sound pathetic.

He didn't give her a chance to worry.

"Yes, tonight."

She nodded but didn't speak. The sound of the waves rushing up on the sand, the trade winds moving through the branches of the trees over their heads, it was soothing.

Summer let go of his hand and reached out. One hand and then the other settled on his chest. She smoothed her hands over the dark fabric of his T-shirt, and she felt the edge of her thumb bump up against the pendant hidden under his clothes.

"I've never seen a guy dance like that before."

"Yeah?" Kai drew in a breath and she smoothed her hands down his sides until she got to his waist and a little lower to his hips.

"Yeah." Summer looked up into his eyes and felt like she was under some kind of spell. Maybe it was the moonlight pulling her like the tide. Or maybe it was the rush and mystery of the ocean that had always been linked to sirens of the deep. "I was so afraid that someone would see," she leaned closer and her hands slipped around to his back, her palms against his waist, her fingers splayed against his skin, "how much it... I mean, what it made me feel."

He wrapped his arms around her, his hands on her lower

back as well. "You want to tell me about it? Because I really want to know."

She was finally, for the first time in her life, bursting with answers, but standing out there on the beach she worried that they'd be seen. "Can we... can we go somewhere... private?"

"How quickly do we need to get there?" Kai's indrawn breath swelled his chest and she felt it brush against her own.

"Soon." She swallowed and kept her voice as calm as she could even as her blood surged through her veins. "Very soon."

Leaning in, he whispered in her ear. "There's a place along the sea wall. It won't take us more than a minute or two to get there. At this time of night, with the moon right where it is, no one from the road or the beach can see us. We'll be invisible to everyone else."

The ache that had been growing inside of her gave her the push she needed as it deepened in her center. "Take me there."

He brushed a kiss against her lips and reached for her hand. "Hold my hand, ku`ulei. Come with me."

She felt the water on her feet as they moved and felt it swirl around her legs like a caress.

"The tide," he explained as they came to a stop, "has gone out to sea, the sand here makes a big enough bar for us to stand on. The waves will still reach us, but they won't..." she heard his breath catch in his throat as her hand reached for the hem of his T-shirt and slipped beneath it, "there's no danger from them."

"I'm not worried." She meant it. He knew what to watch out for. "Are you?"

"I'm feeling a lot of things."

The breath he took in sounded a little ragged to her ears.

And the sound made her feel like she was a woman with

more than a strong intellect. She was a woman who might be able to draw on a measure of power from those sirens. "What things?"

Kai turned and placed her against the rock wall, bracing one hand near her shoulder. "I want to know why you wanted to be... alone."

"I wanted to kiss you again," she smiled. "I've thought a lot about it. Felt a lot of things while I remembered your lips on mine. I'm hoping that you might-"

His lips crashed against hers, his hand cradling the back of her head. It was a kiss and yet it was so much more. The friction he created between their lips was electric. He stepped closer, pinning her hips against the wall and lowered his hand to her waist. The way he held her made it feel like he couldn't bear to let her go.

She returned the gesture, grasping onto his shoulders.

The feel of his body under her hands was incredible. She'd never held a man as fit as he was. A man whose muscles let him cut through the water with the skill and grace of a dolphin, and yet when he held her there was no doubt that he was all man.

She opened her mouth under his lips and felt his tongue sweep across her bottom lip. Summer chased it with her own and when they tangled together, she moaned deep in her throat.

When Kai covered her mouth again with his, she swore she felt him smile.

Summer wound her arms around his neck, her fingertips exploring the back of his neck, brushing against the short cut hair at the base of his head. Touching him just kept getting better and better.

He moved one hand under the hem of her loose shirt and flattened against her belly as his other fingers combed through her hair.

Turning her head, his lips caressed the skin along her jaw and then dipped to the sensitive skin just under her ear. Her arms tightened around his neck and he groaned.

"Ku`ulei."

Her whole body felt like it was alive. The waves that intermittently rushed over their feet pulled at her like gravity, pressing her tighter against Kai.

"What- oh god yes," his lips dragged against her neck and she leaned into his touch.

He pulled away for a moment and she put pressure on the back of his head, urging him back. He met her eyes when she opened them. "What did you say?"

Summer almost giggled. "Oh god yes?"

Laughing softly, Kai kissed her lips and asked again. "What were you going to say?"

She wiggled against him, the ache she felt inside was growing even stronger. She wanted to tell him to forget it, but she knew she wanted to know more. "Ku`ulei. What does that mean?"

"You." He leaned closer, trapping her hips against the wall, her body cushioning his as well. "Lei, like the one around your neck."

She dipped her chin down and smelled the deep floral notes of the puakenikeni flowers mixed in with the ocean salt in the air.

"Ku`u, my." His voice was deep, rich, and she could feel the vibrations of it everywhere he touched her. Her sensitive skin at the back of her neck, the tender expanse of her belly and down to her knees. She could tell that he was as attracted to her as she was to him. She held him close and felt her world swell with sensations.

"Ku`ulei," he pressed a kiss to her lips, "my lei of flowers."

She wanted more, but she wasn't sure she was ready. And

when he stepped back and looked down into her eyes, she saw the same hesitation.

Smiling, she sighed. "All this time I was worried about the waves pulling me under."

He brushed her hair back from her face, and gazed down into her eyes. "Maybe it was the moon that swept you away. It's the moon that commands the tides."

She leaned into him, placed her head against his shoulder and wrapped her arms around his body. "It's all you, Kai."

He led her over to the sandy beach and he sat down, pulling her into his lap. "I just want a little more time with you before we go back."

Summer sat on his lap and leaned in against him. "It is your party and you're missing a lot of it."

"Everyone's having a great time. I doubt they'll even notice."

She wasn't sure that was the truth, but the new week was looming ahead, and she had more than enough on her plate at work. If she had a chance for even a few more minutes, she had to take advantage of that.

"You looked like you were having fun at the party." His fingers combed through her hair.

"I did. I was a little nervous-"

"A little?"

Summer heard the laughter in his voice and poked him in the chest. "Hey!"

"Sorry, sorry!" He gave her a quick kiss on the lips.

She waved it off. "Okay, I had a lot of fun. It's not everyday a hot guy swivels his hips for me."

"I'm glad," he chuckled. "If someone else swivels for you, are you going to choose him instead?"

"Nope," she snuggled into him, "I like the guy I have."

"Good." He wrapped his arms around her. "I like the woman I have too."

"Wahine, right?"

He snuggled closer. "Wahine is woman. Women too."

"I usually make sure to check the picture on the bathroom door just to make sure."

He laughed again. "That sounds helpful."

Summer shrugged. "Unless you're in Outback Steakhouse." She hung her head. "I know. I know. Bad joke. Seriously though, I love learning more about the Hawaiian language. So many of the words just on their own sound like poetry.

"Some of the Hawaiian music that I've heard is achingly beautiful."

"Earlier," he began, "at the party, we talked about the people who are also called Kai by the family."

She sat up a little and looked at him, eager to hear what he had to say.

"I wanted to let you know my full name, that is, if you want to know."

"Yes," she touched her hand to his chest and felt the strong pulse of his heart under her palm, "I want to know."

"There are a number of ways that a child is given a name in the Hawaiian language. In families, there is usually a person well versed in the language who picks the names. Sometimes it's a wish or a hope for the child. In my case it was a dream. My tutu, my mother's mother, woke up on the morning of my birth with an image in her head. When my mother woke up and felt contractions, they took her to the hospital.

"As my mother struggled through labor for hours and hours, my tutu talked her through the contractions with images of the water rushing onto the beach. While she was pushing, my mother was exhausted and started to cry, saying she couldn't push anymore. Her mother took her hand and told her that she had to. That she had a little boy who was waiting for her to give birth."

"She didn't know while she was pregnant that you were a boy?" Summer reached up her hand and stroked her fingers along the side of his face.

Kai shook his head. "I was a very naughty baby. The ultrasound tech didn't have much luck. But sure enough, less than twenty minutes later she had me and my tutu gave her the name that she'd dreamed of the night before. Kaikilaonāoneko'olau. High waters on the Ko`olau sands."

The significance of the words sunk in as the waves rushed onto the beach just a few feet away. Summer brushed her fingertips over his temples and behind his ears, looking into his eyes. Just touching him felt like she was drawing closer and closer to him.

And Kai took her by her shoulders and pulled her physically closer and into a tender kiss.

The night couldn't have ended better.

Frank Ritter snuck into the apartment. He had been gone longer than he'd anticipated and with the streets starting to wake up with the shop keepers and bakers beginning their day he had to make a quick escape from the area.

His mind was reeling, and he felt a knot in his stomach.

When he left the store, he'd been almost halfway back to the apartment when he realized that he'd dropped one of his gloves. It could have fallen anywhere. He just hoped it hadn't fallen at the shop before he left.

He'd tried to double back, looking for it, but there was only so much he could do, looking around bushes and along the street without drawing too much attention to himself. He hadn't found the damn thing, but that didn't mean it was back at the store. Maybe someone had found it and tossed it into a trash can?

Now all he had to do was figure out if he was going to tell his granddad.

After all, if it wasn't found, then there wasn't really a problem.

Looking at the clock, he knew he was late to help his granddad out of bed. He had to help the older man go to the bathroom and give him his meds.

A quick look at his clothes said he was still presentable, but the stench-

"That you, Thom?"

If he kept quiet, he might be able to sneak into the bathroom and scrub off some of the smell, but the first step he took in the dark of the apartment made the floorboards creek.

"Help me!"

There was no hiding now.

Growling under his breath, Frank stopped at the side of the bed and reached down to help his granddad sit up.

He didn't expect the slap until it happened.

The sound echoed off the walls.

"You stink, boy! Have you been out drinking?"

Frank touched his hand to his cheek and then dropped it when his saw his granddad's scowl.

"You have, haven't you? Fucking good for nothing. That's what you are!"

"I haven't been out drinking." Frank had to say something. "I was out doing what you asked."

"You smell like rubbish. Makes sense, boy. Exactly what you are."

"Shut up!" Frank regretted the outburst as soon as he made it. He was better than this. Better than his father who had failed first. "I'm sorry. I'm sorry. I-"

"What's that?"

The question stunned Frank into silence. "What-"

"That thing in your hand."

Frank looked down at the single glove in his hand and tried to shove it in his pocket. "Just something I'm going to throw out and-"

The old man was quick. Frank had to give him that. He looked at the glove and then looked up, straight into Frank's eyes.

Frank looked back as long as he could, but it soon became too much, and he dropped his gaze to the floor.

"Where's the other one? The other glove?"

Before he could stop himself, Frank confessed, telling his grandad that he'd lost the glove on the way back to the apartment. He'd just started telling his granddad that he'd doubled back to look when his granddad went white and clutched at his chest.

The muscles in his neck stood out, looking like thin cords just under his skin, his eyes bugging out.

"Pops? Pops? What's wrong?"

"Get help, son." His hands looked like claws. His voice thin and shrill. "Get. Hel-"

"Pops?"

The old man was still, caught up like a stone statue.

"Pops? Don't do this to me."

He stumbled forward and started to reach out and touch him. He knew he should look for a pulse, but something stopped him.

He still stunk like high hell.

And his clothes. They had to have blood on them. With the mess he'd created, there had to be blood all over him.

If he called for help now. Someone would notice.

Someone would ask what was on his clothes.

One more look at his granddad told him that the old man

was beyond help. Live people didn't look like that. They just didn't.

He gave the old man a sorrowful look before he stepped into the bathroom and turned on the water in the tub. He'd clean himself up. He'd get rid of his clothes somewhere no one would look and then he'd call for help.

His granddad was gone, but he wasn't going to put himself in jail because of it. He'd do right by the old man, but he wasn't going to throw himself under the damn bus to do it.

CHAPTER 12

There was something morbidly satisfying about every damn mosquito bite that marked his skin. They came and died like so many others. Sitting in the shadows of his camp Frank stared at the woods surrounding him.

Everything was taking shape.

Opening his wallet, he pulled out his granddad's picture and looked down into the old man's eyes. "You were telling the truth, old man. You were telling the truth."

He heard his granddad's voice echoing in his head. Heard the words of the man at the VA too.

They're going to deny me, son.

"Your grandfather wasn't in the military."

It was their black eye, but I was the one to suffer.

"I'm sorry, sir. We've gone through the records. Even the lists of guards at the camps. Your grandfather didn't serve in Hawaii during World War II or at any other time."

Lies, son. It's all lies.

That's what he'd been told. That's what he'd known.

But it didn't sink in and feel like it was written in stone until they'd lied to his face. Frank hung his head and felt his stomach aching. "They lied to me, Pops. They lied and then they threw me out of the building."

He shook his head back and forth.

"They threw me out."

"Treated me like trash."

"Well, they're gonna regret it."

"There's going to be hell to pay." Frank got up on his feet, swaying a little as his stomach lurched. "And I'm going to be the one collecting."

He paused, tucking the photo back into his wallet and picked up his bottle of water on the stump beside him. As soon as he'd finished the store-bought water, he'd cut the top of the plastic container off and leave it out to collect water. Rain had fallen in the early morning hours, turning the ground under him into a leafy, muddy mess.

The only creatures who had enjoyed it were the centipedes under the surface.

After the first dozen or so mosquito bites, he could barely feel them on his skin.

When he returned, he'd bring a tent of some sort. He'd bring something that would keep him dry.

The others? They wouldn't care.

Wet didn't matter when you're dead.

It was impossible to miss the SEALs. Physically, they were obviously fit, muscled, and damn gorgeous. When they were out on the private beach, heads always turned. And a number of those heads had eyes that stayed focused on them. Summer and Kai had started out their morning with them, playing around on the sand, but when the SEALs took themselves down to the water, Kai and Summer had moved to the pool.

The crowd there was a different speed. Some of the senior citizens from Aleck's condo complex lounged on lanai chairs and families with small children stayed in the shallow end. The littler tots in their floaties and wings. It was low key and just what Summer could handle.

As she took hold of the railing and walked down the stairs, she turned to look at Kai and watched as he stripped off his t-shirt.

All of those muscles and that gorgeous face. As her lips parted on a sigh, she heard a soft, lilting voice proclaim, "Goodness, Maybell, will you look at him?"

"I'm looking, Jane. I'm old, but I'm not dead."

Summer's cheeks were burning as Kai walked over and slid into the water at her side.

"Sounds like you have fans."

Kai wrapped his arms around her and nuzzled the sensitive skin just below her ear. "I'm your fan."

Summer laughed and gave him a playful shove back. "You're going to get us in trouble."

He pulled her back into his arms and lay his forehead against hers. "This is completely PG," he chuckled.

"I know," she melted against him, "and I'm looking forward to having you over tonight."

Kai stilled against her. "Hey, not fair. If you want me to be good, saying that isn't going to help."

Wrapping her arms around his neck made him smile and groan at the same time.

"You know I love it when you wrap your arms around me."

She heard the low rumble of his voice and she had to keep herself from tightening her arms around him. That would only bring their bodies closer to each other and what would happen after that was pretty predictable.

Over the last few weeks their relationship had been

changing. The way he held her when he kissed her, the words he murmured in her ears made her want more and more with him.

Emotionally too, but it was the physical aspect that might make their pool time a little dangerous. Having little kids around meant they had to be super circumspect, but given the way their mamas were eyeing Kai with appreciative glances she knew they were drinking in their fill of his gorgeous body.

"Maybe we ought to... work on my swimming."

His smile was gorgeous as always, but the look in his eyes was mischievous.

"Kolohe." She smiled when his eyes widened at the word. "Troublemaker."

He shrugged. "Rascal," he countered.

"They both fit. Who am I to argue?"

"You?" He gave her a wink and touched the tip of his finger to her nose. "You're everything."

"Oh, my word, Jane! Didya hear that?"

"Of course, I did, Maybell. I turned up my hearing aids just for this."

Summer covered her face with her hands, but Kai took hold of them and lowered them down.

"Don't hide, Summer. We'll see how much trouble we can get into later, let's work on your floating today."

"Oh my!"

Summer turned and saw one of the old women fanning herself with her Kindle.

"This is just like one of my Susan Stoker books!"

"Shush, Jane! Don't embarrass them. They're lucky to be young and in love."

Love.

Summer looked up at Kai and saw the way his eyes darkened as he looked at her. She knew she was getting very close to love if she wasn't already there, but she didn't want to even suggest such a thing while they were in a pool with a bunch of people nearby. "So, floating?"

Her words shocked him a little. "Are you telling me I have those two lovely ladies to thank for getting you to float?"

Summer gave him a little shove and moved down into the deeper part of the pool. She wasn't comfortable there, but the little kids were in the shallow end and if she flailed, she didn't want to hurt anyone else.

Kai caught up with her easily and with a hand at the back of her head and another sweeping up underneath, he laid her back in the water. He adjusted his hands as they worked. His voice soft. His words encouraging.

It was easier this time. Easier but not nearly comfortable.

Still, Kai seemed to have endless patience with her, and she couldn't have asked for a better teacher. She could have left bad enough alone, but she was living on an island and water… well, there was no escaping it completely.

As a moment of panic settled in her chest and her lower back sank in the water she reached out and grabbed onto his arm like a lifeline.

He didn't let her sink.

He didn't let her drown.

Kai helped her find her center again, eased the tension from her body and she started to float again.

"Let go," his voice crooned to her. "Let go, Summer. I'm right here. I'm not going to let anything happen to you."

Her fear was instinctual, but so was her trust in him. He was always gentle and patient. Always there for her.

Summer made her hand release him and she felt the water against her palm. Relax. Trust. It didn't feel so foreign anymore.

Trusting him was also helping her trust herself.

Closing her eyes, Summer felt the sun on her face and in her heart.

And she floated.

Kai couldn't help but feel he was way out of his league. Summer was a scientist. He hadn't asked her, but he was sure that she had at least a couple of letters after her name. He had to be crazy to believe that what they had together was going to become a permanent thing.

She didn't even talk to him about her work.

Maybe she thought he'd be bored by it?

It couldn't be that she thought he couldn't understand it, at least the basics of it. She didn't treat him like he wasn't smart enough. She just didn't talk about it. So maybe it was okay with her.

For now.

What if he managed to get lucky and have her fall in love with him? Marry him? He could imagine the first dinner or formal event with her colleagues. He imagined holding his hand out as Summer introduced someone. 'This is Doctor X, he's a freaking genius.' And then having to say. 'And this is Kai, he works on charter boats.'

Yeah. She's going to realize really quickly that he just wasn't going to be a good match for her. He just wasn't going to be the man for her.

Then why, he asked himself, why was he even there with her, waiting while she was in the shower, washing off the sunscreen and chlorine from earlier in the day?

The answer was all too simple.

He was in love.

Unmistakably.

Forever.

In love.

And whatever he had to do to show her that he was in this for the long haul, he would do it. He would show her that she was everything he wanted and maybe.

Just… maybe.

He might be enough for her.

"Hey."

Kai lifted his head and saw her standing in the doorway to her bedroom. He hadn't heard the water turn off in the shower.

"You okay?" Her expression was full of real concern. "You look a little… distant."

No. He just felt it.

Getting to his feet, he gave her a smile. She looked incredible. Summer Maitland didn't need a bit of makeup to look like heaven. All she had to do was breathe.

"Feeling a little distant, perhaps." He shook his head. "You look amazing."

"Amazing?" She dropped her chin down and lifted her head back up to meet his gaze. "I guess I wasn't thinking when I pulled out clothes to wear. I don't really own anything prettier than long baggy shirts and a couple of boy shorts in girly colors."

He had to swallow hard to clear his throat to speak. "You don't need to wear anything to look good- I mean-"

They both burst out laughing at his odd phrasing, but she still held out her hand. "You want to come in here… or do you want to sit on the couch and watch TV?"

He'd crossed the room and taken her hand before an answer was necessary and as soon as he crossed the threshold of the room, he gathered her into his arms.

The soft gasp of breath that he heard sounded like the wind.

"Do you have any idea how much I've missed you?"

She tilted her head and looked up into his eyes. "As much as I've missed you. Which is a lot."

"I'm sorry we didn't get to have dinner the other night. The charter came back late. I wanted to paddle the boat back to the marina."

Summer slid her hands up his arms to his shoulders. "You can't be responsible when the engine has a hiccup and I had plenty to keep me busy at the office." She started to move before the sentence was even done. "I'm just glad you could come over tonight."

Her hands lifted to his head, her fingertips tracing long curving paths through his hair.

"I know this probably feels a little silly, but I love touching your hair. It's so..."

"Short? Scratchy?"

"No!" She grabbed a hold of him and kissed him. "Stop."

She leaned in for another kiss, but this time when she moved back, it was less than an inch from his lips.

Summer.

He could feel her warmth against his body and when his blood started to pump through his veins it went everywhere.

Fast.

And a lot of it pooled way down where her hips pressed tightly against his.

Having his dick trapped between them was torture, but it was a torture that he'd gladly suffer every damn day of the week.

"Summer?"

Her eyes were hazy, her lids heavy.

"Summer, we don't have to-"

"Kai."

Her fingers dug into his scalp and the slight twinge of pain made him even harder against her.

"I've been wanting this. I've been wanting you for… for ages."

"Ages?" He slid his hands down over the curve in her lower back and filled his hands with her ass. "You don't feel like you're that old. It must be a science thing, hm?"

He lifted her an inch or two and her thighs parted just enough to fit his leg between hers.

"Maybe," he breathed in and out slowly, "you could teach me a little bit about this scien-"

Her mouth crushed against his and their teeth met for a second before she changed the angle of her head.

Okay, so talking was out.

He could handle that.

His hands squeezed her and pushed her higher on his thigh. The sound he heard was a soft moan and where her breasts were pushed against his chest, he could feel the tight beads of her nipples.

Fuck.

He was so damn hard for her.

"Sum-"

Kai tried to speak but she chased his mouth with her own, kissing him hungrily.

He felt her hands slide down his sides and grab a hold of the hem of his t-shirt. When she tugged it up, he managed to help her with one hand, unwilling to let go of the tight cheek he held onto. As his t-shirt pulled free of his arms, someone tossed it off to the side and he heard Summer grumble under her breath. "It's a shame to cover you up like that. This is what we wish male anatomy looked like on a daily basis."

He couldn't help but puff up a little at her praise. "Well, I do look like this on a daily basis."

Kai saw a spark in her eyes and felt a little out of breath at her open perusal.

"Then I wish I was around you on a daily basis."

He couldn't help how much he wanted to hear that. How much he wanted it to be real.

Kai reached for the bottom of her loose night shirt and caught her gaze with a question in his eyes.

Summer's cheeks colored, but she nodded. And then she lifted her arms above her head and let him pull it off. When it was gone, he went still.

He'd seen Summer in her swimsuit, an athletic pairing of a tank and boy shorts, which he'd never really appreciated until he saw her in them, but nothing could or would ever compete with the sight of Summer's skin bared to his gaze.

Just the slight swell of her breasts and the warm sun-kissed tone of her skin was the most beautiful thing he'd ever seen.

And as he stood there, her shirt in his hands, he watched as she hooked her thumbs into her waist band and peeled her panties down off of her legs.

She left him breathless before he saw her whole body. Just the hint of her naked backside had him throbbing. When she stood up and he saw that the swell of her hips was even more amazing than he'd dreamed it would be, he bit into his bottom lip.

There was a real danger of making a complete fool of himself. He wanted to be mature. He wanted to be desirable. Nutting in his swim trunks wasn't exactly going to cut it. How sophisticated would that be?

He saw it the moment she started to doubt herself. The color in her cheeks paled and her hands, instead of laying easily against her sides, started to move. She was going to cover herself and doubt this thing between them.

She hadn't said as much, but he was pretty sure he could read it in her eyes.

"I've never seen a more beautiful woman, Summer." He lifted her shirt to his face and drew in a deep breath. "And you smell incredible."

She lifted a hand toward the bathroom. "It's just my soap. Jasmine."

"I know what it smells like." He took in another breath and dropped her shirt beside his. "But that's not what I mean."

He took a step closer, his hands making quick work untying the draw string on his swim trunks.

"I want to memorize your scent," he dropped the free ends of the draw string and hooked his thumbs into his waistband, "and breath you in until something of you is always with me." Kai pushed his swim trunks down until they fell on the floor at his feet, his eyes never leaving hers.

Kai saw her shudder.

Saw the way her nipples tightened even more under his gaze.

"And I can't wait to love you, Summer. I feel like we've been headed toward this night for all of our lives, and I want to make sure that you know, this isn't just one night."

He saw her throat work as she swallowed.

Saw the rise and fall of her shoulders as Summer pulled in a breath.

"I… I know…"

Kai was just a step away from her when he stopped. He wanted to know-

No, he needed to know what she was going to say.

An indrawn breath spurred her on.

"I know it's not just tonight."

Kai felt his heart expanding in his chest, swelling with joy.

She gestured at the night table beside the bed. "I bought a box of condoms."

I love you, Summer.

He took hold of her shoulders and kissed her like he was drowning and needed her air. And maybe he was. He was drowning in need for this woman.

Somehow, they made it onto the bed, his hands helping her to get settled against her pillows. There wasn't much room on the bed, but in some ways that was better. He longed to be closer to her.

He needed to be in her.

The moment was surreal.

And yet the sensations in her body told her that this was very real.

Laying there beside him, her body bare, she felt his gaze on her skin like a physical touch.

Kai lifted his hand and touched the side of her face, his eyes searching hers. "Your skin… I've always imagined what silk would feel like. And now I know."

Summer slipped a hand behind his neck, her fingers brushing through the hair at the base of his head, the sensations were delicious.

The heat building between them with just those simple touches… everything.

He trailed his fingers down the side of her neck and she leaned her head into her pillow, giving him more access to her throat.

Chills rolled through her body and when his hand ghosted over her shoulder and along her upper arm she dragged in a breath, struggling for control. She wanted to say something. Wanted to return the gesture.

But the feelings that he stirred up inside of her held her captive and still.

When his fingertips traced the curve of her breast she gasped, her legs squeezing together, but she couldn't tell if her body was trying to find its release or slow it down.

Kai cupped his hand under her breast and then over it, sliding her pebbled nipple between his heated fingers.

Her fingers grasped the back of his neck and held on for dear life.

He leaned over her, his hand shifting against her body so that his thumb could brush over her nipple. Her sigh was barely free of her lips when he took her breast into his mouth.

Her heels dug into the bed as a low, hungry moan filled the air. Her own audible passion as he suckled her, rasping his tongue over her tip.

Summer's free hand latched onto his shoulder and brought him closer as her eyes fixed on the ceiling over their heads. The cream-colored expanse looked as if it was wavering, undulating with the tug of his lips.

"More."

She heard the demand in her voice and stilled. But she didn't have to worry. Kai lifted his head and she saw the fire in his gaze. It wasn't anger. It was passion.

"What the lady wants," he sat up a little more and she wished she hadn't opened her mouth, she wanted his mouth back on her skin, "the lady gets."

And like so many things he'd said before, Kai made good on his word.

He worshiped her breasts. She'd heard the term before but had never understood what it meant. Kai touched her. Tasted her. Buried his face between her breasts and the scrape of his stubble against her skin almost made her come right then and there.

Summer had kept her legs together, her body beside his as he loved her, her thighs and knees rubbing back and forth, holding tight to the anticipation and the need.

It was almost too much for her.

Digging her fingers into his shoulders she drew him closer. "Now. Please. I need-"

He kissed her, drawing her breath from her lips and into his body. Then he looked down at her. "Tell me," his voice was gruff with something she couldn't name. "Tell me, ku`ulei. Are you ready to wrap yourself around me and let me love you?"

Summer couldn't wait another minute. Reaching out, she still had to roll onto her side to reach the drawer and as she pulled out one of the condom wrappers between her fingers, Kai smoothed his hand over her backside and she felt his fingers trace the undercurve of each cheek, dipping just a hint between her thighs.

There would be a time, she told herself, that she'd feel him there behind her. He'd take her in any number of ways, and she would always want more.

Turning onto her back, she gave him the packet. "The lady," she told him, "is hoping you can open that fast, because I want you now."

He pinned her with his gaze as he opened it, and when he lowered his hand down, she looked too.

Kai was as beautiful there as he was everywhere else. She'd done her share of anatomy studies and yes, she'd blushed her way through a number of art exhibits that immortalized that particular part of the male anatomy in oil, clay, and stone. There had also been a few not so exemplary men in her past.

She reached out and Kai caught her wrist.

Summer looked up at him with more than a little shock in her eyes.

"You can touch later," he told her, his voice a little thin, "not now."

Summer saw it in his eyes and the grip he had on himself. She had taken him to the edge.

This was the kind of power she'd always dreamed of and it was all hers.

She lay back against the pillows, lifting her arms above her head. Summer drew her knees up, spreading her legs as she went.

His eyes were fixed on her as he got up on his knees. He moved between her legs, a sensual crawl. Almost a prowl as he knelt between her raised knees.

"I'm never going to forget this." He shook his head, his shoulders rising and falling with his quickening breaths. "I'm never going to forget the moment I first made love to you."

Before she could muster up a single word to say to him, he was there. She felt his thighs under hers. His fingers slipped between her folds, caressing her, and testing her need.

Kai rose up between her legs, bracing a hand on the bed near her shoulder as his other hand guided his cock exactly where she needed it.

The sensation as his head slipped in just past her folds felt as if her body sobbed in relief. He rocked forward and back, his hand guiding him into her until he was sliding in easily between her legs.

He dropped his other arm down at her shoulder, rocking in and out again and again until she felt his hips collide with hers.

She arched beneath him, trying to ease the tight feeling of her body stretched around his.

"This," he sighed, as he moved his hips, rocking against her body, "this is what I've been waiting for all of my life."

"I want the rest, Kai." She met his gaze with her own need swimming in her eyes. "I want more."

And he gave it to her.

The way that man could move his hips, the strength in his thighs, the skill of his mouth against her own. He wrung his name from her. He had her clinging to him, her arms and her legs wrapped around his muscular frame.

Kai had her up and over the edge of release over and over until he found his own and wrapped her in his capable arms.

There was nothing she would forget about that night.

Nothing.

Because it was the first time she made love to him too.

CHAPTER 13

When they reached the crime scene, Summer could see the lines of yellow crime tape and cringed a little inside. She was used to dealing with bodies of a certain… age. Fresh kills always reminded her of the first cadaver that she'd worked on. He was so new, or perhaps it was just the fact that the freezers had done a fantastic job of keeping it cold, that he looked like he could have gotten up and walked straight out of the room.

She wasn't eager to see anything like that again, but the call had come in and Elton had sent her on her way. He was going to his therapy appointment on his own and had released her for the day as if she was his driver instead of his colleague. She was sure she'd never fully understand the man, but for some reason she just couldn't be angry at him.

As soon as she was outside the squad car, Olena left the taped area and met her halfway. "I'm sorry to call you out here, but I'm beginning to think I'm losing my mind." She leaned closer. "If Clive heard that he'd probably write me up or send me for a psych eval. I've been trying to get him to approve bringing you in to consult on these killings."

"Killings?" A strange twist in Summer's gut made her second guess her presence at the scene. "What's going on?"

A strange rattle of sound had both of them looking up at the cabin nearby. Two young men with mussed hair stared down at them. "Hey," one of them called down, "is there really a dead body over there?"

Summer felt a little sick at the eagerness in their voices.

Olena seemed more familiar with the situation. "Go back to bed and sleep it off."

The other young man laughed out loud. "Come on up to my bed and I'll get you off!"

Lifting her badge into the sunlight she let the metal shine light up at his window. "Did you just solicit a Homicide Detective?"

The window slammed shut and the curtains fell over the windows.

"College boys," Olena walked toward the scene.

Summer could see the large tent that had been erected at the heart of the taped off area.

Olena continued on. "Clive was called to the Commissioner's office for a meeting with the top brass. These killings have a few things in common. They've all been found in and around the Downtown area, mostly focused in Chinatown. And all of the victims are Asian of some sort."

"And this one? He's Asian and I guess this is basically Downtown."

"That's what we've got for now."

As Olena held up the tape, Summer ducked under it and crossed to the side of the tent that was open. The side facing the road was understandably covered with a thick tarp. There were standing lights that illuminated the area so they could have sunlight without the curious onlookers. Summer tried to ignore the crowd of news vans crowded at the curb. The last thing she wanted was to be immortalized on film.

Doctor Chang greeted her with a melancholy smile. "Good to see you, Summer. Horrible reason."

"I feel the same way. Do you want to show me what you've found?"

The doctor looked across to Olena. "Are you sure you want to take this chance?"

Summer saw Olena's skin turn a little grey. "What's wrong?"

"Clive is the primary on these cases, case, if you believe that they're all the same killer-"

"Which you do," Summer couldn't help but interject.

"Yes, although Clive has other thoughts. I told him that my gut says they're related to your body."

Summer heard the words, but it took a moment for her to process the idea. "The body from the camp?"

Olena nodded. "I know it's crazy, but it's just this feeling that won't go away."

Nodding, Summer had to ask. "Clive is against it?"

"And he's the lead on this. If I go against him too much, I know he's going to write me up for insubordination."

"Then why are you fighting for this? Why are you bringing me into this?"

Olena looked at her as if she was beginning to regret doing just that.

"I'm asking because I think you need to see it. I've had times before where I had a feeling that there was something I was missing, and sometimes it was simply that I was tired, or we needed more information. It's not easy putting together pieces that might not actually belong together.

"Other times I think there's something your mind is trying to get you to understand. Then you have to make the jump and hope that if you miss you have something to grab on to and hold on for dear life.

"That's why I called you," Olena insisted. "As Homicide

Detectives we're not the only people on these cases. We have fingerprint experts. Blood spatter experts. So many damn experts. I just want you to take a look at this scene and then I'd like you to come back to my office and look at the earlier crime scene photos and see if your kind of expertise is what we've been missing."

Steeling herself for the scene she was about to face, Summer stepped closer and looked at the man sprawled face first on the concrete. There was a good deal of blood under his head, but she wasn't about to get a closer look. "Attacked from behind?"

Doctor Chang answered her in the affirmative. "Looks like."

"Head wounds bleed. A lot." She shuddered and swallowed down the bile that climbed up the back of her throat.

"Will we be able to see photos of this scene alongside the others at your office?"

Olena nodded. "Yes. The initial scene was photographed, and the images are printing back at the station."

"Okay. Okay, thanks." Summer didn't say anything else, settling her own emotions to focus on her work. Normally she took the small pieces and made them into the big picture, but this was different in so many ways. Digging up each individual piece, finding how many layers of sediment, stone, and earth had obscured an object kept the focus on the small, leaving them to make it into a bigger picture of a person, a village, a people.

But here, she had the big picture. There was no waiting for decades to pass before they could dig things up. This was the whole before time had done its number on it.

The clock on the belltower had obviously been listening.

Its loud, resonant boom gave the tarp a wiggle, but didn't affect the crime scene at all.

It sounded again and Summer heard the coroner speak.

"Ask not for whom the bell tolls…" his voice took on a strange tone and then settled back into his normal easy-going tone. "Sorry. Morbid humor. It's a thing."

Summer nodded, not affected in the least, but she'd been distracted.

Snapping her head up, she looked at Olena. "Can we go and see the other photos?"

It seemed as though Olena heard the urgency that Summer felt. The detective gestured out the other side of the tent and they left moments later.

Summer didn't leave the lab that night. She wasn't one to admit defeat. And she certainly didn't like feeling guilty.

And all that she had accomplished that day was digging herself and Olena a big damn hole.

Viral videos.

In her college years, Summer didn't have the funds for a video camera. She'd spent her money on a reliable digital SLR camera to photograph her studies and the scenes that they'd worked. Pictures. Still images.

And maybe it wasn't even the two hung-over horny college guys who had taken video of the crime scene. Surely it wasn't her fault that the tarp didn't cover the whole crime scene?

When the video hit the local news, Olena's partner had just finished meeting with the Police Commissioner, and they'd shown up at the station and told Summer to leave the room. She refused, explaining that she wanted to help. That she believed she could help.

Whether or not she helped Olena with her words, she didn't really know.

They'd all but threatened to have Summer removed from

the building if she didn't leave on her own. It was only Olena's reassurance that she should go that she did.

Now, she was wracking her brain. Trying to go over what she remembered from the few minutes that she'd had to peruse the photos.

A radio technician. A teacher. A lawyer. An apothecary. An electronics repair man.

Chinese. Japanese. Korean. Okinawan. Vietnamese.

And then the body they'd found at the camp. Caucasian.

How was it all related?

Was it all related?

Her phone rang and she knew by the ringtone that it was safe to pick it up.

"Hello."

"You want to tell me what you were doing at a crime scene today?"

Baker Rawlins. Retired SEAL and all-around awesome guy, but apparently feeling nosy as hell.

"Not really, no."

"Too bad, kid. I want to know."

Kid! Well, she was going to let that go.

This time.

"Are you in legal trouble?" His tone wasn't trying to scold. The warning she heard in his voice didn't sound like it was meant for her.

"Not legal. It seems I pissed off some people in law enforcement. Sticking my nose in where it didn't belong."

"And what were you really doing?" She wondered if there was a bit of humor hiding in his voice.

"Well, I was sticking my nose in, but a detective friend asked me for my help. And I was happy to give it to her."

"Her? Good to know." He cleared his throat. "What can I do to help?"

"Nothing really, and I hate saying that because it's the

truth. I've got this puzzle stuck in my head that I'm working on and it's not cooperating."

"Maybe that's because you've got a whole lot of testosterone with badges breathing down your neck."

"Maybe," she sighed, "I just feel bad for Olena. She's just trying to solve these murders."

"Olena Yasui, Homicide."

She paused and looked around the room as if she'd find him standing in the shadows. "I'm not going to ask you how you know, but yes, Olena Yasui. I just know I can help but I feel like there's a wall that we keep walking into."

"Why don't you send me what you have, and I'll take a look over it."

Summer did laugh at that. "I would if I could, but I'm working off of my memory right now. After they ripped us both a new one, they wouldn't let me keep the pictures of the crime scenes so I'm sitting here in the lab trying to go over the images in my head. It's better than nothing right?"

A silence settled between them, but it didn't last long.

"Make sure you get some sleep. You'll figure it out."

"Yeah, I'll try."

"Night."

"Baker?" She tried to catch him before he hung up.

"Yeah, kid?"

"Thanks for checking up on me."

The phone call ended, and Summer set her phone back in its cradle.

There was a puzzle in front of her.

"I used to like puzzles."

The room remained silent.

"And I didn't used to talk to myself."

The room was apparently as stubborn as she was. It didn't answer back.

There was a difference between the puzzles that came out

of a box and the puzzles that she dealt with on a daily basis. When she opened a dig, or went through remains that others had found, the last thing she knew was what it was supposed to look like when she finished.

Even when she thought she had it all figured out there might be nuances that needed explaining. Context was killer.

And so damn important.

Context.

What was there in the crime scenes?

What wasn't?

And what the hell did it all mean?

Summer worked for another hour, taking notes on everything she could remember. Big or small. Colors. Textures. Even the surface under the bodies. She took those notes and let them loose inside her head. Depending how accurate that she had been remembering a few dozen crime scene photos, this might all be for naught, but at this point it was all she had, and she'd use it to help her friend.

Kai had run out of coffee waiting for Summer to come home to her apartment building. He wasn't even sure what he'd say to her when she got there. He just knew that he had to talk to her.

Her phone had gone straight to voicemail when he'd called but based on the crazy things they were talking about in the news, he didn't blame her for not answering. He just needed to see that she was okay. See it with his own eyes and then he could go home.

He didn't have any work scheduled for the next few days, so however long it took for her to come home, he'd be there.

Waiting.

When a pair of headlights swept across his car, Kai eased

onto his feet. His legs were aching, but it didn't come close to the rush of emotion that he felt when Summer pulled into the spot beside him.

He watched her sigh and then lay her head down on the steering wheel. Her shoulders pulled tight, and her hands gripped the aging steering wheel cover like a lifeline.

Kai tugged at the handle on her door and found that it opened easily.

Crouching down between her open door and the driver's seat, Kai stroked the back of her head with his hand, long, gentle, and slow. Over and over.

When she finally spoke, he wasn't sure that he'd heard her correctly.

"What?"

"How mad are you?"

He didn't know what to think and certainly he had no clue what to say.

Summer turned her face toward him but kept her cheek on the steering wheel as if she could barely lift her head. He could see the exhaustion in her eyes, and he could see the hurt in them as well.

"I'm not mad at you, Summer. Worried? Absolutely. When you didn't call me back, I didn't know what to think. I wanted to tell you that I'd be here for you when you needed me. And then I didn't want to wait for you to need me, so I came over to make sure you got home okay."

Her smile was weak, barely lifting one corner of her mouth. "I thought you'd be mad. Mad that I didn't tell you what my job was. Mad that I didn't answer the phone. Just mad."

Kai was hurt that she'd think those thoughts. He'd never lost his temper with her. Never even came close, and while she'd driven up wide-eyed and awake, she was fading fast.

He brushed his fingers through her hair at her temple and

smoothed his thumb over her cheek. "Someone did that to you before? Got mad at you for those things?"

"I just didn't want you think I was-" She yawned, and her eyes started to drift closed.

"Hey, hold on." He shook her shoulder a little bit. "Summer. Turn off the car and let's get you upstairs."

"I just don't want you to be angry."

He knew he wasn't going to get through to her when her brain had been reduced to a one-track mind. "I'm not. Let's get you in bed."

She let him help her up and out of her car before she gave him a cheeky look. "Don't think I'm going to let you keep me awake all night just because you're hot. Not lava hot because that's silly, but easily Jason Momoa hot. Oh," she swayed against him as he closed the door and locked the car, "or Dwayne Johnson hot. You've got that sexy thing going for you."

Kai had to laugh a little and wonder if this is what she was like drunk or just super tired. One thing was for sure, he'd have to keep an eye on her to make sure that all of her flirty moments were directed at him.

"I'm glad you approve." The security guard in the lobby opened the door for him. Kai had already plucked the keys from her hand at the car. The ride up to her floor didn't take much time at all given the hour, but he wasn't prepared for what would happen when they were inside her apartment.

She left a light burning in the living room corner, so he didn't need to worry about his knees or toes as he made his way into her bedroom.

He didn't even bother completely undressing her. That would only wake her up more instead of helping her get to sleep. Her shoes took care of themselves falling right off her feet when she stretched and rolled onto her side.

Taking his arm with her.

And the way she held onto him; he was pressed tight against her back.

She would get no arguments from him. He was just glad that her front door was as easy to lock as it was safe because he certainly didn't want to pull away from her now.

Knowing he was safe leaving his car where it was, Kai snuggled up against Summer, enjoying the way she had literally wrapped him around her.

Settling into the relaxing rhythm of her breaths, Kai fell asleep relieved that she was home safe.

Whatever she was worried about, they would tackle later.

In the morning.

Until then she was safe in his arms and his heart was safe with her.

CHAPTER 14

As she slept, Summer's whole world changed.

She wasn't used to dreaming. When she went down, that was it. The world went dark until it was light, but not that night.

Pictures.

A slideshow of sorts. Images. Victims. Faces.

She saw their pain. Saw their silent cries of horror. Focused on their faces.

Summer tried to shut them out, but she couldn't close her eyes inside of her head.

These men. These victims.

They were just there.

Crying out for help.

And she had nothing to offer them but her own horror.

She cried out and felt warmth wrap around her, distancing the abject terror of her dreams.

A whisper entered the darkness. A reminder.

Pull back.

Look at-

"The whole picture..."

Evidence in her work was a catalogue of bits and pieces, but the answers only happened when you saw a person in their entirety. You could match a medical record to broken bones. You could match dental records to fillings and cavities. You could match any number of a thousand different pieces to an MIA file, but no decision could be made until everything was brought together. Turning remains into a person who had lived and breathed and loved.

Pull back.

From faces to upper bodies.

And further back, finally seeing the victims in the places where they were discovered.

The uniform.

What was it that Olena had said? Connect the cases.

They knew they had a serial killer on their hands, but those victims… those men, were Asians disposed of and likely murdered in Downtown or nearby. What did they have in common with the man buried almost a year before in an old uniform that he'd likely picked up at a surplus store?

Summer moved back to the victims they'd found in Downtown.

What mutual enemy could they have?

What did it all mean?

BZZZ. BZZZ. BZZZ.

Summer opened her eyes and stared at the clock on the nightstand beside her bed. Dear God, was it already six o'clock?

BZZZ. BZZZ. BZZZ.

. . .

Not now.

BZZZ. BZZZ. BZZZ.

Summer smacked her palm down on the off button.

"Are you always so vicious in the morning?"

Startled, she tensed up and almost yelped when she realized she wasn't alone.

But then again, she'd known that Kai was there. At least on some level.

That reassuring distance that she'd felt?

Well, the arm that wrapped around her and turned her on her back was delightfully reassuring.

And the body that pressed against her? Warm and so very solid.

"You stayed?"

He grinned and she was reminded again of how much she loved to see him happy. "You wouldn't let me go." Kai leaned in and pressed a kiss to her nose.

And then against her mouth, rubbing their lips together. "It felt good, being wanted by you."

"Need," she amended the word. "I think I needed you last night."

His smile softened and she found herself more than a bit confused. "You came because you saw the news."

Kai nodded, but she couldn't find anything dark in his expression. Not anger. Not even a little bit of annoyance.

"I should have told you before."

He eased back a little, bracing himself up on his elbow. "Told me what? That you're a crime fighting scientist?"

"I'm not fighting any kind of crime. Olena, I mean, Detective Yasui thought I'd be able to give her some insight on the killer or the victim, but all I did was get her in a lot of trouble."

The smooth skin between his brows furrowed as she spoke. "What kind of lab do you work in?"

She told herself to relax and breathe. His tone was even and there was concern on his face.

"I work in the Defense POW/MIA Accounting Agency. That's a long fancy way of saying that I work with remains of soldiers from past wars, identifying them."

"But that man that was found down at Aloha Tower, he isn't the kind of remains that you'd work with, right?"

Summer hesitated for a moment. "No. He was much more… I don't know how to say it."

"Well, he's not someone you would have to dig up or recover like they do on those real crime shows."

She smiled. "Yeah, like that."

"So why did she think you'd be helpful? Not that I'm arguing with her, or you, but it does seem a little outside of what you do."

Summer was struggling as she tried to wrap her mind around his words and his open expression. "You. You're not weirded out by any of this?"

He shrugged. "Between my mom and my sisters, do you have any idea the hours and hours of real crime dramas they watch? And that means that sometimes I have to watch. The three of them could plan a pretty decent murder if they put their minds to it. I'm just worried that they might try it on me first."

She shook her head. "I seriously doubt that."

Kai's smile grew. "Because they love me."

Summer nodded and then tilted her head to the side when she looked up into his eyes. "Maybe they keep you around for the heavy lifting. They're not kidding when they talk about dead weight." She felt her nose wrinkling up. "I'm sorry, that's gross, right?"

"Dead weight? Maybe." He thought about it for a minute and gave her a peck of a kiss. "I've had my share of trying to carry toddlers. They can become dead weight in a heartbeat. Slide right through your arms to the floor like a sack of rice. Devious little things."

Summer found herself laughing.

"I can't say that I could go through what you do in your lab. I've cleaned and gutted my fair share of fish over the years. My sisters claim it gives them cramps. Liars." He chuckled at the thought of his sisters, "but it's not a big thing for me. I just don't think I could do what you do."

She just shook her head, looking back at him in wonder.

"But I guess someone told you that it was gross."

"Not in those words. A lot of my family from my mom's side. They have a very set way of viewing things. Not only was I stepping out of bounds into a man's field, my grandmother told me in no uncertain terms that God himself would find me wanting. I can still hear her in my head sometimes. '*What you do can only be described as morbid and deeply disturbing. Tearing into the flesh of a body? Disturbing their final rest? You're doing the devil's work.*'"

"I think you're doing the exact opposite. Reuniting families? Bringing soldiers back home to their country? Why would anyone think that was bad?" Kai leaned closer to her and brushed another kiss against her lips. "I think it's pretty badass."

Summer wrapped her arms around his neck and pulled him back for another kiss. For a few minutes she was lost in the love she found in his arms, wanting to say something to him about it, but it just seemed more interesting to feel it than to say it. By the time she kicked free of her blankets and started to wrap her legs around him, a phone rang.

It was his.

Kai picked it up off of the nightstand on the other side of the bed and answered it. "Hey- Mom? Yeah. No. No. I'm okay. I promise."

Summer wrapped her legs around him, hooking her ankles together.

Even with his deepened, natural tan, she could still see a flush of color in his cheeks. "Mom. Mom? I'm fine, okay? No. No! Yes." He rolled his eyes at Summer as he listened to the phone. "Yeah, I guess I can be there," he looked at the clock, "in a half hour? Forty-five? Okay. Okay! Love you. I said I love you! Bye!"

The look he gave Summer when he dropped his phone onto the bed beside her was entirely too hot for words.

And the sound he made when she tightened her hold around his middle and arched against his erection was almost a growl.

"You've got to go?"

"Yeah," he shrugged, "unless you want me to stay?"

"Of course, I want you." The words that tumbled out of her stopped them both in their tracks. "To stay. And… the other way too, but I have to go into work. If I'm not helping Olena I still have a number of things I'm working on at the lab. Maybe you could come over later? Or I could meet you at your house?"

"Really?" The look in his eyes brightened. "I'd love to make love to you in my bed."

Just those few words had blood rushing through her body. "Now, I'm really going to hate leaving for work."

Kai helped her up and stood in the bathroom doorway as she turned the water on and undressed.

"Now I really wish you didn't have to go."

She shrugged and stepped under the hot water with a sigh.

Kai called out to her from the doorway. "I'm going to get going."

"Okay." Summer sighed as she started working shampoo through her hair, massaging her scalp. "I'll call and let you know when I'm almost done for the day."

"Sounds good." She could hear the smile in his voice.

"Thanks for staying last night. It really helped."

"Yeah, talking things out was good too. I thought you didn't tell me about your work because you didn't think I'd understand it."

She groaned at the thought. "It sounds like we should do a little more talking and a little less kissing."

"That would be a huge no. N. O. Not happening. But," he drew out the word longer than it needed to be, "if you want to talk while I'm inside you-"

"Stop or I'm going to pull you in here."

"Oh no!" His mock denial was entirely comical. "Save me from seeing your hot naked body!"

She pulled back the curtain long enough to spray him with drops of water from her fingers. "Go!"

"Fine! Sheesh!" He laughed and then the sound kind of died off. "You know I spent a year being a tour guide on charter buses down in Waikiki and the surrounding area. Aloha Tower used to be a huge hub for cruise ships from the continent, but back during World War II they painted it in a camouflage pattern during Martial Law. Back then the military was everywhere.

"They paid special attention to it because the Harbor was important for shipping and passengers, but also because it was a recognizable landmark."

Summer stood in the shower, unmoving listening to his

words, and maybe he took that for a lack of interest, but that wasn't it. And she was too locked into her head that she couldn't really say much in return.

"I'll see you later, ku`ulei. Be careful, yeah?"

When the front door closed with a soft click, Summer's head tipped up and the pieces started to fall in place.

Rushing through her rinse, she took the fastest shower that she'd ever had before dashing out into the bedroom. She searched for her phone and found her purse sitting on the carpet beside the bed. Whipping out her phone she sent a text to Olena.

SUMMER: Their clothes. They're all wearing old clothes. Not old modern old, like a few years old. I'm talking decades. Look. I know I'm probably not making much sense and I'm probably not your favorite person right now, but I know I'm onto something. Call it a gut instinct. And there's something about the location of the last one. Kai said that Aloha Tower was a big deal during World War II, during Martial Law. Maybe that's the connection! Maybe that first body, the uniform, and the others and their clothes… I don't know exactly what I'm saying here but I think you're right. We just have to find more. Okay. I'm going to get dressed and go and do some research about where their clothes might have come from. There can't be that many vintage stores that have men's clothing from that era, right?

SUMMER: Bye!

By the time she'd reached the seventh vintage store, Summer was ready to admit defeat. There were just a couple left on the list after this, but she was beginning to think that she had finally lost her mind. She had definitely gone into this unprepared which wasn't at all like her.

She'd gone from scientist to crazy person in about four hours.

Pretty impressive really.

The Good Mill Resale store was quite literally a dump. There were boxes and bags of things piled up along the walls, under clothing racks. She quickly began to understand what it felt like for people who were claustrophobic, except she was fairly sure the walls 'could' and likely 'would' close in around her if she had to stay much longer.

The man working behind the counter was the sole employee of the business and his aunt, the owner. The fact that he'd regaled her about their contentious relationship was just another reason she wanted out.

And soon.

"Sir- Todd? I really am sorry about what you're telling me, but I just need to know if you've had any requests for men's clothing from the World War II timeframe?"

He narrowed his eyes at her. "And when was that?"

Summer plastered a smile on her face. "The early forties, sir."

"Nineteen or eighteen?"

She almost laughed out loud but managed to hold it in. "Nineteen Forties, sir."

He thought about it for a moment and the look on his face gave her hope.

Then he crushed it with a shake of his head. "Naw. No one asks for that kind of stuff."

She blew out a breath and struggled to keep it together. She hadn't tried to call Olena with an update. If she couldn't find anything then she'd call after she was done. There was no use reporting it over and over again.

Maybe she'd have better luck with store number eight.

"Then again," the man drummed his fingers on the counter, "there's this guy that kind of helps me out from time to time. I mean he's not like a full-time guy cause we don't sell enough for that, but I pay him a little under the counter if you know what I mean."

She nodded, trying to encourage him to talk.

"But sometimes instead of money, he asks for clothes. The stuff looks old. Like you'd see it on Leave it to Beaver or that show with Barney Fife. He asks for it and it looks like crap to me, so I let him take it." He waved off the thought. "I don't even know what he does with it. From what I could tell, the sizes are all different. But hey," he laughed, "to each their own fetishes, right?"

Summer gave him bits of the profile that Olena had put together. "White man. Late twenties to early thirties? Average looking? Doesn't like rules. A little on the secretive side."

He shrugged. "That's like half of the customers that come in here. But yeah, it sounds like Frank."

Frank. "Sir, I wonder if you'd be okay with speaking to a detective from HPD and maybe meeting with an artist to give us a description of the man you're talking about."

"Not during store hours. If my aunt finds out, she'll kick my ass."

"That's fine. I'm sure we could work around that. But you'd be willing to do it?"

"Sure. It has to be more interesting than standing around here all day."

Smiling for the first time since the morning, Summer thanked him profusely.

"Hey, I didn't really do anything yet."

She shook her head. "I have a really good feeling about this."

Summer pulled out her cell phone to call Olena but stopped when the man asked her to. "My doc says that I shouldn't have cellphones around my pacemaker. My aunt calls that advice stupid, but hey she probably wants me dead anyway. Could you make that call outside?"

"Sure," she looked at the front door and thought better of standing out on the public sidewalk talking about police business, "do you mind if I go out back?"

He gave a vague gesture toward the back of the room. "You can get out that way. Just don't knock over anything."

Easier said than done. It took her longer than she'd care to admit picking her way through the backroom, but she made it to the back door and opened it with a sigh of relief. Fresh air. Lifting her phone, she started scrolling through her contacts.

"You look different in person."

A chill worked its way through her spine as she turned toward the voice. "I'm sorry, what are you talking about?"

His face was normal enough. Like Edward Norton or Kevin Spacey. But not his eyes.

They say the eyes are the windows to the soul and she believed it for the most part. And this man's eyes were angry. Angry and dark.

"Maybe they were right to bring you in. No one got this far trying to find me. And now they'll have to start all over again."

Summer pointed to her phone. "I just called the police. They're on their way here right now."

His smile seemed inhuman. "You're a horrible liar, Summer. Besides, I heard you talking to Todd in the store. White man. Check. Late twenties to early thirties? Check. Average looking? That hurt my feelings. Doesn't like rules. Yes. Absolutely, yes. A little on the secretive side." He looked her up and down before he spoke again. "That part will depend on you, Summer."

He was pressed against her a moment later, the painful

prick of something against her side. "That's a knife, Summer. It's one of my favorites. It's fucking sharp."

She nodded slowly.

"Now that's a good girl. You're listening to me. That's smart."

No, she thought to herself. That's terrified.

"You and I are going to get into my car and you're going to smile like we're good friends and we've done this all of our lives. Like you and me are just driving around, having a little fun. And then we're going to stop and I'm going to tell you where those assumptions have gone wrong. You don't know why I'm doing this? Well, I'm going to tell you."

"And then?"

Shut up, Summer!

Her mind and the rest of her were in a panic.

"And then?" He laughed. "Then we'll see if you're still useful."

Summer tensed, struggling to pull herself together to do something. Anything to get away from him. When she made the decision to move, he'd already anticipated it and cracked her across the cheek with a closed fist and the world went dark.

CHAPTER 15

When Summer woke up, she was in the middle of a nightmare. The pain in her cheek felt like it was radiating through her entire head, echoing off her skull and traveling back again.

It felt like she was in a coffin, but the feeble amount of light that made its way into the space illuminated the dashboard of an old model car. Memories flooded back into her head. How he'd shoved her into his car, barely conscious, and tied her wrists together. A slight twist was all that she needed to know that her wrists were still tied to the grab bar on the inside of the door.

She tamped down the urge to scream as she remembered where she was and who she was with.

"You're awake, aren't you?"

She weighed her options and knew that she was too scared to be a good enough liar. "Yes," her voice was barely there, scratchy, "I'm awake."

He put his hand on her shoulder. "Now that wasn't so hard, was it?"

Summer shook her head. "No."

"Good." His thumb brushed over her skin where the neckline of her blouse had opened up. "That's real good."

"You said you were going to explain things to me." She needed him to talk. She needed to understand.

Because maybe if she did, she might find a way out of this.

She might find a way back to the people she loved.

"Not here. Where we're going, you're going to want light to see the ground as we walk." He pushed open his door and she listened to the world outside. She couldn't hear cars. No sounds beyond nature. Oahu was an island with more than a million people, but there were still hundreds of places that were uninhabited and some unseen by humans. With her luck he was going to drop her into one of those places and leave her to rot.

When he opened the door on her side, she had to move with it or chance having her arm yanked out of its socket. His only reaction was to laugh. "I'd say you think fast on your feet, but we haven't seen that yet, have we? You certainly were easy to corral back at the shop."

Summer seethed inside. Sure. Back then he had a knife pressed in her side. It was enough to keep her docile, but out here-

What exactly did she think she'd do if she got away?

She didn't know where she was. From the thick canopy of trees over her head she wasn't even sure she could see landmarks. So yes, she would be docile and bide her time.

He wanted to talk? Well, he could do that.

"You said you wanted to tell me what you were doing? I want to hear about it." She looked at her wrists where they were tied to the door. "Untie me and we'll go sit somewhere and I'll listen to you."

He took out his knife and cut through the rope. It took a few harsh tugs, and she felt the rope burning against her skin. She didn't make a sound, but she pulled her arm into her chest, cradling it while she turned her head around to look for her purse.

When he reached for her, she leaned away.

"Wait, I need to get my bag."

He reached in and grabbed her elbow, squeezing hard. "Leave it. It'll be safe here."

Something turned over in her stomach, but she had to try again.

"Please? I have… I have medication in my bag. I just need to take it with me."

The look he gave her was flat. Emotionless.

With his eyes on hers he reached into the back of his car and grabbed her purse. Summer reached out to take hold of it, but he was holding it by the bottom. As he yanked it out of the car, everything inside of it spilled out over the ground.

"Look at that!" His sharp tone made her heart kick in her chest. "No medicine!"

"It… it must have fallen out at the store. Outside when you grabbed me and-"

He backhanded her and Summer fell back onto the ground, sliding on fallen leaves and loose soil.

She covered her cheek with her hand and swallowed, tasting blood on her tongue. Where it was coming from exactly, she didn't know, but it was going to hurt something awful as her skin started to swell. Keeping her hand over her face, she looked at the ground beneath his feet. She didn't see her keys.

At home in Hawaii, she kept them in her purse unless she was wearing slacks. And what perfect timing it was that she'd worn a skirt today of all days. Somehow she'd lost the one concrete chance she had of getting out of this alive and in one piece.

Her tracker. It was out there somewhere.

Just like she was.

~

While Olena waited for Summer to answer her phone, Doctor Chang looked over the pictures that she'd laid out on the worktable. When the call switched to voicemail, she shook her head. "Summer. Call me. Please."

She set the phone on the table. "Well? What do you think? Are they dressed in old clothes?"

He stopped looking and turned his head to look at her. "Look, I know most people think I'm as old as the hills, but I was born after the war. You're asking me if remember what clothes looked like during the war?"

"I know this is all crazy and maybe a little off the wall, but you were the only person I could think of who would possibly know if her idea was at all plausible and not go running to Clive or the Chief and get me in deeper trouble than I already am."

He nodded, his expression troubled.

"All teasing aside, my wife has done a wonderful job of preserving a lot of my family photos. The way these men are dressed, they look a lot like the men of that time." He took a pen out of his pocket and pointed out the features on the images. "The collars are very similar. The cut and style of their pants as well. There are definite differences to what we wear now."

Olena smiled and gestured at the stylish red and white palaka print aloha shirt he wore under his lab coat. "I guess they didn't wear a lot of those back then."

He narrowed his eyes at her. "Certainly not if they were in office jobs or store owners. No."

Olena lifted her phone from the table and looked at the screen. No new calls.

"If this was just any day, I'd wait and call her tonight, but I can't help but think that there's a reason she's not picking up the phone. I know she can get overly focused on her work, but she said she was going out to stores to test her hunch."

Doctor Chang nodded. "I think you're right, but the question of the day is what are we going to do about it."

Before Olena could speak, he stopped her with a hand on her arm. "If you call this into Clive and she ends up walking in the door, fine and dandy, you're going to be in big trouble."

"But I can't do nothing!"

Doctor Chang gave her arm a gentle pat of reassurance. "I didn't say that we wouldn't do anything. Just not that."

Olena nodded. "What's your idea?"

Doctor Chang moved to his desk at the far side of the room and pulled his wallet from the back pocket of his slacks. He set it down and pulled out a card with a handful of numbers written on it. When he picked up the phone, he punched the speaker button and called the first number on the list.

The call was answered on the first ring.

"Elton West. Alone in the asylum."

"Not exactly professional, Elton."

"Honestly, Herman? I'm tired of you poaching my scientist. She has work to do here in the lab for me as well. It's another day that I'm having to do everything by myself and-"

"Elton, we don't know where Summer is. We can't get a hold of her."

The silence that followed was deafening

"What exactly are you telling me?"

"We're not sure, but until we hear from her-"

Elton cut to the chase. "What do you need me to do?"

Doctor Chang gave Olena an encouraging smile as he continued to talk to Summer's boss. "Can you look through her work that she left behind and see if she left any notes about where she might have gone, places she might have visited today or was planning to visit?"

Elton mumbled a little and then it sounded like he'd set the phone down somewhere. "Okay, okay. I'm seeing a lot of handwritten notes on the photos, but a lot of question marks. That girl always has questions."

Olena smiled and nodded.

"Look, I don't see any addresses or specific plans for today, but I know that she was here late into the evening. Look, have you tried her boyfriend? The big Hawaiian guy?"

"Not yet. Do you have a number for him? We could try to get a hold of him."

Elton sighed. "I don't have his number. I didn't even ask her for his name. I just called him Aquaman." They could hear papers shuffling. "I should have asked her, right? I should have found out his name. Then at least I could look up his number, but I didn't..."

"Elton, it's okay, man. I think I know where we can get the number. Just let us know if you see or hear from her."

"Yes. Yes, of course. I'll let you know *when* I hear from her. And Herman? If you hear from her first, will you have her call me?"

"Absolutely."

Doctor Chang blew out a breath as he ended the call and dialed another number from the back of the card.

"Hello?"

"Ajax? I'm sorry, I don't know your real name."

"Ajax is fine, Doctor Chang. What can I do for you?"

"I have Detective Yasui here with me in the office, may I put you on speaker phone?"

"Sure. Hey, guys. Doctor Chang is calling, and he's got Detective Yasui there as well."

"The coroner and the hot detective? Sounds like something kinky."

"Cullen, I'm on speaker phone."

Olena's shoulders shook with nervous laughter.

"Sorry about that, sir. Cullen has had his shots, but we're not all that sure he's house broken. What can we do to help you?"

"I'm sorry, but I'm going to get straight to the point here. We're trying to find Summer Maitland."

"Summer? What's wrong?"

"She's been working with us on a project, and she left Olena a message that she'd be out of her office checking on some possible leads, but since that message we haven't heard from her."

"Ajax? This is Olena. Summer mentioned that her boyfriend is related to your fiancée somehow. Can you get us his number so we can check with him please?"

"Yeah," they heard something that sounded like chair legs scraping on a concrete floor, "they're calabash cousins. They've known each other almost their entire lives." There was a moment of silence and then Ajax rattled off the phone number.

Doctor Chang repeated it back to him.

"That's it. His name is Kai."

"Thanks, Ajax. You've been a big help."

Before Doctor Chang could hang up, Ajax spoke again. "Doc? I hope you don't mind me asking, but what's going on?"

Olena picked up the paper with Kai's number on it and pointed toward the far end of the room. Doctor Chang nodded and gave her a smile. As she crossed the room, dialing the number into her own phone, he explained the situation to the Delta team leader. He kept his explanation short. "I'm sure you can see why we need to find her and just make sure that she's okay."

"Yeah, I can understand why you'd be worried. Doc?"

"Yes?"

"How can we help?"

Kai sat on the front step of his mother's house and looked at the dark cell phone in his hands. He'd been surprised to get a call from the Detective that he'd seen on the news with Summer, but even more so when he heard that Summer was out of touch.

What he heard was that she was missing.

He'd been surprised to hear from the detective. It was almost surreal.

Just that morning he'd made an off-handed comment to Summer. Telling her about a random bit of history that he remembered. He tried to impress her.

She'd taken what he told her and put all that information into her amazing brain and then she'd gone out and acted on it.

Had a seemingly insignificant comment put her in the path of a man who had murdered over and over again and gotten away with it?

He had Summer. There wasn't any doubt in Kai's mind. What else could have happened?

Kai had to try one more time.

It was easy enough. She'd been the last call he'd dialed when he'd reached his mother's house, telling Summer he couldn't wait to see her again that evening. He waited through the rings and when he heard her voice rushing through her message, he could almost see her squeezing the message in between a bunch of other things that were more interesting than setting up her phone message system.

"Summer, call me. Please. I hope you're just too busy to pick up the phone, but everyone is looking for you. I just want to know you're okay." The next few words out of his mouth nearly killed him. This wasn't how he wanted to tell her. He didn't want to do it over the phone, but he hoped it would make a difference somehow. "I love you, ku`ulei. I love you."

As soon as he ended the call, he started another one. And this time, it picked up before the second ring. "Kai! How are you?"

"Can you get me on base?"

If Elodie took offense to his curt reply, he couldn't hear it in her voice. "Of course, do you want me to meet you after-"

"I need to go now." He didn't want to say the words, didn't even know if he could. Saying it would make it impossible to pretend it wasn't real. But there would be a time to pretend after they found Summer and brought her home. "Summer's missing. I'll explain more later, but I need to get on base and talk to her boss. He might know more about where she was going today and maybe there will be a clue there that can help us. Can I meet you at the gate?"

"Yeah, sure. I'll leave right now."

He could hear her moving from room to room, letting people know she'd be gone for the rest of the afternoon. It meant everything to him that she didn't even think twice. They'd become closer after they'd been attacked on that charter boat trip, and it was a huge comfort that he knew he could count on her. He yanked open his car door and had it running in a heartbeat even though his hands were shaking.

"Kai? Are you going to be okay to drive?"

"I have to be," he told his dear friend. "I just have to be."

He hung up the phone and tossed it on the passenger seat

as he pulled out onto the road. He had to focus on the road and getting safely to the Joint Base. He didn't have time to be upset.

He just didn't have time for anything but Summer.

When Kai pulled into the parking lot just shy of the gate, he saw Elodie pulling in from the entrance on the other side. He barely took the time to lock the car before he was running toward her. A pair of guards watched his progress across the lot. Elodie pulled to a stop beside him and as he slid into the passenger seat, she gave his arm a squeeze. "I called Scott."

Just those three words took some of the weight off his shoulders. Elodie made a tight U turn in the lot and pulled out and into the line leading to the gate. As they waited through the swiftly moving line, Elodie filled him in.

"They're out at Wheeler Airfield, but as soon as I talked to him, they started packing up."

Elodie pulled up to the gate and before the guard could get out his greeting, she spoke to him. "I'm Elodie Webber. My husband Scott called the gate."

The soldier gave her a nod. "Yes, Ma'am. We were expecting you. You're cleared for access, have a nice-"

Elodie had already pulled away from the guard post. "Oh, I'm going to have to apologize to him later."

"I'll go with you." Kai meant it. He was glad that Elodie hadn't waited for the soldier to say whatever he was going to say because every second was precious.

"Scott says he's going to call in the cavalry."

"I thought Scott and the others were the cavalry."

He saw Elodie's proud smile.

"They are the best, but we have a friend who, believe it or not, is even better."

"If they help bring Summer home safely, I'll believe

anything." As they drove through the base, Kai looked out at the buildings they passed by.

He had always wanted to visit the base and look around. You didn't live on the island and not wonder what it was like beyond the gates, but this was not how he wanted his first visit to go. Not with a kind of urgency that had his gut twisting and his nerves frayed and on edge.

Summer had been ready to drop by the time Frank pointed at the ground and ordered her to, "Sit."

Angry and aching, she would have loved to stare him straight in the eye and tell him where to shove his order. But her legs had other ideas. She barely managed to flop down on the ground without sprawling out like a broken marionette.

He walked over to something that looked like a lean-to. It was certainly leaning. It wasn't until he lifted a flap that she realized there was a camouflage cover tossed over a pile in the shadows.

She could see bottles of water still in their cardboard box. There were other items under the cover, but the shadows made it difficult to see.

That was his purpose after all, so she had to give him credit.

What she didn't give him was credit for a heart. He twisted the top off of the bottle and put it to his lips and took a number of large, greedy swallows.

When he stopped, he smacked his lips and smiled at her. "Thirsty?"

Summer tried to calm herself. She tried and failed to tamp down the rising gorge in her throat. She knew he was likely playing with her, but she had to say something, and nothing ventured, nothing gained, right?

Keeping her tone as even as she could given the depth of her thirst, she nodded. "I could use a drink." They continued to look at each other and when his brows lifted a little, she added one word. "Please."

His tongue swept lazily over his bottom lip as he watched her. What he was looking for, she had no idea.

Frank lifted the bottle to his lips and tipped it up. The water splashed against his lips and coursed down his neck onto his clothes. When the plastic bottle was empty, he tossed it over to her. "It's been raining here off and on for weeks. That should help you."

She kept her face as neutral as she could, but she started to make a list inside her head.

A list of the ways you could kill a person she'd seen in years of watching real crime TV shows and mocking the murderers. Telling herself she could never ever be that evil or desperate to do any of those things.

But she was quickly realizing that she might have been a little self-righteous.

Frank was quickly volunteering himself for a number of painful ends.

Frank opened the backpack that he'd taken out of the car and pulled out a colorful zipper-top plastic pouch. He tugged it open and shoved his hand inside, fishing out a big piece of jerky.

Hunger roared to life inside of her, but she cast her eyes down to the ground praying that he hadn't seen it in her eyes.

His laughter said otherwise. "I'd share with you," his tone was droll, "but you look like one of those vegetarian folks. Wouldn't want to make you uncomfortable."

Uncomfortable. Well, thank you, kind sir.

Yes. He was certainly moving up her list of ends to a level worthy of CSI or maybe even Bones. If he kept it up, she might just find herself all the way into Criminal Minds and then the gloves would be off.

"You said you'd tell me-"

"Bloodthirsty? Maybe we're more alike than you want to think." He looked at the surrounding area, but she kept her focus on him. "This was all my granddad's idea. It doesn't look like much now, but when he built it back during the war... Hawaii wasn't like the States, in fact it was only a territory back then. That's why they let it happen, you know?"

"Let what happen?" The question popped out before she could stop it.

Frank narrowed his eyes at her. "The government locked the rest of those Japs up? They built camps all over the country, but not here. Here, they tossed a couple hundred in a pen and left the rest of them just walking around.

"They were working on the ships in the harbor! Can you believe that? Their bombers blow our boats out of the water and then they let them in the gates to fix them back up again." He stopped talking for a moment and looked at her.

She didn't have a response.

"Can't expect you to understand it, can I?"

"I don't know what you want from me."

"To understand!"

Heaven help her she had no idea what he was talking about. "What you're talking about happened years ago. You weren't hurt by it."

The look on his face changed in a heartbeat.

His expression went from rage to hollow and blank.

If she didn't know any better, she would have sworn she was looking into the eyes of a dead man.

"That's what you think?" His voice was almost a whisper,

but it was the childlike scratch that made her shrink back from him. "I wasn't hurt by it?"

The packet of jerky dropped from his hands, bits and pieces of dried meat spilled across the ground, but her attention remained fixed on him as he rolled back one sleeve and then the other. His arms were a mess. Scars, several different kinds.

"Who did that to you?" No one should have to go through pain and suffering like that.

"Who? Weren't you listening?" He stretched out his arm at the makeshift camp, his scars looking more gruesome with the stark sunlight bearing down on it. "They did! Wandering around like it wasn't their people that had made it all happen!"

"I'm sorry," were the words she said aloud, but there were more inside her head, 'that you feel that way.'

"That's the first smart thing you've said."

She didn't take it personally. This man, Frank, he was lashing out. And as long as he wanted to talk to her, she figured that she had a chance to stay alive.

Someone had to be out there looking for her by now.

Kai's first look at Summer's home away from home wasn't even bittersweet, it was like bile on the back of his tongue. He got out of Elodie's car and walked straight up to the front door, almost walking straight into Elton, her boss.

Elton's wide-eyed shock gave way to hope. "Have you heard from her?"

All he could do was shake his head.

Elton must have seen Elodie coming because he opened the door and held it open for both of them to come inside. "This isn't like her. This isn't good."

Kai had nothing to say. He wasn't prepared to soothe the other man's worries. "Can I see her workspace?"

At first, the older man balked at the idea, but Elodie had his back.

"Maybe we can find something that tells us where she might have gone? Or who she might have met with?"

When Elton nodded and gestured for them to follow him, Kai set his hand on Elodie's shoulder and gave it a gentle squeeze. "Mahalo, Elodie."

She reached up and covered his hand with hers and returned the gesture. "You're family, Kai. Whatever it takes."

Then he couldn't speak past the hardened lump in his throat. The fears that had been building inside of him continued to grow. Until they had some kind of concrete idea of where she was and how they were going to get her back, he knew he wouldn't stop trying.

He just didn't know what to do.

Elton pushed open a door and reached inside to flick a light switch. The darkened space flickered to life as a score of large high-powered fluorescent fixtures lit up.

It took Kai a precious minute to look around the space. A few tables nearest to the door were set up like a static display for tours. At the far end of the room, he saw two flags displayed, the black POW/MIA banner and the American Flag. He could almost see Summer in this space, bent over a table and examining remains, her brow furrowed in concentration.

"I can't believe she's missing." Elton stood beside him and for the first time, Kai could sense a crack in the older man's veneer. He looked almost frail. "Whatever you want to look through, do it."

"Thanks," Elodie moved past Elton and started for the far end of the room, "we'll try not to make a mess."

Elton's chin dropped down to his chest. "She's the only one who knows where everything is anyway."

Kai felt an odd urge to comfort the man even though they'd barely said two words to each other since they'd met. Yet, Kai couldn't deny that he knew what Summer would want him to do. He reached out and touched Elton's arm. "We'll get her back."

The desolate look in Elton's eyes didn't help. "Good. We need her back."

Yeah. Yeah, they did.

Frank kept devolving into rants of some sort or another. Railing at the rain when it started, grumbling at the mosquitoes lunching on him. That part didn't help her either. She could feel her ankles itching and with her hands tied, she couldn't reach down and scratch, so she focused on asking him questions, trying to distract her mind.

"The man you left near the camp?"

Frank's head swiveled around like an owl, locking his eyes onto her face. "What about him?"

"Who was he?"

When he didn't answer, she tried again.

"Why did you kill him?"

The cold focus of Frank's eyes made her itch even more.

"He did it to himself. You need to know that." He tilted his head to the side as if he needed to stretch his neck. It just gave her chills. "He broke into our apartment: me and my granddads."

Okay, that was something.

"It cost us almost everything we had to move here, but it's what Pops wanted. He was old. Dying. We'd been here a few months and taking Pops around was a pain. Sometimes he could barely climb the stairs back to the apartment. A piece of shit place if there was one, but it was what we could afford." Frank shook his head and sank back down onto the camp chair that he'd set out. "We got up to the apartment and the door was open. This scrawny-ass kid was in our place, digging through our stuff. I didn't know what to say, but Pops? He got into it with him. They went back and forth but I didn't really listen in. I was trying to figure out what to do. But that's when Pops noticed what the guy had in his hands."

Frank looked down at his open hands and while he didn't have his eyes on her, she started to work at the ropes tied around her wrists. It was harder to hide her efforts since he'd tied them in front of her, but she had to do something.

"He had granddad's uniform shirt in his hands. The shirt he wanted to be buried in. Pops told him to put it down. Told him he couldn't have it. But that idiot, that thief, laughed and said that… said that my Pops was too small… too weak to be a soldier."

Summer had a second to stop her efforts before he could catch her.

When he looked up into her eyes, she wasn't even sure he saw her. It looked like he was right back in that moment.

"Too weak. Too weak?" His eyes refocused on her face. "And do you know what happened?"

She shook her head, too afraid to take a guess.

"Pops took his cane and he cracked him over the head."

Frank continued on describing the way that the older man killed the thief and as he spoke, Summer went through the injuries John Doe suffered in her head. His story was like a road map of the man's death.

"We showed him."

"And the uniform? Why did you put it on him?"

He looked almost defeated.

"That was Pops too. He called it a statement. An up yours to the military for what they'd done to him back then."

"He was in the military? What branch?"

She couldn't help the rush of hope inside of her. She just had to keep him talking.

"Army, not that they act like it."

The bitter edge in his voice told her to tread carefully.

"What do you mean?"

Frank looked like he was crumbling, breaking into pieces. "Pops died. He died before we finished his plans. And I went to the Army to schedule his burial. They lied right to my face. They lied."

She didn't want to say a word. Summer felt like there was a real possibility that if she said the wrong thing, she might trigger his rage.

"They told me..." His words faded off as his eyes stared off into the distance. "They told me..." He reached behind his back and she nearly swallowed her tongue, but he just pulled out a folded paper and he shook it at her. "They said he wasn't allowed a military funeral because he'd never been in the military."

Summer felt sick. Frank was a scary man on his own, but it looked like he was fighting demons neither of them could see. If his grandfather had built up all of this hate and frustration in Frank, that was bad enough. He'd wound up his grandson and set him loose on the island. Now that his grandfather was dead and couldn't answer his questions, Frank was searching for direction.

And that had led him to her.

She was nauseous and it had nothing to do with the heat or humidity, it was all about fear.

CHAPTER 16

The Delta Team had split up downtown. Trying to make the most of their time and manpower, Ajax split the team into smaller groups of two or three to visit the list of vintage and secondhand stores in the Honolulu area. Ajax, Hi`ilani, and Train. Shado, Commander Chastain, and Baron. And finally, Mace and Cullen went with Detective Yasui.

Their first store had almost been a bust. The tiny woman behind the counter had nearly fainted at the sight of the two Deltas walking through her store. Her cheeks went from red to eggshell white when Cullen's shoulder brushed past a rack of clothes.

She'd been so flustered at the thought of her items being trampled on that Olena had to send the men outside before she could even question the woman.

Yes. Summer had been there. No, she didn't say where she was going.

The one good thing about that first location was the security cameras. As nervous as the woman was about her store, she had the best camera set up that Olena had ever seen. A quick look at the footage told her that Summer had made it into her car safely. It also gave her a direction as Summer drove off down King Street.

That was something.

The second shop was almost like the first. Except the man behind the counter had no problem defending his store, bellowing at the men before they even stepped foot inside. "Don't make a mess!"

Mace took a position at the front door while Cullen walked up to the counter with Olena. She set her phone down on the counter and pointed to the screen. "Have you seen this woman today?"

The man looked down at the image and paused before looking back up. His face hadn't changed, but the pulse at the base of his neck was pounding like a drum. "Nope. Haven't seen her."

Olena reached out and stopped Cullen from reaching across the counter.

Reaching for the edge of her jacket, she pulled it aside, letting the sunlight wink off her shield. "Don't do this. Not today. This," she pointed to the picture, "is my friend."

"Still haven't seen her." The man lifted his chin and almost managed a smile, but it was all bluster.

"You see? That's what I said not to do." Olena knew she might regret her next few words, but she knew that she had to leverage the power she had and also… the muscle she'd brought with her. "This man," she gestured to Cullen standing beside her, "is also her friend."

Cullen leaned his hands down on the countertop and the metal in the glass case groaned at the added pressure. "Don't waste our time."

Olena couldn't believe it when the man lifted his spindly arms and folded them across his chest.

"You don't frighten me."

She didn't even have to look back at Mace, she heard something rattle behind her.

"Oh, this feels like it's about to fall over." Mace's voice was as cool and collected as it was pointed and threatening.

"Good god! Stop that!" The man behind the counter sounded like he was about to hyperventilate. "That's... no don't..."

The shelves stopped rattling and Mace's slow drawl crossed the store. "She's our sister."

The owner looked at Cullen with his dark blond hair and golden tan and then back over Olena's shoulder where she knew he saw that Mace was African American. "Sister?"

Cullen shrugged. "We're a big family."

Olena almost kicked him. "If you want to play dumb. Be our guest." The shelf rattled again, and the owner paled again and pressed his lips together so hard that they quivered.

At the first rattle of metal behind her the man almost burst into tears. "Frank told me he'd kill me if I said anything."

Olena felt her heart skip a beat.

"Don't stop now," Cullen gestured for him to keep talking.

He blabbered and blubbered, making a mess of his answers, but he said enough to send Mace out around the store to the back while Olena wrote down the pertinent information from the owner. She pulled out a glove to pick up a figurine that 'Frank' had picked up from the counter and threatened to drop on the floor to prove his point.

Using her radio, Olena called into the local substation and asked for officers on scene. She'd already briefed her boss and the look that Clive had given her would've melted asphalt. There would be a reckoning for her, but she had to stay in the present, because the present was where she had to be.

Summer had joined the investigation because Olena

allowed and encouraged it. It wasn't everyday that she met a woman who could understand the pressure she was under and didn't feel the need to compete with nearly every interaction.

Her mother had told her that was just the way of things, her father? He'd told her that she was hanging out with the wrong women. Working with Summer was easy and crazy to say, fun. That and they'd both learned a lot from each other.

There was no way she was going to lose her as a friend, but most importantly, they weren't going to lose her at all.

She felt a hand on her arm and turned, looking up at Cullen.

"You okay?"

Olena nodded but that was the only answer she was able to give him. Up until the moment he stepped up beside her and added his own presence into the mix. It was easier to work with him than it was to work with Clive, and she'd been working with him for almost a year.

"If you want, I can take our friend into the back and-" she gave him a cautioning look, but he just smiled and continued on, "look at the security tapes." Cullen looked at the man's name tag and grinned. "What do you say, Todd? Want to be a hero?"

She hadn't been the only one to worry where he was going with that, the man cowering behind the counter slid a dark look in their direction. "If I had security tapes, I'd give them to you."

Cullen's mood darkened along with hers. "What are all the cameras for?"

"Prevention. If people assume that Big Brother is watching they behave better, usually."

"That's not going to help us in this situation." Olena felt frustration building inside of her again. "What else can you tell us?"

His shoulders lifted in a wincing shrug. "He needed money and I needed someone who didn't need benefits. I paid him with cash, and he'd leave. We didn't exactly talk to each other beyond that. To be honest, I didn't even try. The guy gave me the creeps."

Cullen scoffed. "But you kept him around?"

"He didn't argue with me. He came to work, did what I asked him to and then he'd go away. Even better he sometimes took things in trade. I told that to your friend. It was all stuff that I don't usually sell, so that was good."

"What else do you remember about what you told her?"

"Nothing much. I got the feeling she would have asked me more, but she wanted to make a call. I have an issue with my pacemaker, so she said she'd make the call outside."

Outside.

Olena looked up at Cullen. "Where did Mace go?"

He gestured at the back wall and Olena stepped back from the counter, ready to head in that direction, when he walked through the open doorway holding a key ring, dangling from his fingers. "Found this in an alley."

Any hope that Summer might just be taking a long walk or sitting on a beach somewhere crumbled in that moment. Summer was never without that keyring. The sheer number of keys she needed for work were daunting and the POW flag keychain was easy to pick out.

Before Mace could cross the room to hand it to her the phone on the desk rang.

Olena gestured for Todd to pick up the phone.

He shook his head. "It's probably my mother checking up on me."

The phone continued to ring and with a shrug, Olena picked it up. "Hello?"

"Hello. My name is Tex. And I'd like to know why

Summer Maitland's tracker is there and why she isn't, Detective Yasui."

Olena looked around the room at the two cameras fixed to the wall. "What do you mean?"

"You might want to ask Cullen and Mace about me. They'll know who I am. And I'm not looking at you through the cameras in Good Mill. There's an ATM across the side street and a security camera across King Street at the Gym."

She relayed the information to the two men and they immediately vouched for him.

Olena leaned her hip against the counter. "Okay, Tex. They say you're one of the good guys. I'm hoping you're better than good, because we need to get my friend back where she belongs."

She could hear Tex tapping away on his computer, the rapid sounds almost soothing to her frayed nerves.

"I'm accessing the feed on the security cameras in the area as we speak. I'll comb through the feed from earlier today and see what I can come up with."

"That's going to be a great help. I'll start the request on my end so when we get access to the footage there won't be a question about the video feed."

"Great. I'm not in Law Enforcement so you make sure that once we get this guy, we can put him in jail and toss the key. Any details you have on him, text me."

Before she could ask him about his number, her phone dinged for an incoming message.

"That was me," he confirmed. "And yes, you should send the information into your department, but I can guarantee that I can find any computer records before they do. And in some cases," she heard him pause for a moment before typing furiously again, "I'll find even more."

Olena felt like she could breathe a little easier after she heard the even tone of his voice. She couldn't stop the almost hopeful smile at the thought of locking Frank up forever. "Mahalo. I'll send you the information as soon as I step outside."

A moment before she pulled the phone away from her ear, Tex spoke one more time. "Oh, and Detective? We're going to get her back."

~

Summer was exhausted. Riding the line between keeping him talking and shying away from making him angry, she felt like she was dancing on a tightrope. Her head hurt where he'd cracked her across her cheek. There was little she could do to ease her discomfort. She just had to sit there and listen to him and pray that she could make it through this.

Frank had explained about their first kill, or rather, his grandfather's kill.

The shallow location of their disposal was just as shocking.

"He told me to dig," Frank said of his grandfather. "He sat down on the bumper of the car and told me it was my turn, that he'd done all the hard work. That's why I had to dig because it was my part of the job. He told me that he'd dug his share of graves in his time.

"I was tired. I'd worked that day before helping Pops with his errands. I was tired and he wanted me to dig. My hands blistered and then they bled. The dirt was tight packed and almost as hard as a rock. It was only when I started crying that he let me stop.

"He said I could stop, but the rest of the jobs? I had to do those on my own."

Summer lifted her head and almost met his eyes.

"How many?" She barely made more than a whisper of sound. "How many more?"

She knew the number that Olena had told her, she'd seen the reports, the crime scene photos.

Verify.

She needed to know if they were missing anyone.

Frank leaned down to look in her eyes, as if proving that he was the one who would make the decisions, and then he didn't just say that number, he talked her through each and every kill he'd done so far and why he'd picked the men.

It was good to know what happened, but Summer felt as if her skin was crawling.

Frank showed no remorse and didn't seem to care that he'd taken so many lives. He was proud of it.

She knew there wouldn't be a way to reason with him, so how was she going to survive this?

Kai barely looked up when Elodie left the room, he was poring over Summer's notes. It was an unintentional lesson into her personality. He'd seen her easy-going manner when she was with him. He'd felt her passion and tender touch.

What he hadn't experienced was this part of her. The analytical side of her brilliant brain. He'd wondered about her job, but they'd only scratched the surface of it. Even though he knew what she did in the most general of terms she'd never really went into much detail about it.

Having gone through her pictures and notes on the body that she'd helped to dig out of the ground, he could see the horrors of what she had to witness. No one as tenderhearted as Summer could see something like that and not be affected by the stark evil of the man's death.

And yet, it wasn't her perfunctory notes on the man's violent end that had caught most of his attention. It was the way that her notes captured her thought process, and through that, her soul.

The body wasn't just a pile of bones to her. There was life in what she saw. There was a soul in them as well.

Her notes talked about the kind of life he'd probably had. Malnourished as a child. An unset broken bone in his wrist. The pain that he must have felt on a daily basis.

She also wondered about the injustice of a life cut so short. Had he been loved? Had he been close to his family? Or was the injury to his wrist been done by someone close to him? She worried and she cared as she did with the people around her.

The man they'd found half-buried at the Honouliuli site was a person and she cared. That's why she did what she did.

It made him even angrier that someone had taken her. And if he was the person responsible for the death of the man in the photos on her desk, Kai feared that he'd never see her alive again. Would she become a set of photos like this?

He shook his head and rose from the desk with a determined set of his chin. No matter what, Summer would always be the living, breathing person he fell in love with. He just had to get her back so he could tell her just how much he cared for her, and how he'd never stop.

Kai just needed that chance.

"Kai, look!"

He turned his head and saw Mustang come through the door. He was followed by the rest of the SEAL team and once they were inside and the door was closed, Kai wondered at how they seemed to take up the room. Their expressions were calm, but he could see the determination in their eyes and the tight set of their jaws. They looked ready for war and he'd never been so damn happy.

There was just one person missing. "Where did Elton go?"

Elodie shrugged. "I passed him on the way back in, he was headed for the door."

Kai nodded. He didn't have time to worry about the other man as he crossed the room and shook everyone's hand, thanking them for coming.

Midas was the last in the line, but the first to remind him. "You don't need to thank us. We're here to get Summer back."

Jag lifted his chin. "I can't believe of all the places for her to get into trouble it's here, on island."

Pid agreed. "Well, she won't be gone for long. We'll find her and get her back." A thought seemed to cross his mind and Pid looked at Mustang. "Has Tex found her tracker yet?"

Mustang nodded. "He's looking up security footage now. She was at a resale shop looking for anyone who bought clothes from the World War II Era."

"It turns out that the killer has been dressing up his victims as if they were civilians during the war."

Kai heard the voice, but he didn't see the man who spoke.

That changed a moment later when the others stepped aside to let him through. He was military, but he didn't wear a uniform. It was the way he carried himself. The determined set of his shoulders and the sharp look in his eyes that said he could take on anyone in the room and survive. That he'd probably do that and kick some serious ass.

Thank God.

He stopped just short of Kai and looked at the desk with Summer's photos and notes. As the room remained silent, he read over her notes quickly, nodding and murmuring at different times. When he was done, he moved to one of the empty tables and set down the folder he'd been carrying under his arm. Everyone moved to join him even though he hadn't asked for it.

No one wanted to be left out.

"Summer messaged me the information on the bodies

found in the downtown area. She's sharp." Kai heard the pride in the man's tone. "It took me a hot minute to figure out what she was looking at, but I think I know what it is.

Opening the top flap of the worn folder, he started to place a bundle of papers down in order on the top of the table.

Alan Hayakawa – Teacher

David Nakasone – Newspaper Publisher

Kenji Tanaka – Church Caretaker

Walter Yamamoto – Electrician

He continued on and on until eight bundles were laid out on the table. "From July of Nineteen Forty-Three until August of Forty-Four, there were a series of murders in the area." He pulled out a map and laid it out to the side, using his finger to point to the location of each body in order that they were found.

"The information that Summer gave me on the murder victims that Detective Yasui is investigating, I can match them up directly."

He moved onto the second bunch of papers in his folder, laying them on top of the original victims.

Teacher

Online News Blogger

Church Volunteer

Electrician

The pattern placed before them made Kai's skin crawl. "They're doing it all again?"

"I'm sure that Summer was working that through in her head. The detective was likely trained to go from Point A to Point B based on evidence and couldn't quite see the bigger picture. The kind of intuitive leap you'd have to take to see that this wasn't just a serial killer."

Midas leaned forward, bracing his hands on the edge of the table. "More like a copycat?"

The man looked at Kai. "What do you think?"

"Me?" Kai was shaken at the expectation he saw in the man's eyes. "I'm not a scientist. I'm just here looking for Summer. I'm here to bring her home."

"Don't underestimate yourself." He turned to the rest of the assembled group. "There's an unsolved murder of a Camp Guard from Honouliuli. The investigation only got so far. Tensions were already high. It wasn't like the camps on the continent. Here in Hawaii only a part of the population was detained in the camps. The majority of the Japanese residents here continued on with their lives, under Martial Law of course, but everyone was going through that."

"And the people who were in the camps," Kai guessed, "teachers, newspaper men, church volunteers…"

"The main concern as it was declared to the public at large were that those men had the ability to influence others, and many had the ability to communicate with boats outside of Hawaii."

"But if they didn't," Elodie ventured, "then why would someone target these men."

"Frustration coupled with fear. A number of terrifying experiences would put anyone on edge, but the person who did these earlier killings, he took it further. He wanted to end these men and perhaps make a statement of some sort. The death of the guard looks like it was personally motivated. There was vicious, almost unhinged energy in the attack. The same with the body that the Delta Team found at the new Historic Site at Honouliuli."

"Okay," Kai lifted his hands in frustration, "so you're saying that Summer's been taken by the man who killed all of these people."

"No, I'm saying that Summer was likely taken by someone younger than the first killer. Someone who has fixated on the idea of dredging this back up again. The records I found on the original killings stop short of linking them all together."

"They probably didn't."

Kai turned to look at Elton. He hadn't noticed him come back into the room.

"If they had, there might have been more attention put on the killings, but from what I've heard when I talk to the men who were stationed in Hawaii at that time tensions were high. There were many who didn't like the fact that the Japanese here on the island weren't all placed in the camps."

"You call them Japanese, but many of them were born in Hawaii." Kai felt eyes turn to look at him, but he focused on Elton. "They came here to work. Many on plantations. They considered Hawaii their home, not Japan." Kai turned his head, addressing the others in the room. My last name is Akina. And yes, I'm Hawaiian, but I'm also Chinese. And a few more things, or so my mom tells me, making me a bit chop suey when it comes to race, but the people you're talking about were good people. Neighbors, friends, family. Why should they have to be put into a cage when they had nothing to do with the attack? They suffered as well."

Something turned over in Kai's gut and he apologized to the group.

"I'm sorry, I know you're all here to help get Summer back but hearing that… it's hard to distance myself from it."

"You don't have to."

Kai looked up at Mustang across the table.

"Putting the Japanese in camps drew the line between us and them. What we're seeing here, with these men being murdered, shows us that the line is still there for someone. And that line should have been gone a long time ago."

Pid nodded and gestured at a plaque on the wall behind him. It was a unit insignia with the words GO FOR BROKE in shining gold letters on it. "At nearly the same time the camp at Honouliuli was opened here, the Army formed the 442nd Combat Team using volunteers from the Japanese," he paused and looked at Kai, "Japanese Americans. They became the most decorated unit for their size in our history. They charged headlong into danger fighting all over Europe during the war."

Kai swallowed down the lump in his throat. "Many of their families were in camps all across the country, being asked to swear their loyalty to a country who treated them like criminals for their birth. Knowing that Summer is mixed up in all of this is killing me. All she's tried to do is help bring people home to their families."

"And we're going to do the same thing." Midas gave him a knowing smile. "We will."

"Whatever you're doing," Kai countered, "I want in. I can't just sit back and wait."

Slate gave him a cautionary look.

Elodie's soft gasp filled the air and turned people's heads. "I'm not military trained, but I did okay when they tried to kill me, right? We can all help. We can all do our parts. If we're going to get her home, we need to pull everyone together on this."

Slate started to apologize but Kai stopped him. "No worries," he tried to smile, "let's just focus on Summer."

Mustang's phone rang and he pulled it out to accept the call. "I'm putting you on speaker, here."

He set the phone down on the table and everyone moved closer to listen.

"Tex here. I've got a name for you. "Frank Ritter. Based on the information that Detective Yasui and the Deltas got out of the shop owner and a few backdoors to security footage from local businesses and I was able to get a good enough picture for a name. Detective Yasui is taking the Deltas to Frank's apartment to see if they can find out where he's taken Summer."

Mustang leaned closer. "What about a job? Can we go and watch for him there?"

"He was paid under the table, probably had a few jobs but there won't be any record. If the Delta's find anything at his apartment that's out in this area, they'll call."

There was a moment of hesitation.

"You should all know that Summer's tracker was left at the store. I saw enough from the surrounding camera feeds to know that she was out cold when he put her into the car. She wouldn't have left the tracker behind. From here, we're going to have to adjust any plans to find her knowing that we don't have a way to zero in on her. I'll keep digging on my end. If I have more, I'll call."

"Thanks, Tex. Good work."

The call ended a moment later.

Kai was even more confused. "Tracker?"

Mustang nodded. "It's how we found her the last time. She had a tracker on her keychain that would have alerted Tex to trouble. The fact that it was left behind-"

Elodie touched his arm, her concern written across her features. Mustang gently covered her hand and gave it a gentle squeeze.

"Just means we'll have to work a little harder. We're still going to find her."

Elton showed the SEALs where they could wash up, and Elodie went to make a few calls, but Kai stayed in the room with the newcomer, watching him as he pored over the files on the table.

The man was older than the others, but there was no mistaking his powerful build or the fact that he could handle himself. There was just something about him that made Kai want to believe in what he was saying.

"How do you know Summer?"

The other man looked up and Kai saw the knowing glint in the man's green eyes.

"Summer identified remains that turned out to be the father of another soldier on my SEAL team. His son had completed BUD/S and been assigned to my team for a year when the trouble began. Tony had always wondered what happened to his dad. He was sure the man hadn't run off on his family, but without having a clear understanding of what had happened, the questions lingered.

"His son had heard the stories too and when his wife became pregnant, Tony's son started to struggle. The same feeling that Tony had worried over in the back of his head seemed to consume his son. The idea that he'd be lost and never returned to his family ate at him.

"Just as his son was thinking of leaving the military, Tony got a call from Summer asking him for a DNA sample. Tony sent it right away. She'd already cautioned him not to get too excited, that it was a preliminary match and not anything definitive. Still, I could tell that Tony was nervous, but hopeful.

"And when she called and confirmed that the remains they'd discovered were his father's, I'd never seen Tony cry before. Knowing that there was someone like Summer out there, bringing people home to their families, it changed his outlook. He didn't live with that worry in the back of his head anymore and he was the stronger for it. We all were. And that's why I'm here. Anything I can do to help her. I will. And that includes bringing her back home."

Kai felt a weight slide from his shoulders as he held out his hand. "Thank you, sir."

The man gave his hand a good, hard shake. "No need to thank me, Kai. You can call me Baker. Baker Rawlins."

CHAPTER 17

It was near dark when Frank started up again, he'd slept a little in the afternoon, but before he nodded off, he'd tied her wrists to the water tank at the edge of the clearing. It was likely big enough on the inside to fit a compact car if dropped trunk or front first, and it towered over her. Painted drab green like old Army uniforms, it blended into the scenery a little too well for her peace of mind when Frank was digging through the supplies he'd piled up under the camouflage tarp.

And based on the grumbling and grousing he was doing, he wasn't finding what he wanted.

"Damn it!" He turned around and locked his eyes on Summer. "This is your fault!"

She didn't have a word to say in return.

"When I was at the shop that was my first stop of the day. I needed groceries and gas. I had other plans for tonight."

The cold cutting tone of his voice told her exactly what those plans had been.

"I can't just sit here. I need those supplies."

Slowly, Summer let out a breath, trying not to make a big

deal about it. She didn't want to upset him any more than he was already.

Reaching under the tarp again, he pulled out a long-handled flashlight and gave her a look.

While he'd been asleep, she had managed to loosen the rope around her wrists enough that another hour or two of peace and quiet and she could easily remove it.

Sure, that was only part of her problem, but it was something positive and she was going to hold onto that. She had to.

"Get up."

He'd barked the order, but she barely reacted. She was exhausted.

Frank moved closer and glare at her. "I said to get up!"

She didn't want to remind him about the rope. If he came too close or if he took a good enough look, he'd see that she'd worked the knots loose with her teeth and sheer determination.

"Damn it!"

Frank stalked right up to her and grabbed her by the ropes he'd tied around her wrists. Before she could grab hold of it, Frank yanked at it, trying to get her up on her feet. All it did was yank the ropes clear off.

She saw the flash of anger in his eyes before he brought the flashlight down on her.

He missed her head, thank goodness, but he cracked her hard on the shoulder, driving her down to the ground.

The pain radiating from the point of impact was unceasing and Summer knew that he'd likely cracked her collarbone or at least he'd hit it hard enough to ache in a way that went straight to her toes.

"Now, get up."

Slowly, she got to her feet, leaning away from Frank, but his anger made him faster. At least he didn't knock her down.

He just grabbed her by the arm and pulled her around to the far side of the water tank.

She didn't drag her feet, but she wasn't trying to move fast. "Where are we going?"

"Going?" He shook his head. "I'm going to get supplies and you, you're going to wait for me here."

Summer held out her hands and looked at him. "Go ahead. Put the ropes back on."

The look on his face scared her.

"You think I'm going to tie you up when you almost got away?"

"You can tie my hands behind me." It was an offer she could handle. She'd tied her fair share of knots in her time and could probably undo them given time and once he left that's all she would have, time.

Frank shook his head and lifted his eyes up the wall of the water tower. When she followed suit she saw the rungs welded onto the outside of the tower.

"Climb."

"You're joking with me, right?"

His face changed, his mouth a flat line and his eyes cold and empty. He reached into his pants pocket and pulled out a knife, opening it with a flick of his wrist.

She didn't have to look too closely to see how sharp the blade was. The remaining sunlight did an ample job of frightening her all on its own.

"Climb." His tone brooked no argument.

When she reached the bottom of the rungs, she found herself shaking. She didn't know what waited for her at the top of the ladder, but she didn't have much of a say in it.

One rung after another, she climbed up. The only time she stopped was when she finally got a look inside the tank. There was water in there. She couldn't tell how much, but there was more than enough to cover the bottom of the tank.

"Keep going." She heard Frank's voice easily from where he stood on the ground.

"You want me to go inside?" She wrapped her arm around the top rung and hoped she was wrong.

"It's the perfect place to hide you. I have a rope ladder I'll toss down there when I get back. Until then, you're good and stuck where I put you. I don't have to worry about you running away."

"I'll be fine with the ropes. Please, I don't like the water."

"Climb over." She heard him start climbing up from below her. "Do it, or you won't have to worry about ropes either."

Her brain was on overload. Her heart was pounding in her chest.

"Please," she could barely make a noise, "don't make me do this."

"Climb on top of the tank. Now."

Slowly, using her arms for balance, she climbed up on the lip of the reservoir and brought her legs over the edge. Summer tried to guess how far down it was and she was just starting to lower herself down into the interior when he gave her a good hard shove.

And down she went.

Summer had no idea how far she'd fallen, but even though she'd tried to tuck her knees up against her middle, she didn't do it fast enough and the sudden impact of her feet against the metal bottom of the tank made her see stars.

And the water. All of that water!

It splashed up her front and her back and with the surprised gasp of air that she needed, it splashed into her mouth too.

What she didn't spit out, almost drowned her, but she managed to back up against the wall of the tank and center herself.

"You'll be fine in here until I come back." Frank turned on his flashlight and shone it around the interior. She saw leaves and other things floating in the water, but other than that she was alone. "You stay out of trouble and I'll let you climb out when I get back."

Summer wanted to say something. She wanted to give him a snarky comment and act like a badass heroine. Instead, she leaned back against the wall and tilted her head back.

Where she stood, she could see the glowing moonlight against the gray clouds overhead. It wasn't a full moon, but it was enough to see by.

She'd wait for her opportunity to come and then she was going to get out of this horrible predicament.

Until then, she would just have to wait.

Closing her eyes, she left the back of her head leaning against the wall and made sure that her knees were bent so they wouldn't lock up.

She could wait like this. It would be fine.

Something touched her chin.

Something wet.

Lifting her hand up to her chin, Summer felt a third drip and realized exactly what it was.

A pattering sound against the parts of the roof that were still intact, told her that her luck had taken an even worse turn than it already had.

It was raining.

Just great.

Pictures and descriptions had gone to everyone's phones. Including Kai's. The SEALs and Deltas had broken up into groups. A few well-placed news spots had garnered a bunch of tips. Three different businesses where Frank Ritter had worked from time to time since he'd arrived in Hawaii. The fourth team at his apartment.

Kai sat in his car on the street, watching the front door of the building beside Elodie. "Why do I get the feeling I've been sent to the sidelines for the final play of the game?"

She touched his hand. "They're not doing it on purpose. They've been trained for this and you're-"

"Just me. Honestly, after this? If she's as smart as I know she is, she should take one look at me and pick one of the Deltas. Or someone on Scott's team. They can kick ass. Me? I can teach her to swim. Big deal, right?"

He flinched when Elodie pinched him in the side.

"Hey!"

"Hey, yourself!" Elodie shook her head. "You're no slouch, you know? But even better than that. You're good for her. The two of you are good for each other. Everyone who's seen you two together know that you're perfect for each other. Just take a little help from your friends and when we get her back you can pamper her for weeks. I know she'll enjoy that."

Kai was going to say something back to her when he saw movement on the street. Lifting up his radio, he sent a message to the others. "He's here, going into the side door."

He ground his back teeth together as the others replied. Now he just had to wait. Once Frank was inside, Shado followed him up the stairs.

It was a few heart-pounding minutes before he heard a return call.

Three little words that made him take a firm grasp of hope.

"We have him."

Kai and Elodie got out of the car and crossed the street to watch them walk Frank Ritter to one of the cars.

The asphalt was slick under Kai's shoes as he walked and rain battered his head, running in little rivulets down his face. As soon as Frank cleared the doorway, Kai had to remind himself to keep his hands at his side.

Frank didn't seem to have a care in his world. Kicking at the puddles of rain on the street, he almost seemed happy. Beyond happy as he tilted his head back, stuck his tongue out, and shook his head in the rain.

Baron grabbed him by the back of the neck and shoved him in the car, climbing in beside him. On the other side of the car was Mace. Neither man was going to give him an inch of space."

Olena opened the driver's door and climbed in. She gave Frank one chance. "Tell us where Summer is."

"And..." Frank smiled at her, "what will you give me if I do?"

Baron spoke first. "Mercy."

Frank looked like he was going to argue for a moment, but Baron wasn't having it. With his closest hand, he wrapped it around Frank's throat.

"Here's the deal, you little worm." He squeezed his thumb and index finger in just a hair into Frank's neck and all he could do was draw in a short raspy gasp. "I don't have time to waste with you. And you don't want to spend any more time with me than necessary.

"Especially when I have no problem showing you the horror that you caused to others, because I have more skill than you. Anyone from our team could flay you alive for what you've taken."

He removed the pressure and Frank could talk again. He looked straight at Olena. "You're a police officer, you can't let him kill me."

"Well, there's this problem I have," Olena began. "I'm not the one who has you in custody. And these men," she pointed at the assembled group, "are the kinds of soldiers you go to when you want something, or someone taken care of."

"We're the ones they drop into the center of Hell," Mace continued, "and we fight our way out."

"Yeah, sure." Frank was shaking. "But you're not going to let them hurt me, right?"

Olena shook her head. "You don't want to ask me questions like that, because you won't like the answer."

Frank was very quickly getting the idea that he'd met up with the wrong people.

A bolt of lightning lit up the sky and then a roll of thunder shook the SUV.

Torrents of rain smashed into the roof over their heads.

The interior of the SUV was silent for a moment and then Frank started to laugh.

Kai wanted to kill him with his bare hands. "What's so damn funny?"

Frank didn't answer at first, he just kept laughing. Kai tried to climb into the backseat from the front, but someone got a couple of fistfuls of his shirt and pulled back.

Baron grasped Franks' throat and with one little squeeze Frank went silent.

"Now, I'm going to assume that you were dropped on your head as a child. Or maybe you've taken more than your fair share of drugs and fried your brain, but it seems you do understand the imminent possibility of death. So we're going to try this again. You have two questions to answer. Where is our friend Summer? And what the fuck do you find so amusing?"

Baron took his hand away from Frank's neck and laid it on the back of the seat so it would be close enough to use if he had to.

Frank looked at all of them before he focused his attention on Olena. "The answer to both questions is the same thing."

When Baron moved his hand, Frank flinched away.

"I'll tell, I'll tell!" He looked back at Olena. "I just need to know one thing."

Mace looked about ready to murder someone. "What's that?"

Frank's eyes were wild with a kind of frenzy that Kai had never seen before.

"How long has it been raining on the other side of the island?"

As they were driving over to the Windward side of the island, Kai listened to the talk around him. Plans were made. Contingencies on contingencies. He finally understood what it meant to be prepared in the way that the SEALs and Delta Force prepared.

Frank sat quietly in the backseat between Mace and Baron. It wasn't by choice. Baron had a roll of silver utility tape in the SUV and he effectively silenced the man.

Word came through a phone call that Tex had found a large parcel of property sold to a Thom Ritter back in Forty-Two. Deep in the forested area near the H-3 Interstate Highway, the property had been foreclosed over a decade before for defaulting on the mortgage. No one had shown any interest in the property in more than thirty years.

While Tex was listing out the facts, Frank was sitting in the backseat, trying to disappear. Kai had no problem with that outcome, but only after they found Summer. The background information might have been interesting to the others, Kai could only stare out of the window beside him and hope they found her in time.

The way that Frank had explained it was that his granddad had built a bunker and other buildings to make his own base. And once he was done with it, he would have spent his lifetime putting 'them' where they belong. If they were to believe Frank, who was already delusional, his 'Pops' had already taken and buried men in the ground of his property.

Kai hoped that just wasn't true. It was sad enough that there had been a whole new group of killings, dredging up old crimes would be difficult and painful for so many people. And the Ritters, Frank and his grandfather, didn't deserve any attention for what they did.

None.

~

Summer was sure she was close to losing her mind.

It felt like days and days had passed while she was in the water tower. She knew intellectually that it wasn't the truth, but it just felt like that.

"What was that line that LL Cool J said in that shark movie? Touch a hot pan and a minute can feel like an hour, touch a hot woman and an hour can feel like a minute?"

She looked up for a moment as the rain subsided a bit and managed to grumble under her breath. "I'd rather relativity to reality any day."

The water had risen in the tank since Frank had gone. Summer had always been more than a little awed by the magnificent waterfalls that lined the Ko'olau Mountains when it rained. She'd have a new appreciation for it if she survived this. The water had reached her shoulders maybe an hour or so ago and she'd been on her tip toes after that, tipping her head back to avoid accidentally taking more into her mouth.

There were moments when she felt completely off her rocker and other moments when things came into startling clarity. Like the thought of the water getting so high that she might be able to float right out of the tank.

Only to realize that she'd likely fall about twenty feet or more and injure her back.

Or thinking about everything she wanted to do on the island. Before she'd moved to Hawaii she'd made a list about thirty items long that she'd pulled together from island guidebooks. Sure, some of them would likely classify as 'touristy,' but she wouldn't care.

She just wanted to see something outside the lab.

She wanted to see Kai.

To hold him and kiss him and try out a few things she'd never had the confidence to ask her sexual partners, but she wanted to ask him. And she had a feeling he'd probably be more than happy to try them out.

But first things first.

She needed to survive.

And the floor was slowly slipping away.

The heavy pounding of rain started up again and Summer ignored the tears rolling down her cheeks. Slowly leaning back in the water, Summer swore she could almost hear Kai talking to her.

"Lay back. Easy breaths. Let go of all the tension and worries inside and let the water hold you up."

There was enough left of the metal dome that had once been at the top of the tower that she could keep her face out of the pounding rain for the most part, but it wasn't going to be enough soon.

She was tiring, quickly. Stuck in a metal cannister was so very different from floating in the middle of a pool. Or just off of the beach in Waimanalo. With the raindrops pummeling the surface of the water it was almost like feeling waves battering against her in open seas.

She was exhausted. And aching.

There was just one thing that kept her hoping that she'd make it through the evening and to the next day. Kai.

She wanted to show him that she could do this. To see the look in his eyes when she threw her arms around him and thanked him for taking all of that time to teach her.

All she had to do was keep going.

As the teams gathered together along the old access road that was more like a developing mudslide, everyone struggled to hear each other with the sheets of rain coming through from the storm. Tex had pulled up satellite images of the area and found a number of small buildings in two places. It was impossible to tell which group was the one that they were looking for, at least not until they were on the ground.

Kai had already told Mustang and Ajax that they'd have to duct tape him up in the car to leave him behind. He'd even taken off his Local Motion slippers and tossed them aside. Wearing those he'd likely slip and fall in the forested area, but barefoot? He assured them all that he was fine with taking the risk.

Broken into groups they moved off into the dark, rain pummeled forest knowing that time was something they had very little of. Together, they'd cover the most ground and they would find her. That's what they had to tell themselves. There wasn't another option that any of them would accept.

Summer had almost convinced herself that this whole thing was a dream. That she was just waiting for her alarm to wake her up and she'd be home, dry and safe.

Until her head bumped against the metal wall of the tank.

Wincing away from it, her shoulders pushed forward, and her feet dropped down, and Summer got a mouthful of water.

She tried to push it right out again, but some of it slipped down her throat and she choked on it.

It took her a few moments to get her head completely above the water and when she did, she screamed!

"I hate this!! I want to go home damn it!" It was ridiculous, but her shouted words made her feel better. She floated near the wall of the tank and slammed her open palms against the wall along with each of her words. "I'm tired of this horrible, stupid, old can. I want to go home!"

When the last of her words echoed off the metal walls, she sagged in the water. It felt like all of her energy had gone into those last shouted words and suddenly she wanted to take them back.

Her legs began to ache. Muscle deep aches that felt like they might snap right off the bone. Her arms weakened too even though she clawed at the water, trying to grab hold of something solid… and failing.

No.

Not like this.

No.

"Summer?"

That's it. She was hallucinating.

"Summer?"

Well, it was a pretty damn good hallucination.

"Summer? Can you hear us?"

Kai. Mustang. Ajax.

Could it be so easy?

"Summer? Tell us where you are!"

Right, I don't even know where I am! She cackled at the crazy thought.

Her weight threatened to drag her under again, so she

moved her arms, trying to tread water just like Kai had showed her before. She just needed to keep her head above water so she could call out. "I'm here! In some kind of water tank! I'm here!!"

More shouts pierced the air and Summer started to believe that maybe, just maybe she might survive the night.

"Summer? Call out again, ku`ulei!"

"I'm here!" She swore it sounded like they were right under her. "I'm here!!"

She saw flashlight beams over her head and heard the heavy footfalls on the rungs outside the tank. She heard people shouting and people running and she'd never loved sound so much in her entire life.

The first person she saw above her was Kai and then Ajax appeared as well.

"Hold on," Ajax held out a hand, "we're getting something we can throw down to you."

Her strength was slipping away and she knew she wasn't going to be able to grab onto anything, but she just didn't want to look like a total wuss in front of them.

He saw how exhausted she was and the way her body was moving in the water. Kai didn't even bother to tell the others what he was planning to do. One moment he was standing on the top rung and the next he was falling into the water, as far away as he could get from Summer. He didn't want to push her under.

Kai landed in the water and kicked his way back up the surface, cracking his heel on the metal wall. It was the best pain he'd ever felt because he knew he hadn't pulled her under the surface. When he breached the surface, he blinked his eyes and looked around the darkened interior.

There she was, the most beautiful sight in the world.

Kai reached out and pulled her into his arms and just like his lei, she wound her arms around his neck.

He heard her cries and held her closer, murmuring words of comfort into her ears.

"I tried," she told him, "I kept going."

"I know, Summer. You did it."

She touched her cheek to his. "I was so afraid. I'm so exhausted."

He managed to rub one palm against her back. "You're almost done. Almost. Lean on me. Hold onto me, ku`ulei. I'll hold onto you until we're out of danger."

He could hear the others as they figured out someway to get them out of the tank safely, but Kai could hold on. He'd keep her afloat as long as it took.

"You know," he moved them out from under the open sky, taking them into the shadows to avoid the rain as it started again, "as long as I'm with you, Summer. Everything is possible."

He could feel her nodding against his shoulder.

"There's something I should tell you," her voice was muffled against him.

"What's that? You know you can tell me anything."

Kai felt her press her lips against the side of his neck and he gently cupped the nape of her neck with his hand.

Summer tightened her hold around his neck. "I love you, Kai. I was going to tell you before this, but I wanted to find just the perfect moment to tell you."

He pressed a kiss to her temple and held her close against him. "Any moment with you is the perfect moment, Summer. Please tell me you know I love you too."

She turned her head, and he could feel her breath against his skin. "Of course. You've shown me in a hundred different ways. And I'm going to return the favor for as long as you'll let me."

"Let you?" He laughed and held her tight. "You're all I want in my life, Summer."

"And you're my hero," she sighed, her voice nearly a whisper.

"Me?" He sighed. "What did I do? You're the one who saved yourself."

"I did, because you taught me that I could."

EPILOGUE

Waimanalo Beach had been alive with laughter and a whole host of friends and family all day long. There were also a lot of locals that stopped by to kick back and relax as the Deltas and SEALs held an impromptu beach volleyball game. Kai's sisters had enjoyed making a running commentary on all of the flexed muscles.

It was enough to give a man a complex.

By the time the game was half over, he was beginning to wonder if his ego was a lot more sensitive than he'd thought.

Until Summer leaned closer into his side and asked him to go swimming with her.

He was still surprised at how far she'd come in her swimming lessons after surviving those hours in the old rusting tank. Rather than submerging her deeper into her fears it had set her free in a way that he hadn't expected.

But in a way that amazed him and made him love her even more.

They spent the better part of an hour in the water, swimming deeper and deeper in until neither of them could feel the sand under their feet.

Kai watched her face for any signs that she was upset or scared, but he couldn't find any. Instead, they'd splashed each other with water and let the current move them along. When the waves brought them close enough to touch, they did. And Kai found her hands and skin to be equally enticing. When he found her lips for a kiss, the waves pushed them closer together and they had no trouble letting nature push them toward the shore.

Back at his house, they'd brushed the sand off of their feet and left their slippers at the door. Kai packed the remains of their cooler into the refrigerator for later when they were hungry while Summer stepped into the shower.

With the single wall construction of the plantation style house, he could practically hear the water through the walls.

It was a gentle sound.

A comforting one.

Summer was in his home.

He knew that it was only a matter of time before he asked her to marry him. He just wasn't sure how long.

Every time he thought about a plan of how and where he'd propose, they all sounded great and then he'd spend time with her, and those plans would disappear from his mind.

All he wanted was her to be 'at home' with him, but he knew that her apartment near Pearl Harbor Base was closer to work for her and they did spend a lot of nights in her apartment as well.

So many things to think about. Logistics to figure out.

But there was one thing that was at the center of his thoughts and feelings.

How much he loved Summer Maitland.

"Kai? Can you give me a hand?"

A smile lifted his mood and his expression as he walked into the hall toward the bathroom.

As soon as he stepped into the doorway all the air in his lungs left him. Wrapped up in a bath towel, Summer stood before his sink, looking into the mirror on the wall.

The tell-tale bright green bottle on the side of the sink told him why she needed him.

"You know I wear SPF infinity," she groused, "but I still get red all the time."

He made quick work of crossing the space to stand behind her. "You just have haole skin, ku`ulei. Give it some time and your skin will adjust."

The look she gave him as she gazed into the mirror made him shake with quiet laughter. Her brow arched up and her hair slicked straight back from her face made her look elegant and refined, but the red on the tip of her nose made her look incredibly adorable.

"What?" She must have seen where his gaze had landed, and she lifted her hand to cover her nose and ended up wincing in pain. "My nose!"

Reaching for the after-sun lotion, Kai put a little dab on his fingertip and gently smoothed it on bridge of her nose and down to the tip. "Does that feel better?"

"Much better." She nodded and smiled at him in the reflection of the mirror. "Can you do my shoulders?"

Oh the things he'd like to do.

Putting a healthy squirt of the lotion on his palm, he rubbed his hands together to spread it around before he touched her shoulders.

The cooling gel made her tense up at first and then she sighed as he smoothed it over her shoulders and then onto her back where the sun had given her some color.

"Now I know why they call it *sun kissed*." He looked at her face in the reflection and enjoyed the serene look on her face.

Her eyes were closed with her lashes fanned down against her cheeks. Her lips were parted, just barely as if she'd just exhaled.

"Really?"

"Really." He leaned forward and kissed the side of her neck just under her ear. "it just looks like you're blushing."

He smoothed the lotion against her skin, maybe taking a few moments longer than he needed to. Neither one of them seemed in the mood to complain.

When he hooked his fingers into the back of her towel, he gave her a questioning look in the mirror. "Mind if I borrow your towel?"

"Borrow?" She looked askance at him. "But what am I going to use?"

He shrugged and gave it a little tug. "I need to shower too, you know."

"No one's stopping you." She brought her hands up, crossed them at the wrists as she held the towel against her breasts. "Besides, I'm already done and you just put Aftersun on my skin."

Kai nodded and gave the towel another tug and it slipped down a bit, almost pulling it from under her hands. "I'm happy to put more on you after my shower."

She bit her teeth into her lower lip, and he went from being playful to hard in a heartbeat. "So you're saying you're willing to do extra work because you want this towel?"

"I wouldn't consider it work, ku`ulei. Loving you is never work."

Her eyes widened just a little and she leaned back toward him capturing his hands between them. "And here I thought you were going to take a shower."

"Remember?" He worked one hand free and lifted his pendant up so she could see it over her shoulder. "I'm a multi-tasker. I can do a bunch of things, all at once. Shower, love you, make you moan."

He saw the way her throat moved and the way her eyes darkened in the mirror. "Talented," she nodded.

"Handsy," he winked, "and hungry for your kisses."

Kai reached for her and came up empty as she stepped away.

For a moment, he wondered if he'd made a mistake.

That was until he had a face full of towel.

When he tugged it down, he saw Summer laughing at him as she stepped back toward his walk-in shower. "Come on in, Kai. Maybe I'll get a little handsy myself." She held up her hand and wiggled her fingers at him.

Tossing the towel back over his shower, he followed her in, stripping off his shirt and boardshorts as he went.

Summer barely had time to turn the water on before he was holding her hips, backing her up against the cool tile wall, his mouth finding the pulse just under her chin.

"Kai... Kai?"

He lifted his head and looked at the smile on her lips. "Something wrong?"

"The towel," she gestured a hand toward the floor behind him, "what are we going to use?"

He shook his head. "Worry about the towel later, Summer. We need to get wet first."

Her throaty laughter and the flirtatious glimmer in her eyes had him weak in the knees and harder than before. "Oh, you don't have to worry about me, Kai. Love me..."

She wrapped her arms around his neck, and he pressed her up against the tiles, showing her exactly how hungry he was for her.

"Love me like you can't get enough of me."

He took her lips in a kiss, deepening it when she let him

lift her up so her legs could wrap around his waist in an embrace that brought his cock flush up against her mound.

Summer teased his tongue into her mouth as she wrapped herself even tighter around him.

Kai knew he could make her happy. He'd worried about it before. Knowing that she was a respected scientist made him question if she would be happy with him just the way he was, but she'd shown him over the last few months that whatever differences that they had didn't measure up to the things that brought them together.

Using a hand to brace against the tile wall, he used the other to cant her hips so he could slide deep inside of her heat.

The soft moan that came from her throat echoed against the walls and joined his as he felt her walls squeeze him tight.

"This," he spoke to her in almost a whisper as he stroked himself deep inside of her again and again, "this is what I want."

She leaned her forehead against his and he drew her breath into his lungs, sharing life with her.

"You," he thrust harder and felt her arms tighten around him, "you are everything to me."

Her soft gasp reached his ears. "Aloha mai no…"

He couldn't help but smile at her words. "Yes, I give my love to you."

"And aloha aku no," she answered back, giving her love to him.

Kai couldn't help the way he loved her and was truly blessed that she loved him back. "Always, ku`ulei… always."

Delta Force Hawaii

Rescuing Hi`liani

A Hero For Ku'uipo

A Hero for Summer

A Hero for Olena (Aug 2021)

San Antonio First Responders Series

Justice for Sloan

Justice for Miranda

Shelter for Viviana

Justice for Hildie

Justice for Blyss

Shelter for Aylin

Sylvan City Alphas Series

The Tiger's Innocent Bride

Too Much to Bear

The Fighter

Bear His Mark

Center City First Responders

Wild Hearts

Her Rock

The Man For Her (06.29.21)

Mystic Mountain Series

Winter

Xavier

Locke

Three Rivers Express Series

Always, Ransom

Always, Wyeth

Always, Ellis

Orsino Security Series

Her Unbearable Protector

His UnBearable Touch

Their Unbearable Destiny

St. Raphael, CA Series

Finding Home

Playing With Fire

Healing Hearts

Taking a Chance

Shapeshifters of Arcadia

Beneath the Surface

Ellingsford, Montana Series

Stay With Me

Her Gentle Heart

Hold Her Close

Other

Too Much Bear

Home to Roost

Loving Graystoke's Heir

Jesse

The Mechanic

Gingerbear Christmas

Fall in Love

Sanguine Scent (Spellbound Sensuality Series)

ABOUT THE AUTHOR

Who would have thought that I'd start off as a painfully shy child writing stories and end up as a painfully shy adult writing books and publishing them for others to read? Crazy? That's me!!

When I was a little girl, I read every book I could get my hands on and if I didn't have one available to read, I'd get out my pencils and paper and write down stories and scenes. Waiting for my mom to finish working, I'd duck into the ladies' break room and use the typewriter. I'd feel like Jessica Fletcher, happily tap, tap, tapping away until I got to 'The End.' Couldn't quite get the flourish after that and end up tearing the paper, but it was cool and scary to sit down and read the book or give it to my friends to read.

Now my 'typewriter' doesn't clack the same way and the I don't even have paper to pull out of it with a nod of satisfaction, but I have the joy and excitement of sharing my characters and books with people all around the world!

I hope you'll enjoy reading my books, because I'm going to keep writing as long as the characters are feeling chatty!

amazon.com/author/reinatorresromance
bookbub.com/profile/reina-torres
facebook.com/ReinaTorresRomance
twitter.com/rtorresauthor

There are many more books in this fan fiction world than listed here, for an up-to-date list go to www.AcesPress.com

You can also visit our Amazon page at: http://www.amazon.com/author/operationalpha

Special Forces: Operation Alpha World

Christie Adams: Charity's Heart
Denise Agnew: Dangerous to Hold
Shauna Allen: Awakening Aubrey
Brynne Asher: Blackburn
Linzi Baxter: Unlocking Dreams
Jennifer Becker: Hiding Catherine
Alice Bello: Shadowing Milly
Heather Blair: Rescue Me
Anna Blakely: Rescuing Gracelynn
Julia Bright: Saving Lorelei
Cara Carnes: Protecting Mari
Kendra Mei Chailyn: Beast
Melissa Kay Clarke: Rescuing Annabeth
Samantha A. Cole: Handling Haven
Sue Coletta: Hacked
Melissa Combs: Gallant
Lorelei Confer: Protecting Sara
Anne Conley: Redemption for Misty
KaLyn Cooper: Rescuing Melina
Janie Crouch: Storm
Liz Crowe: Marking Mariah
Sarah Curtis: Securing the Odds
Jordan Dane: Redemption for Avery
Tarina Deaton: Found in the Lost
Aspen Drake, Intense
KL Donn: Unraveling Love

Riley Edwards: Protecting Olivia
PJ Fiala: Defending Sophie
Nicole Flockton: Protecting Maria
Alexa Gregory: Backdraft
Michele Gwynn: Rescuing Emma
Casey Hagen: Shielding Nebraska
Desiree Holt: Protecting Maddie
Kathy Ivan: Saving Sarah
Kris Jacen, Be With Me
Jesse Jacobson: Protecting Honor
Silver James: Rescue Moon
Becca Jameson: Saving Sofia
Kate Kinsley: Protecting Ava
Rayne Lewis: Justice for Mary
Heather Long: Securing Arizona
Gennita Low: No Protection
Kirsten Lynn: Joining Forces for Jesse
Margaret Madigan: Bang for the Buck
Trish McCallan: Hero Under Fire
Kimberly McGath: The Predecessor
Rachel McNeely: The SEAL's Surprise Baby
KD Michaels: Saving Laura
Lynn Michaels: Rescuing Kyle
Olivia Michaels: Protecting Harper
Wren Michaels: The Fox & The Hound
Annie Miller: Securing Willow
Kat Mizera: Protecting Bobbi
Keira Montclair, Wolf and the Wild Scots
Mary B Moore: Force Protection
LeTeisha Newton: Protecting Butterfly
Angela Nicole: Protecting the Donna
MJ Nightingale: Protecting Beauty
Sarah O'Rourke: Saving Liberty
Victoria Paige: Reclaiming Izabel

Anne L. Parks: Mason
Debra Parmley: Protecting Pippa
Lainey Reese: Protecting New York
KeKe Renée: Protecting Bria
TL Reeve and Michele Ryan: Extracting Mateo
Elena M. Reyes: Keeping Ava
Deanna L. Rowley: Saving Veronica
Angela Rush: Charlotte
Rose Smith: Saving Satin
Jenika Snow: Protecting Lily
Lynne St. James: SEAL's Spitfire
Dee Stewart: Conner
Harley Stone: Rescuing Mercy
Sarah Stone: Shielding Grace
Jen Talty: Burning Desire
Reina Torres, Rescuing Hi'ilani
Savvi V: Loving Lex
Megan Vernon: Protecting Us
LJ Vickery: Circus Comes to Town
Rachel Young: Because of Marissa
R. C. Wynne: Shadows Renewed

Delta Team Three Series

Lori Ryan: Nori's Delta
Becca Jameson: Destiny's Delta
Lynne St James, Gwen's Delta
Elle James: Ivy's Delta
Riley Edwards: Hope's Delta

Police and Fire: Operation Alpha World

Freya Barker: Burning for Autumn
B.P. Beth: Scott
Jane Blythe: Salvaging Marigold
Julia Bright, Justice for Amber

Anna Brooks, Guarding Georgia
KaLyn Cooper: Justice for Gwen
Aspen Drake: Sheltering Emma
Emily Gray: Shelter for Allegra
Alexa Gregory: Backdraft
Deanndra Hall: Shelter for Sharla
Barb Han: Kace
EM Hayes: Gambling for Ashleigh
India Kells: Shadow Killer
CM Steele: Guarding Hope
Reina Torres: Justice for Sloane
Aubree Valentine, Justice for Danielle
Maddie Wade: Finding English
Stacey Wilk: Stage Fright
Laine Vess: Justice for Lauren

Tarpley VFD Series

Silver James, Fighting for Elena
Deanndra Hall, Fighting for Carly
Haven Rose, Fighting for Calliope
MJ Nightingale, Fighting for Jemma
TL Reeve, Fighting for Brittney
Nicole Flockton, Fighting for Nadia

As you know, this book included at least one character from Susan Stoker's books. To check out more, see below.

SEAL Team Hawaii Series

Finding Elodie
Finding Lexie (Aug 2021)
Finding Kenna (Oct 2021)
Finding Monica (TBA)
Finding Carly (TBA)
Finding Ashlyn (TBA)
Finding Jodelle (TBA)

Eagle Point Search & Rescue

Searching for Lilly (Mar 2022)
Searching for Bristol (Jun 2022)
Searching for Elsie (Nov 2022)
Searching for Caryn (TBA)
Searching for Finley (TBA)
Searching for Heather (TBA)
Searching for Khloe (TBA)

Delta Team Two Series

Shielding Gillian
Shielding Kinley
Shielding Aspen
Shielding Jayme (novella)
Shielding Riley
Shielding Devyn
Shielding Ember (Sept 2021)
Shielding Sierra (Jan 2022)

SEAL of Protection: Legacy Series

Securing Caite (FREE!)

Securing Brenae (novella)
Securing Sidney
Securing Piper
Securing Zoey
Securing Avery
Securing Kalee
Securing Jane

Delta Force Heroes Series

Rescuing Rayne (FREE!)
Rescuing Aimee (novella)
Rescuing Emily
Rescuing Harley
Marrying Emily (novella)
Rescuing Kassie
Rescuing Bryn
Rescuing Casey
Rescuing Sadie (novella)
Rescuing Wendy
Rescuing Mary
Rescuing Macie (novella)
Rescuing Annie (Feb 2022)

Badge of Honor: Texas Heroes Series

Justice for Mackenzie (FREE!)
Justice for Mickie
Justice for Corrie
Justice for Laine (novella)
Shelter for Elizabeth
Justice for Boone
Shelter for Adeline
Shelter for Sophie
Justice for Erin
Justice for Milena

Shelter for Blythe
Justice for Hope
Shelter for Quinn
Shelter for Koren
Shelter for Penelope

SEAL of Protection Series

Protecting Caroline (FREE!)
Protecting Alabama
Protecting Fiona
Marrying Caroline (novella)
Protecting Summer
Protecting Cheyenne
Protecting Jessyka
Protecting Julie (novella)
Protecting Melody
Protecting the Future
Protecting Kiera (novella)
Protecting Alabama's Kids (novella)
Protecting Dakota

New York Times, USA Today and *Wall Street Journal* Bestselling Author Susan Stoker has a heart as big as the state of Tennessee where she lives, but this all American girl has also spent the last fourteen years living in Missouri, California, Colorado, Indiana, and Texas. She's married to a retired Army man who now gets to follow *her* around the country.

www.stokeraces.com
www.AcesPress.com
susan@stokeraces.com

Made in United States
Cleveland, OH
14 March 2026

34491696R00164